Revenge, born of the sea.

"Father!" Samantha choked, and without hesitation stepped in to help him.

"No, lass!" Joe wheezed.

She clawed at Joe. She pushed, shoved, and scratched at him—anything to get to her father, anything to help. How could she witness her family being murdered and not do something—anything—to stop it?

Unfortunately, she had no choice. Another pirate was charging toward them, a foul grin splitting his evil face. Joe grabbed her like a sack of sand. His wound seemed forgotten as he hoisted her up.

"Hold yer breath," he warned, then threw her overboard.

She had time only to close her mouth before the Caribbean swallowed her whole.

What a
Pirate Desires

MICHELLE BEATTIE

BERKLEY SENSATION, NEW YORK

THE BERKLEY PUBLISHING GROUP
Published by the Penguin Group
Penguin Group (USA) Inc.
375 Hudson Street, New York, New York 10014, USA
Penguin Group (Canada), 90 Eglinton Avenue East, Suite 700, Toronto, Ontario M4P 2Y3, Canada
(a division of Pearson Penguin Canada Inc.)
Penguin Books Ltd., 80 Strand, London WC2R 0RL, England
Penguin Group Ireland, 25 St. Stephen's Green, Dublin 2, Ireland (a division of Penguin Books Ltd.)
Penguin Group (Australia), 250 Camberwell Road, Camberwell, Victoria 3124, Australia
(a division of Pearson Australia Group Pty. Ltd.)
Penguin Books India Pvt. Ltd., 11 Community Centre, Panchsheel Park, New Delhi—110 017, India
Penguin Group (NZ), 67 Apollo Drive, Rosedale, North Shore 0632, New Zealand
(a division of Pearson New Zealand Ltd.)
Penguin Books (South Africa) (Pty.) Ltd., 24 Sturdee Avenue, Rosebank, Johannesburg 2196,
South Africa

Penguin Books Ltd., Registered Offices: 80 Strand, London WC2R 0RL, England

This is a work of fiction. Names, characters, places, and incidents either are the product of the author's imagination or are used fictitiously, and any resemblance to actual persons, living or dead, business establishments, events, or locales is entirely coincidental. The publisher does not have any control over and does not assume any responsibility for author or third-party websites or their content.

WHAT A PIRATE DESIRES

A Berkley Sensation Book / published by arrangement with the author

PRINTING HISTORY
Berkley Sensation mass-market edition / December 2008

Copyright © 2008 by Michelle Beattie.
Cover art by Judy York.
Cover design by George Long.
Interior text design by Kristin del Rosario.

ISBN: 978-0-425-22493-9

BERKLEY® SENSATION
Berkley Sensation Books are published by The Berkley Publishing Group,
a division of Penguin Group (USA) Inc.,
375 Hudson Street, New York, New York 10014.
BERKLEY SENSATION and the "B" design are trademarks of Penguin Group (USA) Inc.

PRINTED IN THE UNITED STATES OF AMERICA

10 9 8 7 6 5 4 3 2 1

This book is dedicated to my friend, Fabiola Forcier. Her support of me over the years, through good decisions and bad ones, has never faltered. She's there with encouragement when I'm defeated and congratulations when I'm successful. Thanks, Fab, for the gift of your friendship. I treasure it more than words can ever say.

ACKNOWLEDGMENTS

From the beginning this book was a joy to write, but I didn't do it alone. To my wonderful critique group: Michele, Taryn, and Marilyn, who helped brainstorm with me when I hit a wall or needed clarity. You're much more to me than critique partners; you're dear friends.

To my editor, Allison, for believing in my work and for loving the story as much as I do. Your phone call changed my life. I can't thank you enough.

Prologue

Caribbean Sea
1656

"Miss Samantha, get up! Hurry! For God's sake, hurry!"

Her eyes shot open. The small cabin blurred as she struggled between sleep and wakefulness.

"What? What's the matter?" she asked, trying to focus on Joe's frantic eyes.

Joe, her father's first mate and longtime friend, stood pale and petrified.

She bolted upright. Alarm surged down her spine. "What is it, Joe?"

The last cobwebs of sleep scattered when Joe wrenched her from her berth.

"Pirates, lass!"

She stumbled after him. "What?"

He didn't have time to answer. Cannon fire erupted in the cabin next to hers. The walls jolted, there was the deafening scream of wood splintering, the acrid smell of smoke. Samantha cried out.

Joe took the steps to the main deck three at a time. She

wasn't as quick. Her pale peach nightgown tangled around her legs and wood scraped the bottoms of her bare feet. Keeping up with his frantic pace seemed impossible, though she had little choice. He gripped her arm with one hand and held a pistol in the other.

He pushed the door open with a rap of his forearm.

As the booming clamor crashed around Samantha, men scrambled to get into fighting position. Yelling and cursing came from every direction. Pistols fired; cannons belched deadly shots in a marching rhythm. Smoke from gunfire, cannons, and burning wood poured into Samantha's throat. She covered her mouth and nose with her free hand to block some of it.

The *Destiny* wailed when grab hooks from the pirate ship sank into her polished sides.

Thick fingers of rain-threatening clouds clawed at the moon. The sea, as savage as the pirates intent on seizing the ship, bucked and spat. The *Destiny*, trapped between water and sky, fell prey to the pirates. Samantha knew everything would be lost this night.

A sob bubbled out and her knees buckled. "Joe," she whispered. Fear closed her throat and prevented anything more than a whimper from escaping.

He yanked her back to her feet. "Stay with me, lass."

His eyes, big as the full moon, if not as bright, bored into hers.

"Don't ye move from me side, understand?"

She was seventeen, not stupid. She nodded.

He'd already turned his back, using it as a shield to protect her. Samantha peered around him. She had to find her family. She refused to go anywhere without them.

With the grab hooks holding the ships side by side, pirates flooded aboard like an epidemic. But her father's crew wasn't going easily. Guns from both ships fired as fast as they could be reloaded. Samantha planted her feet far apart to keep steady on the pitching ship. Men yelled, cursed, and fought for their lives. Only a few of them were successful.

Helplessly, she watched friends stumble and fall, their blood smearing the deck. In blind fear, some men jumped overboard. Others were thrown. The *Destiny* hadn't a prayer; its crew was terribly outnumbered.

Samantha's gaze searched the deck. She had to find her father and mother. And Alicia. Tears stung Samantha's eyes. Her sister was so young, barely twelve, with long blond ringlets, innocent eyes the color of a mountain stream, cheeks that dimpled when she laughed. Would she also be lost in this sea of blood?

"No, not Alicia," she fervently prayed.

But her plea remained unanswered.

Samantha finally caught sight of her father, glowing eerily in his white nightshirt, and dared to hope that she wouldn't lose everything she cared about. A shot screamed by her ear. Joe grunted and stumbled. He staggered back and pushed her into the gunwale.

Arched over the side, she stared into the black water, into the rowboat that tugged against the rope like a child wrenching to get free. Had it been only that afternoon that they'd left Port Royal? That evening when her mother had come to give her a kiss goodnight? Oh, God, her mother!

Joe caught himself and stood, though she knew by his grunts that he'd been hit. He turned, and Samantha screamed. Nausea raced up her throat. She cared about all the crew, but Joe was like family. Sweat beaded his entire face, blood streamed from a wound in his chest, and the sickeningly sweet smell of it turned her stomach.

Movement behind him caught Samantha's eye. She yelled a warning. Joe spun and fired. A filthy pirate, dressed in motley, fell dead.

The sight—oh, the terrible sight—scraped away at Samantha and left her empty. Friends butchered and slain, some whimpering as life oozed away, littered the deck. She'd never been so cold. Her heart ripped open, and everything that was vital to who she was and what mattered most tumbled out. Hot tears streamed down her cheeks. She sniffled loudly.

Then she saw her father again. His face pale as his nightdress, he danced around a disgustingly amused wretch, his sword pointed steadily. It was a battle Samantha knew wouldn't end until someone died.

"Father," she choked, and without thinking stepped to help him.

"No, lass!" Joe wheezed. Despite his wound he held her fast.

She clawed at Joe. She pushed, shoved, and scratched at him—anything to get to her father, anything to help. She couldn't possibly stand by and do nothing. How could she witness her family being murdered and not do something—anything—to stop it? It didn't matter if she died in the process. Anything would be better than to go on without them. There would be no life without her father standing behind her, teaching her everything about sailing and the sea. No meaning without her mother telling stories every night, some from books, some that came from her imagination. Without the warmth she'd known all her life—the comfort and love—there would be nothing. She would be nothing.

Unfortunately, she had no choice. Another pirate was

charging toward them, a foul grin splitting his evil face. Joe grabbed her like a sack of sand. His wound seemed forgotten as he hoisted her up.

"Hold yer breath," he warned, then threw her overboard.

She had time only to close her mouth before the Caribbean swallowed her whole.

One

Five years later

It went against every one of Samantha's sensibilities to walk the narrow corridor of the prison. Simply being there had stolen the moisture from her mouth. She loathed having to do this. Upon reaching the only occupied cell, she nearly turned round and pretended she hadn't come at all. Except she had. And, as she kept reminding herself, she had no other options.

Still, it stung her pride just to have to look at him. He was leaning against a musty wall, arms tanned a golden brown and crossed belligerently over his chest. At first glance he didn't look much different from most pirates. His soiled shirt gaped open nearly to his waist, revealing smudges of dirt and enough chains around his neck to anchor a small ship. A gold sash, with its tails hanging down to his right knee, hugged a lean waist. He wore black pants and boots, both of which had faded to gray.

"Like what you see, luv?"

His voice was rich and deep, and it snapped her gaze to his face. A chiseled face that demanded and received her full attention.

Unlike most scalawags, he wore neither hat nor bandana. His hair was the color of a summer sun, and it hung unfettered to his shoulders. A thin mustache topped lips that curled in amusement. His left eye was covered by a shiny black patch. The other, green as the most brilliant emerald, stared unblinkingly.

How she loathed his arrogance, wished she could leave him to rot in the small cell. Unfortunately, she couldn't. She'd put her life at stake coming back to Port Royal. If she were recognized or followed, it would be fatal for her. Her only hope was eyeing her suspiciously from behind bars. No, she'd come here for a reason, and despite the nerves that danced in her belly, she had every intention of accomplishing her goal as quickly as possible.

Sliding into her strumpet role, one of many she'd used to stay alive over the years, Samantha took a tendril of hair she'd deliberately left hanging over her right breast and twirled it between her fingers. Forcing a smile she didn't feel, she laced her voice with syrup.

"Captain Bradley?" she asked sweetly, although she knew the answer. She'd researched his piracy; it was not by chance that she found the notorious Luke Bradley here today.

He looked about the puny prison cell, empty except for him.

"You know, I think I saw him here yesterday"—he shrugged—"but he seems to have left."

"Aren't you a funny one?" she giggled, and narrowly managed not to wince at the shrill sound. "Aren't you due to hang tomorrow?"

His mirthless eye narrowed, and his mustached lip curved. "Luke is facing the gallows. I'm just here for the food."

"Food?" She pretended to miss the jest.

"Well"—his steady gaze roamed her body—"had I known the company would be this good, I might have found my way here sooner."

Her skin turned frigid under his gaze. She bit back the vile retort that sprang to mind. She had little enough time to get him out.

"Oh." She poked out her bottom lip. "I was supposed to help him escape." She shrugged her shoulders. As she spun to leave, her skirt swept the dusty floor. She had taken only one step when she heard him move behind her. She held back a triumphant smile and turned. He'd moved to the bars and now stood barely a foot from her. Her eyes met his, and the victory she'd felt a moment ago dissipated. Her heart leapt to her throat. His nearness sucked the air from the dusty prison. Behind her mask of indifference, which she willed to stay in place, she forced her mind to remember what he was. Despite his surprising attractiveness, he was no different from the swine who had slaughtered her family.

He had a straight nose and cheekbones that rode high and angled toward his full mouth. Though his legends were tall, he wasn't much taller than she. She had only to tip her head a little to look him in the eye. His even stare met hers, and its intensity shook her. She'd have to be careful, very careful, that he didn't guess the effect he had on her.

"Tell me who's looking for Luke Bradley, and I'll think about talking."

She leaned suggestively against the bars. Anything to hurry him up. "Sam Steele."

He arched a pale brow and whistled softly. "Bleed-'em-dry Steele? Why's he looking for Luke? Has Luke been a bad boy?"

Her patience was running thin. "I don't know. He doesn't tell me much." Her forced smile nearly cracked her cheeks.

A coy grin tugged at his lips. "I'd wager, under the right conditions, he'd tell you anything you'd ask."

She couldn't help the heat that burned its way up her neck, nor the anger that followed close behind. Why, if the situation wasn't dire, he'd be hanging from the bowsprit, with large chunks of meat tied to his boots to entice the sharks.

"Who, me?" she purred.

He moved without warning. His dirty hand flew through the bars and wrapped around her bare neck. "You're a terrible actress, luv, and you're no strumpet either, no matter how you're dressed. Why don't you tell me who you really are and what Sam Steele wants with me?"

Talons of fear gripped her heart. He was a pirate, her mind screamed, capable of anything. She took a steadying breath to keep her emotions under control. Emotions could be costly, and she couldn't afford to lose. Pushing aside her fear, she met his gaze.

"What would Steele want with you? You said yourself you aren't Luke Bradley."

He nodded. "Very good, luv. Now, back to Steele."

She seized his wrist. Her blood pounded in her fingers; she was certain he felt it. It wouldn't do to give him any more power.

"Let go of me," she warned, dropping all pretenses. Her fingers dug into his skin. "Nobody touches me without my permission."

He hesitated a moment. Just enough to let her know it wasn't her demand that made him loosen his hold. She slapped his arm away and stepped back.

How she wished she had the luxury of letting him hang in the morning. But she couldn't discard him. Yet.

"Sam needs you. All I know is that it has something to do with finding Dervish. He thinks, as you've sailed with the man, that you know where he is. He hasn't had any luck finding him on his own. Now, we don't have a great deal of time. Do you want your freedom or not?"

He turned, finally seeming to notice the racket that carried through the thin bars of his window. In the street, grenades popped, entwined with the sounds of chaos. Babes screamed. Horse's hooves stamped on the cobblestones. She waited, drumming her foot, while he took the time to examine the situation.

"I see Steele's thought of everything."

"Yes. You help Sam, and he gives you your freedom. Everybody wins. However, you've only ten seconds to decide. That diversion's not going to last forever. Soon they'll discover they aren't really under attack. The guards are indisposed, but only for the moment. Another few minutes and they'll be back from the privy."

He smiled, and bright white teeth flashed. "Well, lucky for Steele I've some time to spare."

The gold chains around his neck jingled as he sauntered back toward her. He idly scratched the corner of his mouth, but his body was rigid. For the first time since this plot began, she smiled. Luke Bradley didn't like taking orders from anyone. Shamelessly, she enjoyed the fact that he had to do just that.

Three pistol shots rang one after another. Her signal. If they were to succeed, they had to go now. She pulled up the hem of her dress, and his green eye deepened to the color of wet moss.

"I've not seen many women wear pants under their dresses. Is that the new fashion these days?"

"It pays to be prepared; you ought to know that."

She lifted her gown a little more and revealed two blunderbusses strapped to her thighs. She slid one from its leather tie and held it out to him. He stretched for it, but she kept the weapon out of reach.

He sighed. "What do you want? A promise written in blood?"

"Just your word, Bradley."

His tongue grazed his front teeth. "You're willing to trust the word of a pirate?"

"We're saving your life. We can take it just as easily."

His laugh had a full-bodied tone to it. It sent her stomach down to her toes.

"Ah, yes, you and the illusive Captain Steele. First, you have to get me out. And I don't know how you can manage that, even if those weapons are loaded. The Royal Navy has waited a long time to hang me. It'll take more than a little smoke and noise to distract them."

"Yes, but Sam wants you alive, probably more than they want you dead."

"I doubt that." He smiled again.

Her hand dipped between her breasts and removed the key she'd taken from a guard. The key she'd snatched a scant moment after the cake she'd offered them had twisted their insides, folded them in half, and sent them running to the privy in a wave of mortification.

Luke leaned against the bars, his arms crossed over his dirty shirt. There was something about him that could make a woman forget herself. She sensed a difference in him, though she hadn't the time or inclination to unearth it.

His gaze lingered on the exposed flesh of her chest. "You're full of surprises, luv. You have any other treasures hidden in there, or am I trespassing on hallowed ground? I don't imagine Steele takes to sharing."

Heat suffused her face. Her ears smoldered, but she ignored the reaction. Luke's lecherous ways were not worth responding to.

"Now don't be running out of here with pistols blazing; you'll ruin everything," she warned.

He glared. "You know, that's insulting. I'm not famous for my stupidity."

Samantha gave him a telling look, took the other blunderbuss from her thigh, and unlocked his cell. She pointed the weapon at him. "Just so you know, I won't hesitate to shoot you if you botch this up. I won't go to prison for you, Bradley."

"Well, now that we have all the niceties out of the way . . ."

The door clanged open. Luke stepped out and walked toward her until the toes of his boots brushed her shoes.

"You do know what you just did, don't you, luv?"

At that moment, she didn't know much. Not with him so close, sharing the same air. She swallowed forcibly, hoping she hadn't made the worst mistake of her life.

"I just commandeered Captain Luke Bradley to help settle a score. Now let's get out of here."

Bloody hell! The phrase kept repeating itself as Luke and the woman crept to the prison door and peered outside. He squinted against the sun's brilliance. Well, if nothing else, he had to admit Steele had one hell of a knack for creating bedlam. The whole village scrambled. Women ran frantically about, their arms laden with crying whelps. Men armed with swords, rocks, and anything else that could inflict damage prowled the town, hunting for attackers that even Luke couldn't locate. While grenades exploded and pistols fired, animals ranging from chickens to mules dashed about half-crazed. The navy, in full uniform, wove among the chaos.

As inventive as the commotion was, the girl was much more entertaining. She'd tucked her weapon back under the folds of her skirt and was combing long fingers through her glorious hair. Waves of chestnut with golden streaks wrapped around her nearly bare shoulders.

If his life hadn't depended on getting out of jail, Luke would've taken more time to appreciate the curves that all but spilled out of the red bodice when she raised her arms. He also would have taken the time to act on the lust that slammed into him and left his blood boiling.

"It's hardly the time for a little primping. Could you save that for after I'm safely away from the gallows?"

She glared at him. "Follow my lead," she said, and wrapped her arm—a little too firmly—around his waist.

He had time only to tuck his pistol within his sash before they stepped boldly from the cover of the prison door.

She leaned heavily into him, forcing him to do the same to her, lest he fall over. She smelled of a sweet summer's day. Sultry words, slightly slurred, slipped past lips that held his rapt attention.

He knew that from a distance they wouldn't be noticed for anything else than what they seemed, just another scoundrel taken with a trollop. Only those who'd look closely would see the rest.

Though her body may have been leaning, it was anything but submissive. And then there were her eyes, cold and hard as ice, shooting him frozen daggers. He'd also bet his good eye her jaw was clamped tightly shut. Though her words were the right ones, the tone could hammer nails. A weaker man than he would shrivel before her. Luckily, he was very adept at wenching.

"You devil," she purred. "We should at least wait until the sun sets."

Luke couldn't remember the last time he'd smiled and meant it. "Aye, but I can't wait any longer, luv." He swung her up in his arms and chuckled at her stunned expression. She might have a plan, but damned if he wasn't going to bend it to suit him.

"Put me down, you filthy rat!"

"Careful, luv. We've a plan, remember? You don't want to draw any unwanted attention." He squeezed her closer. "It was you, wasn't it, that told me to follow your lead? You've not changed your mind, have you?"

Anger flushed her face, gold fired in her eyes. But the curse that came from her delicious mouth made him smile. And it sealed her fate. He leaned in, his quick kiss absorbing the next expletive. Another time, he concluded, he'd linger. It might keep her quiet longer. As it was, the minute his mouth left hers the colorful language continued. Judging by the profanity she spat, one or both of them were going to hell.

"Where's the ship?" he whispered in her ear. "And you might want to bend a little, it's like carrying a length of wood."

She softened, barely.

"There's a boat waiting at the docks. It'll take us to the ship, which is moored nearby."

Smart woman, he thought. Slip out quietly. No, he reminded himself, it wasn't her idea. It was Steele's.

"Put me down," she ordered.

He grinned at her rose-colored cheeks. "Not on your life, luv."

Ignoring her muttered protests, Luke wove through the confusion, her slight weight allowing him to keep a steady pace. However, he couldn't see down so well, and more than once he stepped into something soft that squished beneath his boots. Perfect. He had a beautiful wench in his arms, he was escaping the gallows, and his boots were now covered in shit.

Since his luck had tended toward such things lately, he ignored the smell that trailed them. Keeping his head down enough to look preoccupied and fill his senses with the freshness of the woman in his arms, he nonetheless kept his eye on his destination and his surroundings.

"They haven't noticed us," she whispered.

"Not yet," Luke agreed. Still, he picked up the pace.

Just as they were making their way to the water, its surface glistening under the sun, a man weighing no less than three hundred pounds rammed into Luke and knocked him off his feet. With the bundle in his arms, he couldn't stop the fall.

He landed hard on his arse. His hands went back to keep his skull from splitting on the hard street. The lady's delicious weight landed on his lap, thankfully away from his privates. For the time being, she hadn't succeeded in turning him into a eunuch. Her arm wrapped around his neck, pushing creamy breasts right under his nose.

"Begging your pardon," the man yelled over his shoulder as he ran by.

"No problem," Luke murmured, his eye devouring the banquet before him, "no problem a'tall."

She heaved a breath and immediately realized her mistake. She scrambled off his lap, her face flaming brighter than her dress. "Let's go. The guards are bound to be back soon, and they'll realize you're missing."

He grinned, doubting she'd noticed the squeak in her voice, and followed her the rest of the way to the docks. A fleet of small rowboats waited. He took one and rowed around the inlet, followed by another four boats, which he assumed contained the crew.

There, in the sparkling bay, bobbed a beautiful little eight-gunned sloop. She was as blue as the sea and, as far as he was concerned, equally as beautiful. The mainsail rested around the boom; the lone mast stood arrow straight. The hull rocked lazily with the waves. She wasn't a big ship, but he'd bet she was a fast one. He could almost feel the tiller beneath his palm, the sails full of wind. Not his ship, he thought with regret. Steele's.

But he'd have his own again. Very soon.

His gaze bored into the lady's back. Steele had sent her. Something wasn't right about that. Though he'd never met Steele, he'd heard of him. And from everything he'd gathered, Steele wasn't the type of captain to send someone else to do his work. Which made Luke think. Something was amiss, and before he agreed to anything, Steele had a lot of explaining to do.

The deck of the *Revenge*, the name he'd noted as they'd rowed closer, soon bustled with men.

"Weigh anchor! Hoist the sails!" someone yelled.

Luke spun around to see Steele, whom he assumed is-
sued the command, but couldn't locate him. The small
crew of perhaps twenty-five scrambled about, making their
number look like forty. Everyone saw to their duties. Two
men braced on spread legs cranked the windlass. Their
faces were strained from heat and work as they raised the
anchor from the turquoise water.

The mainsail was released. Ropes groaned as the canvas was pulled into position. The lifeboat, dripping salt
water, was replaced on its perch below the boom. Still no
one appeared to be the captain, especially the young lad
who held the tiller.

With a snap the sails filled, and the ship began to cut
through the water. In its wake were the four stolen rowboats.

For a second Luke forgot Steele and savored the moment.
This was his favorite time of any voyage. He loved to see the
canvas full, to feel the slash of the water underneath him,
and to breathe deep the salty spray while wondering where
this next adventure would take him. Would they find a large
merchant ship loaded with goods? Would they have to out-
sail the navy? Would it be gold, doubloons, or pieces of
eight? It didn't matter. It never mattered, as long as it happened at sea. Everything about sailing called to him. And
without his own ship, he yearned.

Which brought him back to the matter at hand. He
grabbed the man closest to him. "Where's Steele?"

The pirate looked around and shrugged. "Here somewhere," he said, and slipped below.

Bloody hell! Luke spun around. No one said another
word, and he had no way of telling which mangy rat was
Steele. Then he caught sight of the scarlet dress disappear-

ing beneath the quarterdeck. *Oh, no, she didn't,* he thought. Luke moved to follow her, but one of the crew stepped between him and the hatch. Luke shoved him aside, his patience at an end.

The man whipped around and grabbed Luke by the shoulders. "Ye'd best watch yerself, son, this ain't yer ship."

Muscles in Luke's arms were primed and ready, but he held himself back. The man was right; this wasn't his ship. And until he knew exactly what was going on, he couldn't afford to do anything stupid.

"Is it yours? Are *you* Steele?"

He released Luke's arm. "I'm Joe, the first mate."

"Where's Steele?"

Joe took a deep breath, his rounded belly resembling the full sails.

"Capt'n's busy at the moment. Yer to wait ten minutes, and then ye can discuss the terms of yer agreement."

Luke leaned closer to Joe, not wanting any misunderstanding. "I haven't agreed to anything yet."

"Capt'n's been waitin' a long time for this." His eyes moved from the calm sea to Luke. "The crew won't take yer lack of cooperation lightly."

He pushed Luke out of his way and walked to the stern. He ruffled the young whelp's head and took the tiller. Luke's mouth watered. What he'd give to feel the control beneath his palm again. To have his own ship. It had been so long. He shoved aside the thought. First, he had to deal with Steele and put an end to this game.

Luke's stomach tensed with a feeling, a very solid one, that he hadn't really escaped after all. He followed Joe.

"I'm about done waiting for this infamous captain of yours. Tell Steele, if he should show up, that I'm waiting in his cabin."

Luke reached for the hatch, but before he could grab it, a vise of an arm coiled around his waist and hoisted him up until the toes of his boots just tickled the deck.

"Ye won't be goin' nowheres without permission. Capt'n said to give him ten minutes."

Luke wanted to argue, but breathing was a bit tricky at the moment. The huge man was crushing his lungs.

A light ring, like that of a Christmas bell, tinkled from below. With no warning, the vise was removed and Luke thumped to the deck, doubled over, wheezing in air.

"Capt'n's ready for ye," Joe announced with a definite grin in his voice.

From behind the lacy screen, where she'd finished changing into a more modest dress, Sam heard the ladder creak. The hatch slammed closed. There was a thud of boots as someone jumped off the last rung onto the floor of the cabin.

Her parrot, Carracks, ensconced in a cage at the base of the ladder, warned her she had company.

Squawk. "Man in cabin. Man in cabin."

Bradley. She pressed a hand to the butterflies in her stomach, set the bell down on the floor, took a steadying breath, and stepped into the line of fire.

"I heard you and Joe arguing. You're not long on patience, are you?" she asked.

He glared at Carracks. Then her.

"No, and you'd best remember that, luv." He glanced around the small cabin, frowning. "Where the devil is he now? I've had enough of his blasted games."

She skirted past him, the hem of her simple blue gown flirting with the polished floor. In a matter of steps she'd passed the bed to her right and stood beside a neat little table nestled next to the ladder. It had four wooden chairs, and she held on to one for support.

Luke's energy equaled that of a tied-up animal's. She wasn't foolish enough to believe he'd be docile when let loose.

"He's asked me to begin without him. He has a few pressing things to do first."

The chains jangled at Luke's neck with each step he took. "I don't care if he's relieving himself. He can squeeze it, shake it, tuck it back in, and get his arse over here."

Sam choked.

He arched a brow. "What's the matter? You can't possibly tell me I've upset your sensibilities."

She bit her cheek to keep the smile back. "Let's just get this over with, shall we? The articles are in the—Now just a damn minute!"

He took her arm, dragged her a few paces, and pushed her onto the bed. She sat stiffly, her blood turning colder with each shallow breath she took. His legs blocked her from standing. No amount of demanding or cursing moved him. Indeed, it fueled him. He placed his hands next to her hips and forced her back onto the mattress, her toes dangling off the floor.

Squawk. "Stand away. Stand away."

"What's going on here? Why do I get the feeling I'm being led blind where I don't want to be going?"

She wouldn't allow him to badger her. "You had no place else to go, remember?"

"Aye, I do. But that doesn't change what's happening now. Where's Steele?"

This wasn't how she'd planned it. Hadn't she labored over the plan to make sure it would all work accordingly?

The butterflies turned to angry bees. And like her, they wanted out of the current situation. "If you move out of the way and let me stand . . ."

He grinned. Before the smile could die on those cursedly full lips, she'd pulled a dirk from her bodice. She pressed it against his thigh, dangerously close to what he surely considered his most valuable treasure.

"Move away, Bradley, before I ruin all your future encounters with the tavern wenches."

Stepping back, he raised his hands in surrender. But his eye warned that the fight wasn't out of him yet. Indeed, the moment she stood, he grabbed her hand again.

Squawk. "Hands off! Hands off!"

"Let me go, you filthy rat! I told you nobody touches me without my permission."

"Apparently even your parrot knows that." He squeezed harder. She gasped and dropped the knife. It flopped on the bed like a dead fish.

"And I'll tell you that I'm through waiting. I'll let you go when you tell me what I want to know. Where's Sam Steele?"

A knot at the base of her neck took root and grew. It throbbed up her skull and pounded behind her eyes. "Honestly, if you'd just—"

"Where?" he bellowed, leaning in further.

Carracks paced in his cage, ruffling his yellow and red feathers. Sam pressed her lips together. Luke wasn't in charge here. She was.

He shook her, snapping her head back. Lines bracketed his mouth. A storm raged in his eye. "Where's Steele?"

Oh, blast Luke Bradley to the devil himself! She'd wanted him to sign the articles first, but he left her no choice. Her heart clawed in her chest from his nearness. She couldn't stand having any man this close, this overpowering. Cursing him, she sputtered, "You're looking at him, all right?"

He released her, in shock. He shook his head.

"What? I'm what?"

Sam quaked with fury that she'd let him get the best of her. Dammit, hadn't she a plan? He wasn't supposed to know. At least not until he'd signed the cursed articles. Until then he could still refuse to help. Damn him for ruining everything!

"I'm Sam Steele. Are you happy now?"

Squawk. "Sam Steele. Sam Steele."

"Even the bloody parrot knew." Bradley thought about that and then shook his head. "How in the bloody hell is it possible that you're Steele?"

Squawk. "Sam—"

Luke spun. "Shut up, you!"

Carracks stuck his tongue out, then turned his back on them to nibble on his cage. Sam sighed. If only she could turn her back on all this so easily.

"My real name is Samantha Fine, but as that would be a silly name for a pirate, I changed it."

His gaze scanned the room, and as he took it all in, Sam noticed his knuckles got whiter and whiter. Though she saw it every day, she tried to see it from his position. First, the lacy screen she'd bought to ensure she'd always have privacy while changing filled one corner. Second, no filth littered her cabin. She didn't tolerate a filthy ship, and that included her quarters. And of course the bedcovers were neat, except for the wrinkles he'd caused when he'd thrown her down. Though it cost her, she ignored the desire to smooth them. She knew Luke wouldn't appreciate her tidiness just now.

"No, it's not possible," he said. His fevered gaze grabbed hers. "How is it that the fact you're a woman isn't known?"

She sighed. "Every time we take a ship or go into port, a different member of my crew takes the name. That way nobody can tell for certain what Steele looks like." Once again she moved to the table.

"And you remain anonymous?" Understanding softened his words.

"Yes."

"Well, that explains the conflicting stories I've heard about Steele. Once he was fat, the next time gaunt. Some said his hands were all gnarled, making him useless as a captain."

That was Trevor, her cook. She remembered how much it had pleased him that day to be Steele. How he'd preened about, his watery blue eyes more alive than she'd ever seen. She must remember to give him another turn soon.

While Luke's anger seemed under control, Sam pressed the issue. "Now that you know, can we get on with the articles?"

He scowled. "I don't know anything, yet. Why Dervish? What's Steele—" his gaze clouded. "What do *you* want with Dervish?"

So much for his anger being under control. However, her reasons for going after Dervish were her own, and she had no intention of sharing them with Luke Bradley. He knew all he needed to. Her past remained hers, the pain not one to be shared with a pirate, with a man no better than those who had killed her family.

"He stole something of mine," she said sharply.

"And you'd be wanting it back?"

Her spine stiffened as biting memories surfaced. "What he stole cannot be taken back or replaced. It's not treasure I'm after; it's revenge."

Long, slender fingers, a musician's fingers, toyed with

his mustache. "Which explains the name of your ship. Not very original, luv." He crossed his arms over his chest and leaned against the wall. "So am I to assume that because Dervish turned his crew against me and left me for dead in the sea, you thought I'd be game to help you in this little venture of yours?"

"Yes."

"Ah." He turned a chair and straddled it. "Are you not aware that it's been years and I've not taken my own revenge yet? If I haven't done it for myself, why would I do it for you?"

She'd thought of that, of course, though his words scared her. He had to help. She wouldn't accept anything less. She pressed the only advantage she had. "To get his ship. I can see by the light in your eye you're wanting your own ship, Luke."

He turned his head to the small window and the sea that rocked behind it. "Aye, but not his. Besides, it's not just him I'd have to deal with, but his crew as well. I want *a* ship, luv, but any will do."

"Don't be ridiculous." She shoved her chair aside. "You form an attachment to a ship. You've sailed on that ship; surely she means something to you. One is not as good as another."

"Ships, luv, are like women. You always think the one you have underneath you is something special until the next one comes along. Suddenly, it pales in comparison."

"You are vile," she spat.

He shrugged. His indifference didn't help bank the fire within her.

"Can we finish this now?" She took the papers from the table. "The articles will explain everything."

He took them, and she paced while he read. His shallow

breathing echoed in the confines of her cabin. Her own rattled unsteadily in her chest. She couldn't think about the possibility of his refusal. It had been too long already. They needed to find Dervish so it could finally end.

The papers snapped in his hand. "I'll not agree to this."

She smiled at the mortification on his face. "Let me guess. Number five."

" 'No crew member is to get drunk while on board.' No, I won't bloody well agree to that. It's madness."

"You can drink your life away when we go ashore. But on my ship we drink to stay alive, not to get drunk."

He snarled at that.

She waited, her hands wringing, her ears focusing on the slap of waves against the hull and the thud of boots overhead. He was wading through the papers as if they were mud. Finally, when she was near ready to explode, he flicked the agreement onto the round table.

"This doesn't explain your reasons for seeking out Dervish."

"Nor will it," she said firmly.

He leaned back in his chair. "You're not giving me much motivation, luv."

"You read the contract. You'll get a larger share of plunder on my ship than you'll find anywhere else."

His pointed gaze probed hers. "Why is it you take so little? As captain you're entitled to more."

Sam sighed, resigned to the fact that she'd have to answer some of his questions if they were ever going to get on with things.

"I take only what the ship needs for its voyages and a very small sum for me. I'm not here to make a fortune, Luke."

He smirked. "Your selflessness wouldn't seem so distorted if your sole purpose wasn't to find and take a life."

She gnashed her teeth, weary of both him and this conversation.

"That's my business."

"Hmm . . . perhaps for now it is." He propped his boots on the table.

Sam glared at him, wishing with all her might that she didn't need him.

"Well, since I'm already free and you're not likely to risk your pretty ship and your equally pretty neck to take me back, and since I couldn't care less about Dervish or *his* ship, what's in it for me?"

"I already told you. A larger share of plunder."

He crossed his ankles as well as his arms. "Not good enough."

She took the chair across from his, so there was no mistaking her. She leaned in, braced on her forearms. For a few charged seconds they stared, measured.

"This is to be my last voyage as Captain Steele. Once Dervish is taken care of, I'm finished. So"—she leaned back in her chair—"if you don't want his ship, how about taking mine?"

TWO

The ship was quiet. The crew was asleep, some men below in the hold amid barrels of water, rum, and food, and others spread out on deck. Willy, her carpenter, always chose a place underneath the lifeboat. Aidan, the youngest member of her crew, preferred the bow. Their snores ranged from purrs to rumbles and kept Sam company on her watch. There was no wind and the water lapped lazily at the hull, like a kitten with a saucer of milk. A full moon, unobstructed by clouds, cast its reflection on the sea. Samantha watched the yellow ribbons dance on the current.

"Keep starin' like that and it'll put ye to sleep."

Because she'd recognized his steps, having memorized all of the crew's, she turned with a smile on her face.

"You should be asleep, Joe. You'll need your wits about you in the morning."

She accepted the mug he offered her. The coffee was thick as mud but it was wet, so she drank it.

"As will ye. There wasn't much chance to rest this afternoon."

Sam rolled her neck from side to side. Her shoulders were tight and achy, but there wouldn't be any sleep until morning. Once the sun pushed itself above the horizon, she'd fall into her berth.

"We haven't talked all day. How did Luke take the news?"

Joe wasn't only her first mate; he was all that was left of her family. Willy, too, had survived that horrible night, and as much as she appreciated his work and loyalty, she hadn't known him as long and therefore her feelings for him didn't run as deep as they did for Joe.

She grinned. "That I was Steele? Shock at first. Fury was certainly there. But Luke kept it all tightly bound. He's smart, Joe. We'll be wise to remember that."

Joe's ruddy cheeks creased when he smiled. His pale blond hair shone in the moonlight, giving the illusion of a halo.

"Aye, but not half as smart as our Steele." He sipped his coffee. "I saw 'im come from yer cabin. He didn't look pleased."

"Well"—she rubbed her palm on the smooth wood of the tiller—"that's to be expected."

Joe stepped closer, the buttons of his shirt straining to close over his girth. The smell of cigar smoke, a cloak he always wore, was familiar and comforting.

"Ye did it, though. Got yerself Luke Bradley."

She ignored the pride that filled his eyes. Springing Luke from jail to help her kill another man wasn't an action worthy of the fatherly love in Joe's warm gaze. In fact, it made her feel very close to the horses' droppings Luke had stepped in earlier. She sighed and rubbed at the knot at the base of her neck. Soon. It would be over soon. Then maybe she'd be able to do something worthy of Joe's admiration. And her own.

Her free palm closed over her stomach. The nerves that had jumped there all day had abated, but the memory of how they'd clawed at her remained. "I have to say, Joe, I was worried. I don't think I breathed until he'd signed the contract."

The familiar creaking of rigging and lines, the gentle rock of the ship, eased the nerves she felt coming back. Sam drew a breath. The articles were signed. She'd locked them in her table before slipping out of the cabin. Luke had questions. She'd seen them in his stance and in his hesitation to let her pass.

"Are ye sure ye trust him, lass?" Joe straddled a cannon. His coffee steamed under his beard, giving it a ghostly look.

Sam took a last gulp of coffee and set the empty mug aside. "No, but we need him. And I should tell you I've promised him the *Revenge* when it's all done."

The understanding in his eyes was the same she remembered from that dreadful night.

"Not a day goes by, Joe, that I don't remember it all—the noise, the smell of fear and death." She paused. "Being thrown overboard."

His eyes shone and he took his time with his next swallow of coffee. "'Twas the only thing I could think of. Yer father wouldn't have settled for less."

Which was the truth. Joe had been designated her and Alicia's companion when her parents were busy or stayed ashore long past the time their children were tucked in bed. Her father would have wanted her safe. But why, her heavy heart asked again, did it have to be without them?

"I'm just glad you followed me in. And that Willy was still alive. It took so long for Dervish to leave that I was sure everybody would be dead when we went back."

"I'd like to say the rest didn't suffer, lass, but we both know better."

She did. They'd bobbed in the water, listening as the pirates had plundered and raped the *Destiny*. The gleaming wood the whole crew took pride in had lain splintered. The sails had wept where they'd been ripped and shredded. And through it all, over it all, were the screams of the crew as they fought off their enemy. Limbs and dead bodies had rained down around them, slapping the water before sinking into watery graves.

Sam shook it off. "And when it was all done, they cheered like it was a damn party. 'Long live Dervish and the *Devil's Wrath*.' I swore then and there that animal would pay."

Joe swung a thick leg over the cannon and cupped a hand under her chin.

"He will. If it's the last thing I do, I'll help ye see to it. I stayed not only out of respect for yer father. Ye was too young to be on yer own. Yer still all alone, Samantha Margaret, and I'll not be leaving ye until that's changed."

"I'm older now." She attempted a smile, which she was sure looked more like a grimace. "I'm Sam Steele. I can take care of myself." She raised up on her toes to kiss his cheek. "Although I appreciate your being here."

Because the mood was too heavy, she began to hum a little ditty she knew always made him smile. It worked. He leaned against the gunwale.

"Not scared Luke'll turn us against ye?" Joe teased.

She threw him her empty mug, and he caught it in one of his big fists. "You're harder to get rid of than the barnacles that cling to the hull. Willy seems content enough. Aidan and Trevor as well. If we haven't had a mutiny after four years, I don't expect one now."

Joe's voice lowered and all humor escaped him. "Aidan, Trevor, and the others, they'd be dead without ye. They're not goin' to be forgettin' that anytime soon."

She pushed aside his comment. They'd all had to claw their way out of hell. It had taken nearly a year, but she'd gotten out. "Then we'd best concentrate on Luke." Sam looked around the ship. There were shadows of sleeping men, of guns at rest, and of the gently swaying lifeboat, which hung beneath the boom. "Is he sleeping below?"

"He's there, but not sleeping. Got himself propped against the wall, his pistol resting beside him. I'd say he sleeps with one eye open, but then he wouldn't sleep, would he?"

"Joe!" She shook her head.

"Just messin' with ye." He ruffled her hair. "I'll be up at dawn, then ye can get some rest."

He disappeared below, and Sam turned back to the water. She let her thoughts drift along with the sea. Her past was never far out of her mind, but their conversation had brought it to the surface.

Upon rowing back to Port Royal, Sam, Willy, and a wounded Joe had collapsed on the beach. They'd treated Joe's wound as best they could, then slept under the palm trees until dawn. With the sunrise, Sam and Willy had tried to get Joe's wound examined. But they had no money, and nowhere to go. A local man, a plantation owner, had found them. He'd taken them back to his sprawling house, which was surrounded by fertile fields. Joe's wound had been tended; the men had been fed and offered work.

Mr. Grant, the plantation owner, had taken her on as a

worker as well. Though her heart was lost at sea, she would at least have a roof over her head and food in her belly. If only it had been that easy. It wasn't long before the true nature of Mr. Grant was unveiled. He wasn't a kindhearted man out to help three lost souls. He was after slave labor.

The men were tortured and beaten. Food was not a certainty; it was leverage. Anybody who moved a toe out of line, or dared complain of sixteen hours in the baking sun and pelting rain, was left without a meal. And those were the lucky ones.

"Not much of a lookout if you're asleep."

Sam jumped, a terrified scream lodged in her throat. She managed to squelch it before it woke her crew. Her hand clasped over her mouth to keep her heart inside her body. Blast him for catching her so off guard and for making her jump like a fool.

"What in blazes are you doing, creeping up on me like that?"

His pearly teeth shone in the moonlight. "I wasn't creeping. I walked over. It was you who was asleep on duty."

Her spine stiffened. She wiped her wet palms onto her skirt. "I was not asleep!"

"Very well. You were looking with your eyes closed. I can't say I've tried that method, but seeing how it seems to work for you, I think I'll give it a try."

Sam rubbed her hand over her gritty eyes. "Why aren't you asleep?"

"Why aren't you in your cabin, resting properly?" he countered.

"I always take the night watch."

He propped his elbow on a gun and leaned forward.

"How is it you've garnered such a reputation if you sleep during the day?"

"Joe can handle the crew, and he wakes me if he sights another ship."

"Ah."

He said nothing else, but continued to stare at her. His gaze stripped her, left her feeling exposed. She'd learned what power a man could wield over a woman, and Luke was no exception. Although it wasn't violence she saw in his eye, it was equally dangerous. Her conversation with Joe had left her vulnerable, and she decided to ignore the challenge in Luke's eye. She turned to the sea.

Luke chuckled. "So Captain Steele isn't as hard as her name implies."

"What do you want?" she asked wearily, looking over her shoulder.

He lowered his arm, stepped around the cannon. His walk was predatory.

"Why didn't you tell me straight away in the jail you were Steele?"

He touched her, a slender finger circling the back of her hand. The hand that gripped the tiller tighter and tighter until she was choking it. He was testing her, she knew. Well, it would be a cold day in hell before she quivered before a pirate again.

"I couldn't chance you revealing me. And, if you recall, we were in a hurry."

His head dipped as though he would kiss her. She arched away, her body stiffening.

"Step away, Bradley."

"I see where your parrot gets the attitude." His gaze wandered to her chest. "Do you still have your knife handy?"

She did, but her hand was shaking too much to reach for it. Ever since the plantation, she'd managed to stay clear of men. At least in personal matters. Her crew were workers, nothing more. Their loyalty was appreciated, their labor needed. Best of all, they left her alone. Partly because she'd saved their lives, but mostly because Joe had threatened terrible things if they ever laid a hand on her.

Still, she'd never given them any notice on an intimate level. Her first experience being close to a man had left deep, blistering scars. Keeping her emotions cold was the only way she'd managed to survive these last four years on the ship.

Sam braced herself, terrified that Luke had the power to chip away at her resolve.

"As a matter of fact, I do. But I can't help but wonder why you keep pushing me. With a snap of my fingers the crew will dump you in the sea. You do remember what that's like, don't you?"

His expression hardened, though he tried to hide it behind a cocky sneer. "Aye. But then you won't be finding Dervish, will you, luv?"

"So is this the way of it, then? You continue to push me, reminding me I need you, while I contemplate the logic of not heaving you overboard?"

He grinned, a real one if the gleam in his eye was any indication. "That about sums it up."

She turned away before he could see the smile that itched to escape. The man was insufferable. It must be exhaustion that was making her enjoy the bickering between them.

After checking the compass and ensuring they were going in the right direction, Sam looped a rope over the tiller so she could step away for a few minutes without the ship veering off course. The gunwale was smooth beneath her palms as she looked out into the darkness.

Light footsteps followed her to the side.

"You love the *Revenge*. Why would you give it away? Especially to me?"

She kept her gaze locked on the sea, preventing him from seeing the moisture in her eyes at the thought of saying good-bye to her ship. "Because I won't need her anymore. And if I know one thing about you, Luke, it's your love of ships. I know you'll take good care of her."

"And your crew?" he pressed.

The male scent of his skin, windblown and musky, drifted under her nose and made her wonder about things that had previously petrified her. She took a step back.

"It will be up to them if they want to stay under your command. But none of them have ever expressed a desire to captain her. Assuming you're fair, I don't see why they wouldn't stay on board."

"And you'll be going where?"

She glanced over. He had one hand on his hip, and his shirt gaped open revealing a long, lean chest. Her mouth became unusually dry. "That's personal."

He took another step to close the slim distance between them. Before she could move, he'd taken her hand and pressed it to his lips. The action was at odds with the pirate behind it. Although, having heard of Luke's way with women, it shouldn't have surprised her. Nor should it have curled her toes.

"And if I have my way, Samantha, things will be getting much more personal before we're through."

With nothing more than a smile and a good night, he left her. Her hand was warm and tingled where the warmth of his lips and the soft brush of his mustache had touched. The marching rhythm in her chest pounded loudly in her ears. And he'd walked away without even a hitch in his arrogant stride.

"That's Captain Steele to you," she said, though by the time she'd come to her senses and formed the words, he'd slipped beneath the main hatch.

When dawn crept over the horizon, Sam's eyes felt like pools left behind at low tide—full of water with a layer of grit all around. The more she blinked or moved them, the worse they grated. Even the pink and purple slashes on the sky's canvas weren't enough to keep her interested. She was bone-tired and ready to sleep. She'd spent a long night thinking of Luke's kiss. Too much time, she argued with herself.

She heard the shuffle of boots at the same time she smelled freshly cooked eggs and ham. Her exhaustion was forgotten as she turned. Trevor smiled and offered her a plate.

"Trevor, you're a saint. This smells delicious." The eggs were scrambled and fluffy; the ham, a deep pink color.

He'd only had his fiftieth birthday, but the years on Mr. Grant's plantation had taken their toll. Thick creases were carved into his cheeks and at the corners of his eyes. A white scar ran down his right forearm and led to hands that had been smashed until the fingers bent abnormally at the middle knuckle. As a sailor he wasn't very useful. But as a cook, he was priceless.

Trevor ducked his bald head, but not before Sam saw his smile. His pride had taken more of a beating than his hands. She was glad she'd been able to give it a little nudge by hiring him.

"Thanks to your idea of not springing Luke until midday, I was able to go ashore for all sorts of supplies. We should have enough eggs for a few days."

They all but melted on her tongue. And the ham was smoked and flavorful. She passed her empty plate to Trevor.

"You know you don't have to wait on me. I was going to get it myself before heading off to bed."

"It's no trouble, Captain. I was coming up anyway, to check the weather." He took her empty plate and went back to the galley.

As a lie, it was a sorry one, but she let it pass. Trevor had served her breakfast every day since he'd been on board. She made a point of going down to the galley early for the other meals. It wouldn't do for the rest of the crew to see her getting special treatment. There was a rule on the *Revenge* that she lived by. She might have the title of captain, but each member of her crew was valuable. No one was worth more than their fellow man. Or woman.

"Off to bed, are you? Want any company?"

Of all the men to wake up, why did Luke have to be one of the first? She hoped he wouldn't see the frayed ends of her nerves poking through her skin. And she prayed feverishly that he wouldn't realize they were all his doing.

"I prefer to sleep alone." She looked hopefully for signs of Joe or Willy.

"I can take it, you know. I've captained my own share of ships."

"Perhaps, but it's Joe's duty. Not yours."

His gaze hovered over the tiller. His lips flattened for a brief moment. She hadn't meant to hurt him, but now that it was said, she saw the merit in angering him. It kept things at a safer distance.

When he raised his head to hers, there was nothing in his eye to reveal what he was feeling.

"What is my job, exactly? I believe you failed to mention that yesterday."

He'd moved close enough that his shirt rubbed against the arm of her coat. She ignored his deliberate attempt to taunt her. She'd thought of him the whole damn night; that was as much power as she was prepared to give him.

"You can run the bilge pumps."

His lips pursed. "I could. But I won't."

"It may not be the best duty, Luke, but it's vital. If we sink due to taking on water, there'll be no saving you this time."

"You may be more comfortable to have me below and out of sight, but as I've been a captain, I won't work below deck. Get another of your crew to run the pumps."

The last thread of her patience snapped. She was exhausted, and the more time she spent around Luke, the less in control she felt. And where the devil was Joe?

"First, I'll be sleeping, so I don't care where you are. Second, every member of this crew is important, and we all take turns with the pumps. Third, as you so clearly pointed out, you're a *former* captain. On this voyage, *I'm* captain, and as long as you're on *my* ship, you'll be obeying my command."

Luke leaned in close, close enough for Sam to notice the black ring that circled the deep green of his eye. His gaze clutched hers and refused to let go.

"The way I see it, me, you, and Joe should be taking turns at the helm. You didn't disagree with me yesterday when I suggested we go to Tortuga first. I've been there enough to find the damn place with my eye closed."

"You will not be taking the helm," Sam managed between gritted teeth. "And you will *not* be giving me orders."

"If you didn't trust me, why in blazes did you spring me in the first place?"

"Mornin' Capt'n," Joe said cheerfully as he joined Samantha. His voice lost all humor when he turned. "Luke."

"Ah, our first mate. Samantha here was just about to run off to bed. You and me shall captain this ship together while she rests her pretty head."

Sam fumed. How dare he disobey her!

Joe, finally seeming to catch the undercurrents between Sam and Luke, moved closer to her side.

"Is that a fact?" he asked.

Luke's eyebrow arched as he waited for her to choose. Lord, she was too tired for this. It took all her will to keep her head upright. But hadn't he pushed her enough? He'd forced her to reveal she was Steele before she was ready. He had yet to address her as captain. And he touched her every chance he found.

She'd had enough. It was time to get some control back.

"Luke is to man the bilge pumps. Wake me when we get to Tortuga."

She brushed past them both, ignoring Luke's mutinous stare. She felt his anger latch onto her coattails, trying to drag her back for another argument. Deliberately keeping her head held high, she grabbed the hatch, careful not to rip it from its hinges the way she wanted to. Once in her cabin she undressed, muttering the whole time.

"Damn Luke. Damn his arrogance."

Squawk. "Damn Luke. Damn Luke."

There. Even Carracks had him figured.

Sam fluffed her pillow, crawled into bed, and fell into a restless sleep.

Oliver Grant stepped into the dank shed that stood in the middle of the large-leafed green crop that had propelled

him from small merchant to respected—and wealthy—
owner of one of Port Royal's largest plantations. The small
structure was a haphazard construction of rotten boards
with a leaky roof. But it wasn't designed for comfort. Its
placement, if not its sturdiness, amid the fertile fields where
his slaves worked was ideal.

Taking a white linen handkerchief from the breast pocket
of his suit, he dabbed at the moisture on his forehead. Thick
slabs of sunlight angled inside from every direction and
crossed the dirt floor in a battle of golden swords.

Nathaniel, his overseer, stepped forward. He was a brute
of a man whose head reached nearly to the roof of the shed.
His hands were the size of dinner plates and could crush hu-
man bones in seconds. It was why Oliver had hired him. He
dragged alongside him an average-sized black man. Blood
oozed from cuts along the slave's arms and bare legs. He
wore nothing but a loin cloth.

"Sir. He was found hiding in a small village on the
other side of the island." Nathaniel cupped the man's jaw
and jutted it upward.

Oliver didn't care to know the names of his slaves, but
he knew faces. The one that looked at him now, with chocolate eyes surrounded by a rainbow of bruises, was definitely
one of his. Or had been until four years ago.

The smell within the closed walls was a mix of sweat,
blood, and fear. Oliver didn't mind the last, but the first two
gave him a headache.

"Where's my ship?" he demanded.

"I—I don't know, sur."

Oliver's gaze roamed the walls around him where whips,
chains, and knives hung in glory. A few were stained with
blood, as a reminder to those who were brought in. Lying,
disrespect, and stealing were not tolerated on his planta-

tion. The slave's eyes widened fearfully—large bulging white orbs.

"You and thirty men escaped here four years ago. You're the twenty-fifth man I've located. My ship, however, is still at large, as are five of my slaves."

The man shook his head. His voice quaked as he pleaded. "I didn't see no ship. I ran, sur."

Oliver had already learned from those who'd been recaptured that a large white man had chopped away the locks with an axe in a effort to free them. Some had fled blindly in the night, others had stayed behind in fear. Nobody had seen which direction that man went, or who he was with. But Oliver knew. Only a handful of white men were in his employ, and one of them had been Samantha's friend. Both were still unlocated. Obviously they were together, but where?

Oliver rubbed at his left arm, where tingles ran from his shoulder to his fingers. He rotated it to get the feeling back and stepped to the wall. The slave begged for mercy behind him. Enjoying the thickening smell of fear, Oliver trailed his hand over a scythe, and then an axe that had been sharpened to a bright silver. His fingers closed over a pick brought from the ice house. Lifting it from the wall, Oliver turned and pressed it against the man's throat. The slave squealed like a wild boar.

"Four men and a woman are missing, as is my ship. Where are they?"

Sweat poured like water from the top of the slave's head. He trembled and wept. With the pick at his throat he could do no more than whisper and beg, plead that he knew nothing, that he hadn't seen anything.

It was the same song and dance he'd heard from the others. Furious to be no closer, Oliver plunged the pick into the man's throat, then stepped away before he could be dirtied by blood. There was a gurgle as the man attempted to breathe. His eyes rolled back. Nathaniel let go and the man slumped to the floor, dead.

"Nathaniel, I expect the search for the remaining five to continue."

"Yes, sir."

Oliver glanced at the dead slave, then at his overseer. "I will be most displeased if we cannot locate them. Most displeased."

Nathaniel nodded. "Yes, sir." Then, knowing his place, he stepped back into the shadows.

Sighing, Oliver tugged his vest down, checked his tie, and ran smooth hands down the front of his suit. Then, whistling, he opened the door.

Hands went back to work and heads lowered as he stepped from the shed. He kept to the small dirt path that cut between the healthy growing plants of his crop. Oh, he'd find her yet, he vowed again. No whore was going to leave him for dead and get away with it. Samantha had cost him time, energy, and far too much money. He glanced back at the shed. Waste, he thought with a click of his tongue. She'd pay for that, too.

Three

The door creaked open. Sam shot up in bed.

"Don't come near me," she threatened. "I've got a weapon."

He laughed. The sound was as evil as his heart. "Silly girl." He closed the door behind him. The lock clicked loudly into place.

Cold sweat ran down Sam's back. She knew why he was here. She began to shake.

"Get away from me!" She pressed herself into the corner of the bed as the shadow of hell stepped closer. His steps made no noise; he'd already taken off his boots.

"Be a good girl"—he unfastened his pants—"and this won't take but a moment."

They'd been through this once before. Sam had sworn then that it wouldn't happen again, even if she had to kill him. The hammer she'd stolen weeks ago was hidden in the folds of her nightdress. She'd slept with it every night since he'd last been there. Weapon aimed high over her head, she flew out of bed.

Her breath stuck in her throat. The hammer was slick in her palm. Fear blurred everything as she lunged toward her attacker. One good blow, that would be enough. Then she could run away. But somehow the hammer vanished. One second she was ready to kill her attacker, and the next the weapon had dissipated like fog. Her fingers were use-lessly empty. Then he had her by the arms, his fingers dig-ging into her flesh.

"No," she whimpered. Not again.

"Samantha! Samantha!" He shook her.

She thrashed against him, desperate to escape. There were no tears. They were frozen inside.

"Get away from me. I'll kill you. I swear I will."

Though her fists shot out, she hadn't the satisfaction of hearing them connect with flesh.

"I don't doubt it, but not today."

It was the voice that seeped through her nightmare and chased the evil away. A deep voice that ran smooth as honey.

Squawk. "Hands off. Hands off."

Her head snapped back, and she opened her eyes. Luke Bradley stared back at her. He still held her arms, but his grip had softened. She blinked, and the last traces of the night-mare slithered away. Mr. Grant was gone. He was really gone. She took a shaky breath, trying to regain a normal rhythm.

"Go away," she pleaded. It would only be seconds, she knew, until the shudders would take her. She'd had enough of the nightmares over the years to know the order of things. First the dream and waking bathed in sweat. Then the shud-ders that racked her body. Finally the exhaustion and weakness. He'd already seen the beginning. She'd do anything to prevent him from seeing the end. She shoved away, embarrassed at how limp her arms were.

"Not until you tell me what the hell that was about."

"Where's Joe? How did you get down here?"

"I waited until his attention was diverted. Now what's going on?"

"It's none of your concern," she managed before the tremors began. Then there was no stopping them. She felt as though she was covered in ice. Her teeth rattled along with her bones. Luke's eye widened in surprise and Sam lowered her head, hating the weakness she was incapable of halting. So much for taking back any control.

The mattress shifted under his weight, and before she could look up, he'd wrapped her in his arms and pulled her close. He smelled of wind and sea. His chest was smooth under her cheek, the chains around his neck cool compared to the heat of his skin. Because it was too easy to lean in, to let him share the burden, to let anyone share the burden, she pushed herself away.

He was stronger and his grip was firm. "Just take a bloody minute, will you?" he growled, and squeezed her back against his chest.

Any protest was muffled against him. Then, as the shudders slowly ebbed, his warmth seeped into her cold skin. Every muscle in her body melted. It was like sinking into a bed of cotton. She closed her eyes and forgot, for one precious moment, that she was in the arms of a pirate.

Luke's hands were unsteady as he held her against him. He'd come down here to watch her sleep for a few minutes before waking her, so that he could see her without all the walls and barriers she hid behind. But he'd barely pulled up a chair to sit when she'd begun to thrash and cry out. The depth of pain and fear had shocked him. So had the urgent need to shelter her from it.

Women, up till now, had been either a source of pleasure or a sliver that got under his skin and irritated the daylights out of him. Never had one roused the torrent of feeling he'd experienced as she clung to him. He felt helpless, useless. Shaken.

He held her while she was still too weak from her dream to really put up a fight. Absently, he stroked her spine. The damp material that clung to her back made his jaw clench in anger. He had a fair idea what had caused the nightmare, and the truth of it sickened him. His hands curled into fists as the picture of Samantha suffering such a fate formed before his eyes. He pulled her a little closer.

A few minutes later her breathing slowed and her slender body sagged against his. Her smell was pure, and it made him want things he had no business wanting. A strumpet was one thing. Samantha Steele was another ocean altogether. She might be a pirate, but as far as he could tell, it was only work to her. It wasn't in her soul, the way it was in his. He'd heard regret in her voice when she'd said Steele was a good pirate. Wasn't she repulsed by the idea that he himself was one?

He knew the moment her sanity returned. Her perfect little body went rigid. Her voice cracked like a whip.

"What are you doing here?" She pushed Luke away and pulled the bedcovers to her chin. Ribbons of curls framed an angry face.

The knot in his stomach loosened as he took the chair he'd set beside her bed. The good captain was back. "I've come to wake you, fair lady."

"You're not welcome in my cabin. Get out."

"Now that, luv, is not the way to make friends." He crossed his arms over the gold chains. The color hadn't returned to her cheeks, and even the yellow rays coming through the small window didn't take away her pallor. Her knuckles, white as a virgin's thighs, clutched the covers as though her life depended on it.

"Besides," he added, "you wanted me here just fine a few minutes ago."

The bedcovers fell away in her agitation. She rushed out of her berth. Her window wasn't large, but it was well placed. As Luke stood behind her, the midafternoon sunlight flooded into the room and traced her form nicely. The curves beneath the white cotton gown left him breathless. A dip at her waist, a gentle rounding over the hips. Luke's gaze feasted while his body heated. Though she'd revealed more in the gown she'd worn yesterday, there was something in the simpleness of her nightdress that sparked his blood. It shocked him just how much he wanted to drag her back into her berth, to lose himself in those curves.

"I was dreaming, and you took advantage!"

The chair scraped the floor. Visions of them together blinded him and made walking uncomfortable. "Luv, you haven't seen me take advantage. Yet."

She froze in place. "Try it, and you'll be marooned on the most barren island we can find. If I don't kill you first."

"That's the second time you've threatened me."

He moved close enough to see her pulse leap in that inviting little curve at the base of her throat. She might be Steele on the outside, but he was getting another picture of what lay beneath. Fire. Lots of it. And damned if he wasn't willing and ready to get burned.

Squawk. "Step away. Step away."

Gold sparks flew from her eyes. "If you don't like it, leave. This is, after all, my cabin."

"That's something else we need to discuss."

She grabbed a pale blue bedcover and pulled it against her chest. "What?"

"I don't like sleeping with your crew. And since I'm half in command of this journey, I should be allowed half the cabin."

Her mouth gaped open. He was suddenly very glad the idea had come to him.

"You are not in command, Luke. You're simply supplying the bearings."

Squawk. "Damn Luke. Damn Luke."

Samantha turned the same red as her parrot's head. Luke resumed his chair and propped his boots on the berth. The fact that the parrot knew his name put some wind in his sails. It meant she was thinking of him. And talking about him.

"You lied to me, got me here under false pretenses. The least you can do is share your cabin."

He toyed with his mustache, a grin on his lips while he watched every emotion, from disbelief to outrage, flit across her face. While she stewed, he enjoyed the cooler temperature of her cabin. He chuckled. It must be a sin, he figured, to be having this much fun.

"Besides, your parrot likes me."

Suddenly she stilled and smiled. It was a serene smile. And he didn't trust it.

"All right. You may share the cabin."

"You're smiling; that's not good. What's the catch?"

"I don't sleep at night. That's when you may have it. During the day, you're not allowed here."

Damn! He hadn't thought of that. He stood up again, not ready to accept defeat. "Fine. But one night, Samantha, you will be here. With me."

Her chin shot up. "Not on your life."

The fear from the nightmare still lurked in her eyes. But he also saw something else. A wise man, however, knew when to play his cards.

"Why? Seems to me we have a lot in common."

She threw the cover at him. "Get out! You're nothing like me, and it's daylight. It's my cabin now."

His gaze wandered over her one more time. She ducked behind the screen.

"You'll want to be getting dressed, Samantha."

"Captain Steele, for the last time," she growled from behind the screen.

Squawk. "Sam Steele. Sam Steele."

"Carracks!" she ordered.

The bird quieted and dipped his head into his feathers to scratch.

"By the looks of the sun, I couldn't have been asleep more than a few hours. Are we there already?"

The surrender in her voice surprised him. She'd agreed to use Tortuga as a starting point for Dervish's trail. Why, then, did she sound as though she'd rather wade into shark-infested waters?

"Yes, luv. We're coming up on Tortuga."

The mood, when Sam climbed on deck, was boisterous. Men sang raucous songs about warm rum and hot women, stamping their feet or clapping to the fast-paced rhythm. Sam knew, from past experience, that it was what they'd be doing until dawn the next day. It was always with a heavy heart that she chose to anchor in Tortuga. But as much as she despised it, the crew needed the break from the monotony at sea. And their spirits, as well as their pockets, were always much lighter after a night on the island.

Since they'd been there less than four weeks ago, Sam had hoped not to see it again anytime soon. A good day was when she could put the blasted place to her rudder. But there it was. Named for its shape, which resembled a large sea turtle, Tortuga was anything but serene and innocent. The island was a festering pit of debauchery.

Though no more than twenty miles long and four miles wide, what it lacked in size it more than made up for in vigor. And that was what Sam hated. It was also the reason she was about to take the wind out of a young boy's sails. Again.

Aidan had worked under Mr. Grant, and he'd been the first Sam had sworn to save. There'd been no taking away the brutal slash marks on his eight-year-old back, but she'd vowed he wouldn't accumulate any more. His face, so brave despite the pain she'd witnessed him endure, reminded her each day that she'd done the right thing by becoming Steele. She wasn't about to ruin him all over again by sending him onto Tortuga. Though he'd never begged, or even asked, she knew he wanted to go ashore. To be part of the men. Longing was etched in his every feature as he leaned over the gunwale.

His cheeks were pink, partly from the Caribbean sun but mostly from the anticipation of going ashore. His hands, growing with approaching manhood, held fast to the ropes. Hair the color of straw and just as matted clung to his head. She was certain he'd overheard the men recounting their stories, no doubt creating longer and more colorful tales with each telling. It was no surprise he'd want to see it for himself. At twelve, he was bound to be curious.

The lines creaked as the lifeboat was lowered into the blue-green water. A few blue fish fluttered beneath the surface and disappeared under the *Revenge*. The breeze was soft and carried with it the smell of roasted pig. Her mouth watered. There was *one* good thing about Tortuga.

"Ready to go ashore, Captain." Willy said.

Willy was wiry, with a beard that must have weighed nearly as much as he did. His arms weren't much bigger than hers, but she'd seen him lift heavy beams and barrels, and knew his stature was deceiving. One of his front teeth had rotted away, and he often spit through the gap where it had been. Nevertheless, he kept the sails in order, the masts upright, and the ship afloat.

The light in the crew's eyes had little to do with the sun they were facing. Gone were the drab clothes they normally wore. In their place were brightly colored sashes, long coats that were far too warm to wear on such a day, and fancy hats with a flock of multicolored feathers protruding from around the rims.

"They make a lovely sight, don't they?" Luke asked from behind her.

The scene in her cabin sprang to mind, and she bit down on the wave of embarrassment. Since she couldn't change what had happened, she would pretend it meant nothing.

She turned. He hadn't changed a stitch. The sight of him, with his pistols tucked into his sash, and that insufferable grin on those full lips, left her feeling restless and out of sorts. It was the island, she concluded. It always affected her this way. If a part of her brain screamed she was a bloody liar, she ignored it.

"They do at that." She forced herself to smile. "Gentlemen, you may go."

They cheered and fought as to who would go first. It

would take two trips to get everyone ashore. Those who'd pushed and shoved their way into the boat shouted insults at those left to wait. Among them was Aidan.

Sam sighed. She was doing this for the boy's own good. Even if he'd never see it that way.

"Aidan?"

He turned, the look of wanting still ripe in his eyes even if his voice was heavy with disappointment.

"I'm to stay on board, Captain?"

The "again" was left unspoken. It was seen, however, in the droop of his narrow shoulders. She'd never explained to Aidan her reasons for keeping him away from the men. He assumed it was because she considered him too young. That was only part of it, and she didn't know how to tell him the rest. It was cowardly, but she'd always found excuses not to talk about it. And now, with Luke hovering behind her, she latched on to another way out.

"Actually, I won't be staying on board this time, Aidan, and I need you to man the *Revenge* for me. Can you do that?"

Despair turned to hope in a heartbeat. His brown eyes sparked like flint, assuaging the guilt that was brewing in her stomach.

"By myself?" he asked.

The boy was all but dancing in his worn boots. His hair was wild and in need of a brush, his teeth were desperate for a scrubbing, but he looked like she'd handed him the moon.

"Well, Trevor wasn't keen on a trip and he'll be below, but you'll have full rein on deck."

"Oh, right," he muttered.

"I'm trusting you to take care of my ship for me," she said.

He nodded, kicked the gunwale, and turned away.

The lifeboat returned, and Sam's attention shifted to the remaining crew who were practically leaping overboard to get in. When only she and Luke were left to board, she moved toward the ladder. In his usual lazy manner, he ignored the curses of the crew yelling for him to hurry, and stepped in front of her.

"What's the real reason you're coming with me? Tortuga doesn't seem as though it would agree with you. Besides, I hardly need a keeper the way the lad does." He gestured to Aidan. "I'm capable of finding Dervish's destination without you."

"And leave you to your own devices? I'm not that foolhardy. You're likely to vanish."

"Hurry up! We don't have all bloody day!" Willy called from the water.

"You're forgetting something," Luke said, creeping closer to her side.

"And what might that be?"

"If I leave now, I'll lose the chance to own this ship." His lips curled into a grin. "Not to mention I'd miss the opportunity to seduce you."

Sam glared. "Watch your step, Luke. I can always change my mind and shoot you."

He laughed, then stopped her heart when he leaned in and his breath caressed the sensitive area behind her ear.

"I look forward to you trying," he said, and climbed down the ladder.

Muttering very inventive curses, Sam followed.

"Yer sure about this? I can go with ye, as we've done before," Joe said to Samantha once they were on the beach.

Behind him the rest of the crew raced through the white

sand. Sprays of it shot up in their haste. Their singing floated along with the campfire smoke.

"I'm sure. Besides, we can't all be hovering around Luke or we won't learn anything."

Joe cast Luke a warning look and moved down the beach, his boots sinking in the pearly sand.

"So what's the rest of this plan of yours?" Luke asked, toying with a piece of driftwood he'd picked up.

"I plan on staying close to you, Luke."

He stepped near enough to touch, but didn't. The wind gently tugged her hair and swept it across her shoulders. His fingers quivered to reach out, to feel the silkiness slip between them.

"As my woman?" he asked, letting his voice caress her the way he wished his hands could.

Her hesitation wasn't long, but it was enough to encourage him.

"As your shadow," she corrected. "I want to make sure you hold up your end of the bargain."

"Ah. Well, as you've told me, you've tried this direction before and weren't able to gather any useful information. What makes you think they'll tell me with you lingering about? You may not realize it, but you've a face no man with blood in his veins could possibly forget. Not to mention your—"

She narrowed her eyes. "It's not the same dress, Luke. I'm wearing my hair differently. Last time I had on a large hat and spoke with an Irish accent."

He couldn't resist her. Her mind worked in the same way as his. How could he not be drawn to that? His boots shuffled in the sand and he brought his toes to hers.

"Tell me, Samantha, does anyone ever get to see the real you?"

"No."

Lord, he wanted to touch her. Her skin glowed a soft bronze color; her hair was unbound and grazed the delectable swell of her breasts. The breath that whispered against his face was uneven and seductive. He leaned in.

"I will," he said, a whisper away from her lips. "I'll see all of you, have all of you." He hovered, though it cost him. He wanted to sink into her, to taste and devour. But he'd learned enough about Samantha to hold back. If he forced her, he'd be no different from the man in her nightmare. Still, it was a bittersweet pleasure to be so close, to feel her quick breaths on his lips, to smell the freshness of her skin.

She shivered when he pulled back. His vanity soared.

"Disappointed?" he asked.

Her face turned the color of the sinking sun. "Not on your life," she answered.

"I told you before, we'll be getting personal. Before this little venture is over, you won't only be asking for my touch, you'll be begging."

He marched away, lust fogging his brain. Sand pulled at his boots but didn't slow him down. He'd let himself get caught up in her. Now he had but a few seconds to clear his head before she caught up. A few seconds to figure out his strategy. For as much as Samantha thought this little jaunt was about finding Dervish and getting revenge, it was about so much more to Luke. The key remained keeping Samantha unaware of just what that was.

Oliver never came to his own beach, to this far section of his land where the crystalline waters folded into a small bay, because it reminded him of all that had been stolen from him.

He shouldn't have come. Truthfully, he had no idea why he had. Except that the last few times Nathaniel had come back with another of the treacherous slaves, he'd never been left with such an unsettled feeling afterward. The *Jewel of the Sea* was close. Dammit, he couldn't explain how he knew, he just felt its nearness.

The tiny bay was calm and empty. His ship. He could envision her frolicking in the warm surf, waiting for him to take her to sea. Lord, he'd missed her. And he'd have her, he vowed. The *Jewel* and the whore. He'd take Samantha at least once before he finished with her. The need for revenge clawed through him, a hungry beast starving for blood.

The pain came fast and savage, and clamped around his heart. He gasped, staggered. With a shaking hand, he gripped one of the posts that anchored the pier. Leaning heavily against it, he concentrated on regulating his breathing. In and out, nice and steady, just like the tide.

The pain lasted longer this time, and his face was wet with perspiration before his heart was able to function without agony. He forced himself to calm down. He hadn't spent a week unconscious and months learning to walk and talk again only to die now. That had been years ago, four to be exact. But he remembered it like yesterday. And it still had the power to infuriate him.

In the distance a whip cracked, followed immediately by an ear-splitting scream. Oliver smiled. That should teach the man, whoever he was, to adhere to the rules of his plantation.

Feeling no remorse for the cries that continued with ten consecutive strokes of the whip, Oliver walked to the end of his pier and gazed out at the water.

The sea was a sight. Blue-green water, so clear he could

see to the rocks below, filled his bay and spread out into the Caribbean. Shards of light bounced and carried on the gentle undulations. It was mesmerizing and, as long as he didn't think of his ship, soothing.

However it *was* his ship he thought about. Those thoughts had led him here. He'd fallen in love with the *Jewel of the Sea* the moment he'd set eyes on her. Except for his wife, Justine, nothing had lodged in his heart as firmly as she had.

He heard the labored breathing at the same instant he heard footsteps rushing toward him. Looking over his shoulder, he saw his lawyer. Curious as to what vital information Isaac had to impart in such haste, Oliver turned.

"Isaac, what brings you by in such a state?"

The attorney leaned over, arms banded around a waist as thin as a sugar cane. It took a few minutes, minutes Oliver figured he was very generous to extend, before Isaac had enough breath to speak without wheezing.

"Sir, pray forgive my intrusion. I came as quick as I could. I meant to come sooner, but was fully engaged in a legal matter and could not pry myself away. And then it was so late, and I didn't wish to disturb you."

Oliver rolled his eyes. "Yes, yes. As you're here now, tell me what urgency has propelled you."

"It's the *Jewel*, sir. I believe she was in port yesterday."

Oliver's breath caught in his chest. Was that why he'd felt her presence so keenly? Hope seeped into cracks he'd thought long sealed.

"Are you certain?"

Isaac nodded his head, and two of the curls left on his otherwise bald scalp waved from side to side. "Fairly, sir. She was painted blue and was too far away to see her name clearly. But, sir," he said and squeezed Oliver's arm, "I'd stake my life it was her."

"Did you see anything else? Anything a'tall?"

"No, sir. She was sailing away when I happened to look out my window and saw her."

"What direction was she sailing?"

"East by northeast sir."

Oliver turned back to the sea. She *was* here. It was the first time there had been any sign of her. He felt it. He knew it was her. Now all he had to do was round up a crew and—

"There's more, sir. That pirate, Luke Bradley?"

Oliver frowned. "Yes?"

"Well, sir, seems he was sprung from jail. Yesterday, sir."

"Do you know the time?"

"No sir, but I'm sure the governor would."

Yes, his friend Governor Madison. The same governor who, upon occasion, could be bribed to overlook certain missteps. Was it a coincidence his ship was sighted on the same day a notorious pirate escaped the gallows? Perhaps, but Oliver didn't believe in chance. He trusted facts.

Absently he rubbed at the scar on his head. Thirty sutures it had taken to close the wound. The doctor had said he'd been lucky, though he hadn't felt it at the time.

Now, as the water curled against the supports of the pier, the lapping sound a soothing embrace, he finally felt lucky. Very lucky.

He didn't know who was captaining his ship, and he didn't care. But some of his men were on that ship. Perhaps through them he could finally find Samantha. Regardless, he'd at least have the *Jewel* back. Once he had her in his possession, it would be only a matter of time until he located Samantha as well.

Four

A fog hovered over Tortuga. And though it equaled walking through a lacy veil of spider webs, its smell wasn't unpleasant. The aroma of slow-roasted meat wafted from kitchens where wild oxen and boars were being smoked. Torches of candlewood, Tortuga's main lumber crop, burned brightly in doorways and illuminated the narrow streets. Mixed with it all was the acrid smell of tobacco, the most profitable harvest of the island. It was little wonder the people Tortuga attracted were so diverse.

Pirates, buccaneers, whores, and farmers frequented the heart of the island. A woman with painted lips, her skirts raised to mid-thigh, squealed as she ran past them. She stopped and allowed her swaggering companion to catch up. The chase, to Sam's wonder, appeared to be part of the excitement. If she ever had the misfortune of such filth pursuing her, she'd find the closest hole and hide. She threw a glance at Luke's smiling face. Or she'd find something sharp to send the scoundrel back where he belonged.

Horses plodded along, ridden by men too drunk to hold the reins and likely too blurry-eyed to see where they were headed. Nobody walked, they staggered. And belched. And cussed.

She stepped to Luke's side, and her heart stuttered when he flashed her a grin. The heat from their moment on the beach was still there. It radiated between them like sunlight off sand.

Captain Steele could resist Luke. She wondered, desperately, if Samantha could do the same.

His gaze was embracing the sights before him. The cocky grin he'd given her was replaced with a genuine curve of his mouth. He breathed deep and sighed.

"God, I missed this place," he said.

While Luke headed in the direction of a certain tavern, he noticed Samantha kept her eyes to the cobblestones and stayed clear of the filth that littered the streets.

She stepped over a small puddle filled with little green chunks and pressed a hand to her throat.

"Now, see, Samantha. You really need to find pleasure in the little things."

"Little things?" She dodged a hurtling bottle, which crashed behind her. "I'd hate to know what you consider a big thing."

Luke snickered. "Well, as it happens . . ."

Samantha held up her hand and shook her head. "Never mind."

"I can't be that bad. It was you, after all, who came hunting for me."

"A means to an end, Luke. Nothing more."

"So you say."

Into the meaty part of town now, they were jostled and shoved. Sweaty men, rank with rum and filth, crashed into them. Luke simply shoved them back. Some, he noticed as he kept going, were lucky and had their fall broken by another hapless drunk; others fell and stayed down when their thick skulls struck the cobblestones. Samantha simply moved behind him and used him as a shield.

"Do you have a particular place in mind?"

He stopped and faced her. A flush rode under her skin. Bronze hair spilled over her shoulders. Gold teased her eyes. Her dress sailed low while her breasts rode high and firm. They made him think of creamy waves. And yet she was strung tighter than a corset. Her arms were rigid at her side, her chin angled high while her mouth was pinched with distaste. She didn't trust him, and it should have angered the hell out of him. But damned if it didn't make him grin.

"As a matter of fact, luv, I do. But before we go any farther, do you plan on smiling anytime soon, or are you going to scowl the whole time?"

The attempt was bitterly lacking and stretched pale skin over fine features.

"That's a girl," he said.

"Let's just get this over with," she muttered, and gave him a shove.

Despite the fact that Dervish's crew had left him for dead, Luke did have friends among his former comrades. He knew Samantha wouldn't believe that. She wouldn't take to any kind thoughts aimed his way. Still, the fact remained that there were a handful of people he could trust when needed, and it was one of those he turned to now.

"Luke! Saints in heaven, I thought you was dead."

Luke grinned at the greeting. "For a moment I was, but then she asked me to move, as I was getting heavy and she couldn't breathe."

His friend choked up rum, then swallowed it again. His bulging gray eyes watered as he fought to breathe normally.

"Don't be doing that when I'm drinking, man. I've got more mayhem to see to before they point my arse skyward."

"Skyward?"

"Ever know me to be ordinary, Luke? I plan on getting meself buried cheeks up."

Captain, a name he'd given himself, was a bear of a man. His silver hair was grizzled and stuck out every which way. It would take three of Samantha to circle his girth. Legs resembling sturdy logs moved quickly, and before Luke knew it, his hand was crushed within a fist that easily doubled his.

Throbbing fingers aside, Luke was pleased to have found his old friend. It had taken five deliberate passes before going into Doubloons. Grinning, he acknowledged he'd done that for Samantha's benefit. He'd savored her discomfort, her grumbling and cursing as she'd traipsed behind him. Doubloons was Captain's preferred place, and if he was to be found, it was going to be there.

"So, Luke," Captain said, slapping him on the back. "Last I heard, they had you locked away in Port Royal. What scalawag rescued you this time?"

Since he had no intention of telling Captain he'd been rescued by an agitated, vengeful woman, Luke did what he did best. He lied.

"I dug my way out."

Captain raised a woolly eyebrow.

"With the heel of my boot," Luke added, saying the first thing that came to mind. He was relying on his friend's drunkenness to keep him from questioning the probabilities of such an action.

"Luke!" Captain roared. "That's bloody brilliant! Always knew nothing could keep you behind bars."

Luke glanced over his shoulder to the door and exhaled his relief. Samantha was obeying his order to wait five minutes before following him in. He had some time.

"Listen, Captain, I need your help."

He steered his friend to a small table. Thick candles with wax tears running down the sides stood on a small silver plate. They flickered with the breeze his and Captain's movements made.

"Have you seen Dervish lately? Do you know where he's headed?"

"I was wonderin' when you was going to pick up that loose end. It's been years, Luke."

And if it hadn't been for Samantha, it never would have happened.

Captain finished his rum and wiped the trickle that slipped from the corner of his mouth. Over the din of music, bellows, and arguments that echoed within the four wooden walls, Captain leaned conspiratorially over the table.

"He was here not three days ago," he whispered.

When loud whistles and crude offers carried from the tables near the door, Luke knew his time had run out. He needed to get what he was after.

"Where is he headed?" Luke asked.

"Well, I think . . ." Captain's attention turned to the commotion Samantha's entrance had created.

"Captain"—Luke moved his head to block his view—
"about Dervish . . ."

"Yeah," Captain continued, "his ship's slowing down,
Luke. He'll have to careen soon. Might be your chance to
get even."

Luke's gaze narrowed. That was perfect. It would be far
easier to deal with Dervish when his ship was stopped for
repairs and most vulnerable. He played with his mustache,
rubbing the coarse whiskers as he thought out a plan.

"Mother of God, Luke. Take a look at that."

Captain shoved Luke's arm with a meaty, scarred fist
and succeeded in tipping half of Luke's rum onto the tee-
tering table. Luke could already hear the whistles, the
crude calls aimed Samantha's way, and his stomach pitched.
He had to hurry Captain along before things got too far out
of control. What had she been thinking, dressed like that
in a place like this?

It took three firm shakes of Captain's arm to draw his
attention back. When his friend's ravenous gaze turned
back to him, Luke's world tilted and left him skidding.
Captain looked at Samantha the way he would any harlot.
Mutiny filled Luke's heart and burned a jealous trail he felt
down to his fingers. They formed a fist before he'd realized
it. Jealousy was new to him and not the least bit pleasant.

"I tell you, Luke, I get teary just looking at her, and I'm
not discussing me eyes, if you know what I mean."

Twisting in his chair, Luke looked toward Samantha.
That damn red dress rode low, exposing far too much bo-
som. Her wavy hair shone in the candlelight. It was the
kind of hair a man dreamed of being cloaked in. Oval eyes
framed with long lashes took everything in. Lips meant for
kissing curved into a bright smile and put every man in
heat.

What the hell was the matter with them? She may have looked like a strumpet, but any man worth his salt should see she didn't belong there. It was in her stiff limbs, her forced smile. The way her eyes darted about the room. He bared his teeth when one of the locals grabbed her arm and dragged her to an empty chair.

"See what I mean, Luke? She's a beauty, ain't she?"

Words formed but died on Luke's tongue. The man who'd pulled Samantha into a seat had placed another next to it and was sitting too damn close to her. The other foul men around the table were laughing and drinking. And none of their gazes left her chest. The fact that only a few days ago he'd have done the same thing didn't make him any happier.

A sound kick landed on Luke's calf and had him seeing stars.

"What?" he turned his attention back to Captain.

"Thought we'd finish our discussion. About Dervish," he prompted.

Right. Luke rubbed at his face, disgusted he'd forgotten his goal. She'd insisted on following, hadn't she? She could bloody well take care of herself.

"Where is he headed?" Luke asked, finishing his drink. The rum burned, but not as hot as his temper, when he turned just long enough to see a buccaneer sling an arm over Samantha's shoulder. She smiled, an unspoken invitation he'd never have believed could come from her. He saw black.

"Well, I'll tell ya. Seems—"

Samantha's scream shot Luke to his feet. He spun around. She was being pulled into the middle of the room where a few swaying couples were practically clawing at each other under the pretense of dancing.

"Order me another rum," he said to Captain. "I'll be right back."

He didn't think, didn't take the time to weigh the wisdom of his actions. It was going against everything he'd planned. He was supposed to get word of Dervish, then take Samantha back to the *Revenge* with as little incident as possible. But just now, drawing attention to himself was the last thing Luke was worried about.

He cut a path through the din, his gaze fixed on her back. As Luke approached, the drunken pirate turned them in a circle. Samantha's eyes narrowed when she saw Luke stomping toward her. He nearly reached out and strangled her when she fastened her fake smile into place.

"Buy a lady a drink?" she asked.

"Get out," he growled. "You're ruining everything."

"Hey, get your own wench," the man complained when Luke clasped Samantha's wrist in his hand.

Luke could have shot him dead. Hell, he would have, if Samantha hadn't smiled at her dance partner before stepping away from the vermin. She moved closer to Luke. Only the fire burning in her eyes gave away her true feelings.

"I'll not leave. God knows what you'll do if I'm not here to keep an eye on you. Besides, *you're* the one who's forgetting the agreement."

Because she was right, he growled, "You're distracting. How am I supposed to find out anything if they're too busy gaping at you?"

"Really?" She damn near glowed. "Well, that's the nicest thing you've said to me yet."

Blood pounded in his ears. "Do you want Dervish or not?"

"Luke," Captain said as he joined them.

To her credit, Samantha didn't cower when the giant's shadow all but consumed her.

"Are you looking for Dervish, too?" Captain asked.

Samantha smiled, and it infuriated Luke that this smile wasn't nearly as forced as the one she'd given him moments before.

"Actually, I am."

Captain beamed. "Well, so's Luke here. Did you know that it was thanks to Dervish poor Luke's only got one eye?"

Samantha turned to Luke, angled her head, and peered at him from under raised brows.

"No, actually. I didn't know."

"Captain, this one's mine," Luke said. He slipped an arm around her small waist and tugged her roughly against his side.

"Bloody hell, Luke. I saw her first."

The men around the table beside them groaned and grumbled, but were wise enough not to interfere with Captain.

"You're too good for her," Luke said, and hauled Samantha outside.

His ears rang as he stepped from the tavern, but it was nothing compared to how they sizzled once Samantha started her tirade.

"Let me go. Those men knew me. You're not the only pirate who has been here before. They were drunk, but harmless."

"Harmless? Ha! Then why did you scream?"

She rolled her eyes. "He pointed out a spider that was crawling close to my hand. I did what most women do. I yelled."

"Well, you might have tried to keep your mouth shut. I thought you were in trouble."

"Did it ever occur to you that I got along just fine before I met you? And did you even find out where Dervish is?" she demanded as he pulled her back toward the beach.

Dammit!

"Wait here," Luke said, "and don't move so much as a toe."

Luke stalked back to Doubloons, cursing her the whole way. If she hadn't acted like a damn woman, he'd have what he needed by now. He could have seen her safely back to the *Revenge*, then gone back to Doubloons to get blissfully drunk.

"Luke, back so soon? I thought that was one strumpet that was too much for you," Captain said.

"I'll finish with her later." Luke grabbed a mug from a passing barmaid. "Dervish?"

Captain heaved his forearm on Luke's shoulder, nearly buckling his knees. "Going to Santa Placidia."

It was a small, insignificant island that nobody bothered with. Tucked between walls of rock was a virgin beach which opened up to a small, shallow port. The perfect place to unload a ship for careening. And better yet, the perfect place to seek revenge. Luke listened eagerly while Captain told him the rest. When he'd finished, Luke was feeling happier than he had in months.

"Captain, my friend, let me buy you a drink."

Five

Exhaustion was weighing heavy on Sam when the rest of her bleary-eyed crew finally staggered aboard the following afternoon. She'd taken her usual night watch and declined Aidan's offer to take the morning one for her. It wasn't because she didn't trust him. She'd be on board, he'd be safe enough. No, Aidan wasn't the problem.

The fact that Luke had traipsed back to town after seeing her to the *Revenge* the previous night was. Not only had he refused to discuss his irrational behavior, but he'd also left her stewing and wondering. What was he doing? With whom? She knew those questions would plague her until Luke returned. Sleep wouldn't come until he did.

It unsettled her that she cared. She'd known what Joe, Willy, and the rest of her crew were up to. Hadn't she allowed it, despite her hatred of Tortuga? Why should Luke be any different?

Because she hadn't risked her neck breaking him out of prison for him to waltz around Tortuga getting stone drunk and whoring with whomever he pleased. And if that didn't make a lick of sense, so be it.

"Welcome back, gentlemen."

Her greeting was answered by a series of grunts and shuffles. Luke, last to come aboard, was maddeningly wide-eyed and alert.

"Joe, get the crew in order and haul anchor. We've wasted enough time. I'm going to sleep."

Her first mate looked at her questioningly but was smart enough to keep his thoughts to himself. He did, however, spare a scowl for Luke.

"You're trusting his word, then?"

Sam pulled her tired bones together and demanded they stay upright a few minutes longer. "If Luke says Dervish is headed for Barbados, then that's where we're going. I asked him to find Dervish's destination, and he did. I'm not about to second-guess him now."

Luke's smile, when he faced Joe, was blinding. Ignoring the fact that she'd just fed his ego, she left Joe in command and disappeared below. She fell onto her berth fully dressed. If a lingering voice whispered in her ear to be careful where Luke was concerned, she was simply too tired to pay it any mind.

The *Revenge* was quiet that afternoon. There was just enough wind to keep the ship cutting along without extra effort from the crew. Which was a good thing, as they were mostly asleep, spread out on deck. Willy was squeezed underneath the lifeboat to escape the unrelenting brilliance of the sun. One of the boatswains was balanced on the base of the bowsprit, arms and legs hanging limply at his side. Joe was at the helm, but his eyes were glassier than the shimmering surface of the sea.

It was an opportunity Luke didn't intend to pass up.

"Why don't you get some sleep?" he said to Joe. "I can take it from here."

"Good effort, Luke. I don't think so."

The need to take the helm was staggering. It had every nerve in his body primed and humming. But Joe couldn't know that.

"You prefer walking in your sleep, do you? Look, I just thought you'd rather lie yourself down and rest for a while. She's quiet," he said, referring to the ocean. "Besides, it was me who found out where Dervish is. I can read a compass and get us there."

Deliberately, he stretched, taking his time so as to give Joe an opportunity to think about what he was missing. "But if you don't need me, I guess I'll go get myself some sleep. Seems a shame, though. I'm not really tired."

"Joe, I can keep an eye on him."

Luke spun to face Aidan, who, despite his manly words, was fidgeting in his boots.

Joe smiled warmly. "I guess you could at that, son."

Aidan grinned. The boyish delight at Joe's praise overpowered his uncertainty.

"All right, me boy," Joe said, "I'll leave ye to keep an eye on Luke. Ye come fetch me or Capt'n Steele if anything comes up."

"Aye, sir." Aidan straightened and all but saluted.

Joe faced Luke and all humor vanished from his face. "Don't do anythin' stupid, Luke. We have what we need, now. Yer of no further value."

"So nice to know I'm wanted."

Joe grunted and shuffled off. Luke didn't care where he collapsed into sleep. He'd gotten what he was after. His hand was embarrassingly unsteady as he reached for the tiller.

"Luke?" Aidan asked, his dirty palm outstretched.

Luke grinned and ruffled the boy's messy hair. Then he dug into his pocket and pulled out a shilling, dropping it into the boy's waiting palm. Aidan's bony fingers curved over the coin and he beamed. Luke returned the smile.

"Thanks for your help, son."

Then, with the boy beside him, Luke took the helm. He couldn't have said which of them was happier.

Oliver wasn't able to secure an appointment with Governor Alexander Madison until the following afternoon. Oliver's ship was sailing further away, and the overnight delay had taxed his patience. He kept that anxiety well hidden, however, as he followed the butler through large carved doors into an open courtyard. A circle of blooming red rose bushes encompassed a small terrace, which was furnished with an iron table and four straight-backed chairs. The governor, with his long, gray curly wig and an afternoon overcoat in peacock blue, turned at their arrival.

"My dear Oliver, how lovely that you came to call today. Please"—he gestured to a chair as the butler stepped forward to hold it out—"join me. I was about to indulge myself with a small nip of brandy."

Oliver made himself comfortable as the butler silently slipped off to get their drinks. Behind the sickeningly sweet roses, thick palm trees spread long, leafy fingers over them, producing a refreshing bit of cool shade.

"I'm glad you had time to meet with me on such short notice," Oliver said.

The butler poured them each a healthy dose of the brandy and then, upon Madison's request, left the bottle.

"Tell me, Oliver, how are things at your plantation?"

Insignificant, nonessential talk had helped Oliver slide his way among the rich and powerful, gathering allies the way the governor gathered roses. Today, he resented every word. Underneath the table, his knuckles were white.

When the obligatory chatter was finally finished, Oliver jumped to the heart of the matter.

"I heard that pirate escaped yesterday. Bradley, was it?"

Alexander nodded into his glass, then swallowed. "I was told upon my arrival back in Port Royal. I can tell you, my friend, I was most distressed."

Oliver pushed his glass aside and leaned forward. "Were any of your men hurt, sir? Nobody seems to know exactly how it happened. Only that there was a commotion and he slipped out in the midst of it. The jail wasn't harmed. Did he have a key, then?"

"No, but his accomplice did."

Oliver grabbed the decanter and poured them both another shot. He swallowed his in two gulps.

"He had help, then?"

The governor, blue eyes twinkling, leaned back in the chair, crossed his arms over a fit chest.

"It's most embarrassing, Oliver. When I heard the whole tale, I immediately asked for everyone's silence. But, as a friend, I feel you may get a good laugh out of it. I know I did."

At the start of the governor's tale, Oliver thought he'd wasted his time. It was of no significance to him that some strumpet had come to see the pirate. Nor that she'd flirted shamelessly with the guards. But when Madison said she'd brought along some baked goods that rendered the guards so violently ill that they'd left their stations for the privy, *that* had Oliver's blood sputtering.

Samantha had been so pretty when he'd taken her back to the plantation that he'd wanted her nearby. He'd given her a position in the kitchen so he could see her more often. But the damn tart had refused his advances. Indeed, she once smacked his hand with a spoon when he'd run it down her perfectly rounded backside. Two days later the chocolate cake she'd baked for dessert had turned his insides to slop and he'd been wretchedly sick.

He'd taken away her apron and moved her to the fields that very night. After she'd spent a few days at hard labor, he'd come to her bed.

Thankfully, Madison's table prevented the man from seeing Oliver's instant arousal. She'd been so tight, so bloody spirited, he'd ridden her like a bucking stallion. And had loved every damn minute of it. Which was why, after that one taste, he'd been desperate for another. In his lust, he'd underestimated her. Not a mistake he planned to repeat.

"You think she poisoned the goods?" Oliver asked, though he knew. Just as he knew who had done it.

His ship had vanished the same night she had. Now guards had been poisoned the same way he had been. It was her.

"Unfortunately, yes. Oh, they'll be fine," the governor acknowledged with a wave of his hand. "After a few hours in the privy they were right as rain. But damn embarrassing all the same." He leaned forward, black eyebrows coming together in a worried frown. "You won't repeat what I've told you, will you? 'Tis bad enough Bradley got away without the true reason being told."

Smiling, Oliver took two of his best cigars out of his

breast pocket and offered one to Madison. He bit off one end, spat it into a spittoon, and lit the other end. Smoke curled into his lungs.

"Of course not, my friend. As always, what is said between us remains in confidence."

As the governor then began to expound the details of his recent trip to Cuba, Oliver shut him out. The *Jewel*. Samantha. Soon they would both be back in his possession.

It started out as a wee gray speck on the horizon. Luke took the looking glass, and within the small circle saw the speck take shape. His mouth watered.

A ship!

Judging by the angle, they were headed straight for each other. It was too far away to be certain, but Luke figured it to be a merchant ship. One gun deck, up to sixteen guns. Twelve if they were lucky. His skin prickled. For a pirate ship, the *Revenge* didn't have nearly the amount of weaponry he was used to, but he'd been outgunned before. It added a little excitement.

"Aidan, looks like things are about to get more lively."

"Sir?" the boy asked.

Luke handed him the looking glass and pointed it for him. "See that ship? In a few hours, we're going to be having the time of our lives."

He'd managed to contain Aidan's immediate need to wake Joe. They had a few minutes to spare. Besides, he wasn't ready to let go of the helm yet. There was nothing better than having a ship beneath his palm. Nothing more thrilling than feeling her obey his command; than knowing that with her, the horizon was always within his grasp. And it had been too long, much too long, since he'd been in this position. The tiller pulled at his hand, and Luke tightened his grip.

Since Aidan was all but dancing in his desire to fetch Joe, Luke agreed it was time. They had to have a plan in place before the other ship could see them too clearly. Aidan stomped away, the heels of his too-large boots dragging on the deck. Luke heard Joe's grunts, and all too soon he was forced to relinquish control. It didn't sit well. The knot of pride was a hard one to swallow.

"Fetch Capt'n Steele, son," Joe said.

But Luke was already on his way. "Wake the rest of the crew," he told the boy, and quickly closed the hatch before Joe could come after him.

Squawk. "Man in cabin. Man in cabin."

Luckily Samantha was tired enough that the bloody bird didn't wake her. Luke crept to the cage, wondering what a parrot tasted like.

"Before we're through here, birdy, you'll be learning some other words." He turned back to Samantha.

Shafts of light spilt from the window in a myriad of slender fingers. One of them danced on Samantha's face. Her lips, the color of pink coral, were slightly parted. From between them slipped a soft breath. Eyelashes rested on creamy cheeks. Hands, relaxed and open, lay at her sides. The bedcovers lay just over her breasts, and if he hadn't known her better, he'd say she'd done it deliberately to tease. As it was, the effect was the same.

He filled with a need to pull the covers down slowly, and feast. He'd seen enough to know the banquet would be bountiful and succulent. And keep him smiling for days.

But, woman or not, she was the captain and he needed to wake her. Since she'd been gracious enough to leave some space, Luke eased onto the berth next to her.

She was warm and soft, and he shifted closer. That was its own kind of torture. Her hair smelled of soap and wind. He gazed down on her, peaceful in sleep, her luscious body pressed close, and began to count. He figured he had until at least twenty.

She awoke at seven.

It wasn't a slow awakening, the kind he'd love to see after a long night of lovemaking, her body exhausted and limp. She bolted to a sitting position even as sleep still blurred her eyes. She gasped loudly, then turned to see what had jarred her awake.

Luke wiggled his eyebrows.

"Hello, luv."

She shoved her rich hair out of her face and glared daggers at him.

"What in blazes are you doing here? Again?"

He pushed on the mattress and hungered after the heat that warmed his hand. Her heat. "Testing the bed, as I've yet to sleep on it."

Her nostrils flared, but rather than the ranting and cursing he'd been looking forward to, she reached under her pillow and pointed a pistol between his legs. He scurried back.

"I believe you were told last time that this cabin is off-limits to you during the day."

"I was," he acknowledged, and stepped another inch farther away from the weapon.

"Then what are you doing here? Other than the rather sad excuse of trying to seduce a sleeping woman."

He stepped away from the berth. "It seems your beauty

rest is to be postponed yet again. There's a merchant ship headed straight for us."

That the light in her eyes faded didn't surprise him. That she put away her pistol, did.

"How much longer?"

Luke watched her carefully. "We've got time. An hour at least."

She nodded and frowned, looking at the sunbeam that cut across her berth. "I didn't get more than a few hours' sleep, did I?"

"About two, luv."

She sighed. "Fine. You've done your job. You can leave."

"It seems to me, luv, that as we're about to leaden our pockets, you should be much happier."

Samantha eyed him and shook her head. "Nobody says we're going to win, Luke. It's never a certain thing, trying to take another ship. We can be hurt, killed. They could outgun us. The *Revenge* could sink," she added softly.

One day soon, Luke promised himself, he was going to get to the bottom of this sadness and reluctance to be a pirate. Especially since she was a reasonably good one. Though not as great as himself, of course.

"That's fine talk before going into battle, Samantha. Shall we tell dear Aidan to save himself the bother and just jump overboard now?"

"Shut up, Luke."

Squawk. "Damn Luke, damn Luke."

"Besides," he added, having fun now that she'd insulted him, "you've never gone into battle with Luke Bradley on your side before."

Before she could move, he leaned down and gave her a smacking kiss. "Now let's get going, Samantha. The fun's about to begin."

Six

The ship on the horizon was gaining steadily. It wouldn't be long before they'd be seen clearly through a looking glass. If they didn't do something soon, they'd lose any chance of commandeering the other vessel. Where the hell was Samantha? Luke slapped the looking glass in his palm. She had ten bloody seconds to get up on deck or he'd be going down to get her.

"Joe, where do we stand?" he heard her ask.

Finally. Luke jumped down from the bowsprit and stopped dead in his tracks. Then, with a head full of fury and shock, he barreled to the helm.

"Just what the devil do you think you're doing?" he demanded.

Samantha turned to face him. "I'm about to find out how much time we have and just who is coming toward us. As first mate, Joe would know."

Her little dagger hit the mark. He didn't need a bloody

reminder that he wasn't anywhere near commanding this ship. Or any other, for that matter.

"And as a member of this crew, which I am whether you like it or not, I want to know why you're dressed in all these trappings. Just how do you think that'll help when the guns start firing?"

Every man on deck stopped working. Maybe they'd never dared question her authority, but damned if he was going to sit back and let her ruin it all. Clearly her reputation had been exaggerated. She didn't know blazes about running a ship.

Joe stepped forward, his fists tight and ready. Samantha stopped him with a quiet word and the palm of her hand across his stomach. Then she fixed her attention on Luke. She stood every inch a lady in a demure light yellow gown, her hair arranged on top of her head, with half the curls looking ready to spill from their pins. Whispers of wind made them dance against her cheeks. Late afternoon sunlight gilded the deck at her feet.

She'd have blended into Port Royal, Havana, or any other fine city. Only the tempestuous storm raging in her eyes painted another picture.

"I'm hoping, Luke, that guns won't be necessary."

He snorted. "Planning on asking politely if they'll simply give us their cargo?"

She moved a folded parasol from her side. Though he figured she'd love to whack him with it, she only held it across her waist.

"What I plan on doing is heaving a few of the empty barrels we have stored below into the water. We've also got some dishes and cutlery we can spare. They will be tossed in as well."

She circled him now, and he felt very much like prey.

"Willy will tear the smaller square sail. We'll drag pots and an old mattress behind to slow our speed."

She stopped in front of him.

"And just so you understand what I'm meaning, I'll say it all very clearly and very slowly. From all appearances it will look as though we've been attacked and our ship is crippled. Aidan and I . . ."

At her words, the boy appeared at her side, a young man ready to defend his captain.

"We'll be waving white handkerchiefs and holding back tears while the rest of you lie about as though wounded. A few moans here and there wouldn't hurt."

Samantha looked over her shoulder at Joe. "Does that about cover it?"

"Don't forget we're to be armed and ready, and when the other crew comes aboard, we jump, ready to fight."

His gloating expression made Luke feel like a child who'd been too simple to figure it all out himself.

"See, Luke, we've done this a time or two. And usually the guns don't get fired because we've managed to catch them ill prepared. Seeing as how you've signed the articles, you know that though Dervish is my first priority, I can't expect my crew to sail with me for free. Be that as it may, I prefer to compensate their loyalties with as little violence as possible."

Her lips curved. The gesture was rich in satisfaction.

"I'll take your silence for an apology," she said, then dismissed him by giving him her back.

By the time the ships came within hailing distance, all the pieces of the puzzle were in place. Men were sprawled on the *Revenge*'s deck. Joe, Willy, and a few others were draped over the guns. Trevor and three more appeared to be tied up in ropes, unconscious or dead. Four men had remained below, armed and ready should the need arise.

From his position by the lifeboat where he lay spread on his stomach, Luke watched from between his folded arms. Samantha and the boy were at the gunwale. She waved her handkerchief with one hand and kept an iron grip on Aidan with the other.

The captain of the merchant vessel stood on his deck. The size of his ship had Samantha shielding her eyes from the sun to look up at him. She was too bloody small and delicate to be standing there all alone. Luke wished she'd listened to reason and let him take that position. Not that he could pretend to be a woman, but he could have feigned an injury. The results would have been the same, and she would have remained safe below.

He didn't think on the whys of that. There'd been women on a few of the ships he'd sailed on, though none of them a captain. Their safety hadn't concerned him any more than the rest of the crew's. But Samantha's, for a reason he couldn't fathom, did.

"Ahoy, there. What happened?" The captain's stance was wide. The musket he pointed at her gleamed in the sun.

"Pirates!" Samantha wailed. "They took everything."

She hugged Aidan closer, as much for his protection, Luke figured, as for effect.

"My son and I are the only ones who escaped without wounds."

The man looked past her to the deck. Luke closed his eye to a slit. As long as the captain was on guard, they had to be careful.

"Small crew."

She nodded, and Luke noticed her fingers were digging into Aidan's arm.

"Can you help me get to Barbados? We can't stay out here, and I know nothing of sailing."

The desperation in her voice was so real that Luke almost believed her.

Some of the captain's crew had gathered round him, whispering among themselves. But the flag Samantha had raised, the one that matched theirs, snapped so that Luke couldn't hear. Their expressions, however, were cautious.

Luke's blood was coursing. It tingled in his fingertips. He looked forward to a good battle, but not with a woman at the forefront. Sweat trickled into his eye and stung.

Samantha's arm swept to encompass her ship. Luke saw her face was pale, her body strained. She looked exactly as she pretended: scared, alone, miserable. And he knew, without question, it wasn't all an act.

"I need to see that these men get a proper burial. I can't simply throw them overboard. It's"—she shuddered— "uncivilized."

Well done, luv, Luke thought.

"Ma'am, you can't leave them there, either. The smell alone will be horrendous long before you get to port."

"Oh, my!" she whimpered, turning back to the captain. "I hadn't thought of that."

Her knees buckled, and she took Aidan down with her.

Luke held his breath. Every muscle twitched in anticipation. The pistol under his belly was ready.

"Ma'am? Are you all right?" the captain asked.

She said nothing, simply kept Aidan in the circle of her arms and wept. The waiting while the captain of the merchant ship decided their move was endless. The breeze waltzed between the two foresails. Water gurgled between the ships. Sweat from the men lying around him rose in unseen currents as the tension mounted. They were hidden hunters, ready to strike and catch their quarry unawares. As one of them, Luke's mind toyed with all possible ways the battle could go.

"Prepare to board!"

The command washed excitement down Luke's dry throat. The contest had begun.

Grab hooks arched through the air. They scraped across the deck and dug into the sides. Samantha hurried Aidan to the quarterdeck, always using herself as a shield between the boy and the men.

Luke counted ten sailors coming across. All carried muskets and extra shots. The captain came on board first. A quick hand signal, and his crew dispersed. Luke's plan to keep the captain in his sights died when one of the boarders stopped and blocked his view. A boot kicked him in the shoulder. Luke moaned and muttered a curse, then eased one hand under his belly. The pistol slid warmly into his palm.

"You! Are you hurt?"

He sprang to life. With the grace earned through years of practice, Luke launched himself to his feet and pointed the weapon at the sailor, whose face drained of all color.

In a cresting wave, the crew of the *Revenge* leaped up, pistols raised, teeth bared.

"P-pirates!" someone stammered.

A quick look showed most of the sailors' weapons shaking in their hands. Every face was the color of a freshly laid egg. Every face but the captain's.

His was red. Luke saw the fury boiling within the man. Hell, he didn't blame him for feeling like a fool, so long as he didn't act like one. Especially since he was close, far too close, to Samantha.

"Captain?" a man asked from behind Luke.

The rest of the crew still on board the merchant ship had weapons raised. There were at least double the number of the *Revenge*'s men. Sweat trickled down Luke's back. He shifted his gaze just quickly enough to notice Samantha had Aidan tucked behind her, and she'd produced a blunderbuss from somewhere. She stood defiant, her weapon aimed. It scared the hell out of Luke. He knew she'd die for the boy, and prayed it wouldn't come to that.

The captain's voice was coated with bitterness. "I will not be taken by these curs," he said, then lunged for Samantha.

Bedlam erupted on the deck.

Shots cracked in the tropical heat. Luke narrowly avoided one that splintered into the lifeboat at his back. He ducked, rolling to the deck, and fired at the sailor who had him in his sights. The man gasped, dropped his musket, and collapsed to the deck. Luke dragged himself behind the lifeboat and, using it as cover, reloaded.

He raised the barrel over the side of the boat and took stock. There were too many bodies lunging and fighting to be certain, but he figured the *Revenge* was holding its own.

"Get them!" the captain shouted over his shoulder, and Luke spun toward him.

His heart leaped, then dropped like an anchor. The captain had cornered Samantha on the quarterdeck and was inching closer. Her pistol was rock solid as she kept it pointed at his heart. *There's a girl.* Another shot exploded into the mast to Luke's left. Wood fragments burned across his cheek and his ear rang. Luke fired. He hit his target, who staggered over the gunwale and splashed into the sea.

Fists were flying now, and he saw Willy land a heavy

one into an opponent's stomach. The sailor doubled over
and fell hard on his knees. Another was coming straight
for Luke. Luke dodged the fists, then cracked his attacker
over the head with the butt of his pistol.

It didn't take long for the merchant crew to realize that
though they had more men, they weren't nearly as good at
fighting. Muskets dropped, clanked onto the decks as arms
were raised in surrender. Luke bolted for the quarterdeck.

He wasn't quick enough. The captain had reached Samantha and grabbed her arm.

"Let go your weapon, wench!" he ordered.

"No," she answered, then to Aidan added, "Stay down."

Luke grinned at the authority in her voice until the
man banged her arm on the gunwale. He didn't hear the
bone break, but the thud of her arm being repeatedly
struck against the solid wood curdled his stomach. Then
she shouted and her blunderbuss rolled to the deck. Aidan,
ignoring her screams to stay put, crept around her and
grabbed it.

Now both Luke and Aidan had the captain in their sights.

"Let her go," Luke growled, so angry that for the first
time he could remember, he wanted to hurt someone not
for treasure or self-defense. But simply to inflict pain.

The captain shifted Samantha in front of him. "No. You
will not loot my ship."

Luke glanced over his shoulder. "Who, exactly, is going
to help you with that?"

Other than ropes creaking and the sea licking the hulls,
there was silence. The merchant crew on board the *Revenge*
was being tied up. Joe and Willy were aboard the other
ship, taking care of those men. One they'd missed made for
the guns. Before Luke could do more than yell to Joe, the

shot was fired. It exploded into the *Revenge*, rocking her and everyone on board.

Samantha gasped in horror.

Outraged, Joe barreled toward the perpetrator, even as the man cowered. Joe lifted him by the collar and heaved the scoundrel overboard. The blinding rage in the captain's eye said he was out of supporters, and he knew it.

"I will not," the captain said low in his throat, "be taken by pirates."

Luke treaded very carefully, knowing both Samantha and the boy could easily be hurt. "Don't be a fool, man. This could have all been done nice and easy if you'd only surrendered." He pointed to a few men who lay in pools of blood. "Those lives were lost because of you. Don't make us take yours as well."

The man's eyes narrowed, and he gripped Samantha tighter. Aidan's gun was shaking, but Luke kept his attention on Samantha. It was about keeping her safe. Her face was pale, and her bright eyes shifted from him to Aidan.

"I won't be the one doing the dying next time. It'll be her."

His arm wrapped around her neck. Samantha's eyes widened and her breath wheezed out. The arm that wasn't choking her pointed a pistol at Luke. Luke took one step before Aidan cocked his weapon. The sound splintered the silence. The captain's gaze cut to the boy, as did his weapon. Samantha wriggled frantically.

"Not Aidan," she rasped.

Later, he'd be insulted by that. Luke yanked the boy behind him, taking the weapon from his stiff fingers. Once again the pistol pointed at Luke's heart.

Samantha suddenly threw herself to the side. She and the captain lost their balance and staggered. He righted himself quickly, grabbed her, and threw her against the gunwale, where her head cracked against the wood. It sounded louder than a pistol shot to Luke.

Luke leaped. He knocked the man down and they rolled to the deck, a mass of tangled limbs. A fist knocked his head to the side. He swallowed the metallic taste of blood and swung out. The skin over his knuckles split as surely as the man's lip. Luke struggled to stand, but was grabbed by the ankles and pulled down. His cheek bounced off the smooth deck, where he had a second to smell the tang of polish. Before he could catch his breath, a boot smashed into his ribs.

Stars fell before his eyes. His breath lodged in his lungs, where it burned to come out. By the time it did, wheezing between his cracked lips, he was rolled onto his back. A knife, long and shiny, was arching toward his throat.

Then his attacker was knocked aside by a parasol to the head.

Luke rolled away as Samantha lunged for a second attack. Sweating, panting, and hurting more than he'd like, Luke scrambled to his feet. His stomach lurched when the captain's blade sliced into her forearm.

Blood dripped off the knife. Luke grabbed the pistol at his feet, aimed, and despite Samantha's being within a foot of her attacker, pulled the trigger.

Seven

Squawk. "Man in cabin. Man in cabin."

Sam winced. Her head throbbed. Even the slightest noise resounded like cannon fire. It hurt to swallow and the cut on her arm raged. She was bone weary and emotionally exhausted. She didn't need Luke. She needed to be alone.

"What do you want now?" she asked, not bothering to get up from her perch on the side of her berth.

"To ensure you're all right." His gaze cut to her wound. "Are you?"

She shrugged, though it cost her. Fire flashed up her arm at the movement. Her breath hissed between her teeth before she could stop it.

Luke stepped from the ladder, past Carracks's tirade of "Damn Luke," to her side.

"Lie down. I'll find some water and cotton to bandage that up."

Joe had already gathered the supplies needed. He'd insisted on tending to her until she'd ordered him back to

work. It was, after all, his turn at the helm. He'd cursed
and complained about stubborn women, and had been only
slightly mollified when she'd let him carry the necessary
items down to her cabin. She pointed to the table where
Joe had left everything.

"It's all there, Luke. And I'll tell you the same thing I
told Joe; I can do it myself. Why don't you make yourself
useful and help Willy patch the ship so we can make it to
Barbados without sinking?"

Water splashed onto his boots as he carried the bowl
over. It was a sign of how weary she was that she wasn't
driven to wipe it up.

"And I'll tell you, luv, that I'm not leaving. Now shut up
and rest so I can see what the damage is."

She didn't lie down. With her emotional fragility, it
would have seemed far too intimate. Instead, she scooted
back and pressed her spine to the wall. Luke poured a shot
of rum and held it out. Before her fingers could take the
cup, he'd raised it.

"Here's to your health," he said, and finished the drink
in one gulp.

Then he poured another and handed it to her. "Drink
this, it'll numb the pain."

The rum was warm. It slid down her tender throat.
Directly behind that balm, however, was agonizing pain.
Hundreds of hot needles plowed up her arm as Luke
washed away dried blood. Sam turned her head and bit her
lip. She squeezed her eyes shut, thinking of calm seas and
blue sky. Anything but the fire in her arm.

"It's going to need sutures."

His tone, heavy with regret, drew her attention more
than his words. She opened her eyes and was confused by

the expression on his face. If she hadn't known him for a rogue, she'd have sworn he looked genuinely concerned.

"I figured it might. Get Willy, he can do it."

Luke threw the rag into the bowl. Red water swam up the side, spilled over, and landed on his pants.

"I'll not get the carpenter to do a hacking job on that arm," he said disgustedly. "We'll be in Barbados tomorrow night. I know someone there who can tend it, and do a better job than that butcher would."

Sam jumped to Willy's defense. "Since he's been mostly responsible for keeping my ship in great working order, I think he can do this." The drums marching in her head increased their rhythm. "Just get Willy. The sooner he finishes, the sooner I can get to sleep."

It was hardly surprising that Luke ignored her. Instead, he finished cleaning the wound, then wrapped it in clean cotton. His fingers brushed her skin with each wrap around her forearm, and Sam expected to see sparks. Surely something so strong that it sent pulsing heat to every part of her body would be visible.

"There. That'll keep it together and clean until we get to port. Now . . ." his lustful gaze slid over her from head to toe. A mischievous grin pulled at his swollen mouth. "Anything else need tending?"

Warmth spread all over her and gathered disturbingly between her legs. Sam jumped from the bed.

"Other than being tired and having a splitting headache, I'll live."

He leaned against the ladder, mischief sparkling in his gaze.

"No 'thank you, Luke'?"

Sam rolled her eyes. "Thank you, Luke. Go away."

She was turning down the covers when he made his move. From behind her, his hands snaked into her hair, his thumbs rubbing at the base of her skull. Her initial jump at the contact was soon soothed by the wonder of long fingers. It felt far too good to resist. Her head lolled forward. Tingles danced along her scalp as his hands worked their magic, easing away the tension and pain until she felt weightless. She swayed.

"Time for bed, luv." He scooped her up.

He could have put her down straightaway, but instead he held her close to him. His shirt was still damp with sweat from the battle. Dried blood ran from his mouth to his chin. He looked every bit the fearsome pirate.

Yet that wasn't what she saw when she looked him in the eye. Luke had never hit her or threatened her. He'd located Dervish when she'd failed to. He was gentle, irritating, and arrogant. A strange combination that worked for Luke Bradley. Added to that was the very real fact that she wanted to be around Luke. Especially now.

Their lips were mere inches apart. His hands tightened, pressing her closer to the gentle rise and fall of his chest. Wicked promises lay within his dark gaze, promises that should have scared her but only made her hungry. She wondered what his lips would feel like on her own. Not the smacking kiss he'd given earlier, or the others to keep her quiet. A real one. How desperately she wanted to feel his softness, to discover the things he could show her. Without realizing, she leaned in.

"Easy, darling. This isn't the time or place." He dropped his forehead to hers. "But it's coming."

His breath and words caressed her as he laid her down. She felt the loss of heat immediately. He tucked her in as a parent might a child, though desire was still ripe in his eye.

"Get some sleep, Samantha. I'll help Willy with the ship."

"What about you?" she asked. "Judging by the bruise on your cheek and the blood on your face, you must have been hurt as well."

He paused, as though surprised she cared, then shrugged. He rubbed his belly with a swollen hand. "Nothing serious," he answered.

Only when the hatch closed behind him did she breathe. Dear Lord, what was getting into her? Luke was a pirate. He, like Dervish, lived to take from other people, to pillage and destroy. Hadn't she seen today, on her own ship, the damage that pirates wreaked? Hadn't she dirtied her own hands with innocent blood by being part of it all? How was it she'd been able to forget all that when he held her close?

She rolled to her side, on her uninjured arm. Her heart was heavy in her chest. Two men had died on her ship today. Unnecessary deaths. Her own crew had suffered injuries, as had her ship. And for what? For a few pieces of eight? Some flour, salt, and fresh meat? Extra ammunition so they could do it all over again?

A tear slipped from her eye and wandered warmly down her cheek. She was sick of it. All she wanted was for Dervish to pay, and then maybe, just maybe, she could finally put her family's massacre to rest and have a normal life. But in the meantime she was no better than the man who haunted her soul. She might not gain any satisfaction from hurting and looting, but she did it all the same. A means to an end, perhaps, but a dirty one.

She shut her eyes against the pain. Not from her arm, but from the reminder of everything she'd lost, everything she ached for each day. And everything she'd become. How could she hold piracy against Luke when she'd stepped knowingly into the same role? She had to find Dervish. Thanks to Luke they were close, so very close. It had to end soon. Before revenge and death gnawed away any more of her soul.

The hatch opened silently and Luke crept down the ladder. He must have thought her asleep by the careful ways he tried not to make any noise.

"Man in cabin. Man in cabin."

He tiptoed to the cage, and whispered threateningly, "I'll have you for supper if you don't shut your beak."

"You touch my bird and I'll see to it the sharks have *you* for supper."

He turned, frowning. "You're supposed to be sleeping."

"If you'd stay out of my cabin, perhaps I could."

His face was clean again, and now he was shirtless. The bronze skin beneath the curtain of chains looked smooth as polished wood. Her fingers itched to touch, so she dug them into the covers.

"Willy didn't want my help. Cursed me blue, then enlisted three other of your men to help instead. So I cleaned up, and thought I'd—well, I figured I'd just . . ."

Luke looked around helplessly. The gold sash trailed down a lean thigh, swaying slightly with his movement. Something warm spilled from her heart when she realized what he was up to. No one, save her family or Joe, had ever shown concern for her. Her heart did a silly roll.

"Spit it out," she said, longing for the words she'd never heard from a man before. Words that would go a long way to heal the inner scars she'd created today.

He glared at her, catching on to her tactics. "You know damn well, so there's no need to be telling you. Now, why aren't you asleep?"

"You haven't given me enough time."

He muttered something, then suddenly went quiet. "You've been crying."

Sam wiped the tear she'd forgotten she'd shed. It would have shamed her for Luke to see it if he wasn't squirming in his worn boots.

"I was thinking about those men who were killed today. By our own pistols."

His casual shrug bothered her.

"We gave them a chance," he said. "Wasn't our fault they had a foolish captain."

No, it wasn't. But it didn't take away the facts. No amount of scrubbing would ever wash their blood from her deck. Or her mind. Because she felt her eyes burning, she turned onto her side, her back to Luke.

"I'm tired. I'll be up later."

His breathing wasn't exactly ragged, but neither was it normal. Just off cadence enough for Sam to recognize he was troubled. Funny how well she'd come to know him already.

The bed sagged under his weight. Sam didn't move as he settled in behind her and pulled her close. Her mind screamed "pirate." Her heart calmly replied "comfort."

His heat enveloped her, his breath caressed her neck while his arm slid boldly over her waist to tuck her in close. She couldn't bring herself to order him to leave. For some reason, Luke wanted to be there as much as she needed him to be. It was as simple as that.

Sam closed her eyes, expecting the battle to run over and over through her mind, as they usually did. Instead, there was nothing but the reassurance that for this moment, she wasn't alone. Sighing deeply, she sank into an untroubled sleep.

* * *

At the first groan of the hatch opening, Luke turned. Samantha lay snug against him, and he was ready to blast the man who'd dared interrupt her rest. And his rather colorful fantasies.

Squawk. "Man in cabin. Man in cabin."

Joe shushed the bird with a quick command and stepped down. He stopped when his gaze fell on Samantha's berth. His eyes turned mutinous.

"Get the hell away from her, ye mangy, flea-bitten rat."

Luke grinned, though he knew his life was at stake when Joe stalked across the room. "Easy, mate. Our fair lady simply needed her rest."

He'd kept his voice low so as not to wake her, and Joe did the same, though his face flamed and his breath puffed from the effort.

"Aye, she did. That don't explain yer presence in her bed. Get out so's I can kill ye without harming the capt'n."

"I'll get out when I'm ready, and not a minute before."

Joe swelled like a dead fish on a hot beach. "I'm telling ye yer ready now."

Luke sighed. "Look. Have you not noticed we're both dressed? She's had a hard day, all right? I'm not about to take advantage of that fact."

It took a few breaths before Luke saw Joe's fists open at his sides. Anger was replaced with regret.

"I know it. She hates taking ships. Bloody shame there had to be bloodshed. That'll make it worse."

It was damned aggravating to have Joe tell him so easily what he himself had struggled to figure out.

"That's right. So you'll let her be."

Joe looked back to Samantha and exhaled deeply. "Would if I could, but it's her turn."

Luke arched his neck and saw Joe was right. Dusk had fallen outside the little window without his realizing.

"Let her sleep. I'll take her post tonight." Luke slid reluctantly away from Samantha. The loss of her heat and softness was a tangible thing.

The first mate was shaking his head. "She's a capt'n, Luke. Ye know better'n I what that means. She'd be cursing me to hell itself if I let her sleep through. Duty bound, she is, to keep up her responsibilities to her crew."

It really was galling the way Joe knew her so well. Luke grimaced. "I'll wake her. She'll be on deck in a moment."

They stared each other down, each trying to win this silent battle over Samantha. But Luke, with a fair chunk of pride on the line, fought to win.

"I believe that until Samantha relieves you, you're in charge on deck, are you not? If she doesn't shirk her duties, do you think she'll be happy to know you've ignored yours by being down here?"

Joe sputtered. " 'Twas only to come wake her."

"Anyone else could have done that. Besides, I'm here, so I'll do the waking."

"She don't like nobody else in her cabin."

His pointed look said he still wasn't pleased Luke had changed all that.

Luke glanced down at Samantha. Her lips were slightly parted, her face flushed in sleep. The body that had pressed against him for a few glorious hours remained curved onto its side, one hand in front of her face, the other tucked underneath her ear.

No other man had ever been in her cabin. Interesting. So

he was gaining more ground than he'd realized. She trusted him, at least a little. Maybe she hadn't at first, but she did now. Why else would she allow him to be where she'd not let anyone else?

But like a starving man, a little wasn't enough. Not nearly enough. Luke intended to have it all.

The silence that coasted on the waves was a blessed relief after the noise that had bombarded Sam most of the day. The hole in the ship was patched, for now. Willy's thudding hammer and screeching saw were thankfully at rest.

The plunder had been divided after the evening meal, and it had felt like endless hours as each man boasted how he was going to spend his share. And each one, it seemed, had to tell his story louder than the one before. But now it was just her, the sea, and her nightly mug of coffee with Joe before he retired.

Tonight something was different, though. Joe was uncomfortable, extremely so. His feet toyed with a coiled rope on deck and he swallowed repeatedly, though he'd yet to drink from his mug.

When she'd followed Luke above deck earlier, after he'd awakened her, she'd seen the dismay on Joe's face. All day she'd felt the lecture coming, and knew by the way Joe was acting that the time had finally come.

"Miss Samantha," Joe cleared his throat. "We need to talk about Luke."

She'd done nothing wrong, yet his tone made her feel as though she was twelve years old. There would be no distracting him, no matter how uneasy he was. When Joe got a thought into his head, it came out only one way. Through his mouth.

"Say your piece, Joe. It's been gnawing at you all day."

"That it has. How did ye know?"

She laughed. "By the way you glared at Luke, ready to skin him alive if he stepped too close to me." Her voice lowered. "By the look in your eyes when you looked at me."

Joe took a long, slow drink. "I've had a terrible feelin' ever since he's come aboard. I don't trust 'im."

"Yes, I think everybody knows that, especially Luke. But we were running in circles without him. Now things will go much faster."

"That's what I'm afraid of," he muttered into his mug as he drank.

Sam shook her head. "I thought that's what we both wanted. To make Dervish pay."

"Aye, that I do. More'n me life. 'Tisn't what I meant, though." He shoved the rope aside. "I'm seein' somethin' between ye and Luke. And with yer parents gone, the task lies with me to discuss, er, certain things."

There was no telling which of them was more embarrassed. Sam studied her shoes.

"He saved my life today."

Joe snorted. "He could've killed ye!"

Samantha looked him in the eye. "But he didn't."

"Ye were but a foot away. When I saw Luke point and shoot, me heart stopped dead." He shook the disturbing thought aside. "But yer distractin' me. 'Twasn't what I was talkin' about."

No it wasn't, and she'd known it. "You're referring to him sleeping in my cabin? I told you there was nothing to that. You saw us yourself, fully dressed."

"Aye, Samantha, I did. But yer only foolin' yerself if ye think that was nothin'. I can promise ye Luke thinks there was a mite more to it than that."

There was no point arguing with him. There was no way to explain to Joe what she herself didn't yet understand.

"Ye know what he's after, don't ye?"

Sam's stomach lurched with a wave. Dear Lord, he went straight to the heart of the matter. She took a breath for courage and faced him.

The light from below squeezed through the latices on the hatches and skimmed over Joe's features. His eyes were lost in shadows, but she felt their conviction. His mouth was set and his hands were locked in a battle against each other. There was no mistaking his nervousness. And there was no hiding from it either.

"Whose intentions are you questioning, his or mine?"

Joe took a breath that strained three buttons on his shirt.

"His." He sighed worriedly. "And yours."

"I see." She took a large gulp of coffee, wishing that for once he'd laced it with rum. "Joe, you know what happened on the plantation. I'm not innocent any—"

He held up a scarred hand. "Yes, ye are. What that man did to ye was unspeakable. It was robbery, plain and simple. He stole a part of yer innocence, but he didn't take it all."

As Joe seemed to be gathering steam, Sam leaned back and let him finish.

"There's more to what happ'ns between a man and woman than what that animal showed you. 'Twas what was between yer parents."

He stepped through the curtain of darkness. Understanding tumbled from his eyes.

"'Tis natural ye should look to find it. But Luke's not the man."

Sam toyed with her empty mug, needing a release from what was bubbling within her. "After what Mr. Grant did, what makes you think I want another man to touch me?"

Joe angled his head to the side. "Don't ye? I've noticed ye've allowed him closer than anyone else. I've eyes, lass. I see ye looking out for 'im. I see the way ye perk up when he's on deck. And I see the hunger in his eyes."

Sam's stomach twisted in a knot.

He rubbed the beard that covered his lower face. "I hate that look, it drives me mad. He'll hurt ye, Samantha. He'll take what he wants and leave, that's the way of 'im."

It was, and she knew it, though it hurt to have someone else say it.

"I know that, Joe."

"'Tisn't wise to follow this course. If he gets his hands on ye, it won't be him left hurtin' in the end."

Tears spilled from her eyes. She was so afraid of her emotions for Luke. If he wasn't in sight, she wondered where he was and what he was up to. If he was on deck with her, she found herself grasping each word or brief touch, tucking them away in a secret part of her heart.

She knew to the bottom of that very same heart that he was nothing more than a liar and a thief. The blood she had on her hands was nothing to what he had on his. It was men like him who had ripped her family from her life. And once she was gone from the *Revenge*, he would go back to pillaging and plundering. And whoring. She'd be nothing more than another conquest.

Yet woven amid the wanting and the knowing was a certainty that no matter what she thought or believed, their coming together was inevitable.

"I'd envisioned a life for myself, Joe, before my parents were killed. There would have been a wedding to a fine man, babies, as much love as a heart could hold. We'd have a home where our children would grow strong and secure in the warmth of family." She swallowed the lump that had formed in her throat. "Just like what I'd been given as a child.

"But it died with my family. Everything changed after being in Mr. Grant's employ. After that horrible night."

The bloody image shot forth in her memory, and Sam staggered from the impact. He'd raped her only once. The second time he'd tried, she'd been ready. The hammer had done its job. She hadn't lingered to ensure he was dead, but the amount of blood pouring from his head onto the floor had terrified her out of the room. After she'd told Joe, he had snuck back to make sure. Mr. Grant was still alive, but Joe hadn't expected him to live much longer.

Joe shook his head. "Luke's not yer answer, lass. 'Tis a mistake. One ye'll regret."

She released the tiller to Joe so she could pace. "I know he's a pirate, Joe. Dammit, I know that. But he's shown me tenderness. A tenderness I'd never have thought possible from him. A tenderness I never realized I needed." She squeezed her eyes against the pain pushing at the walls of her chest.

When she opened them again, Joe was shaking his head. "Well, he's not likely to show his true colors yet, is he? It's a ruse, to get yer defenses down." He grabbed her as she stepped in front of him. " 'Twould break me heart to watch ye suffer again.

"The pain I used to see in yer eyes tore me in half, lass. The little girl who followed me every move so I'd teach her to sail died on that plantation. Ye stopped smiling." His hand cupped her cheek. "I'd never seen such empty eyes."

Tears trickled down her cheeks.

"Yer just startin' to chase away those shadows. We're so close to Dervish. Soon as he's dead, ye can move on and do yer family proud. Getting tangled with Luke will only suck ye back under."

Sam stepped back, away from Joe's touch and his words. She circled around him and took the tiller back.

There'd been a time she never would have thought herself capable of wanting a man. But lately it wasn't Mr. Grant's pawing hands she saw when she closed her eyes. She didn't think of pain and indignity, she thought of being held in Luke's comforting embrace. She saw the desire in his eye, yet felt his resistance. He wasn't pushing her, but giving her the time to wonder and want.

"He's not Mr. Grant, Joe. Luke won't take anything I'm not willing to give."

Joe cringed. "No, he'll hurt ye more, and it won't be only yer body this time."

She looked up at the moon hanging in the sky like a ripe banana and drew a ragged breath.

"I've told myself everything you're telling me. It doesn't seem to make any difference. I'm not sure I have the will to fight what's coming." She faced him again, hoping he wouldn't turn from her if she chose to give herself to Luke. "I'm not sure I want to. Can you understand that? Please?"

He wiped her cheeks dry, then tucked a finger under her chin and raised her head to his. His eyes were as stormy as hers. "If he hurts ye, he'll see the same fate Mr. Grant did." Steely determination hardened his features. "I promise ye that."

Justine Grant wouldn't listen to reason. She adamantly shook her head, refusing to hear him out.

"Oliver, you're not well enough. What if you should have more pains while you're at sea?"

Inside the wood-paneled walls of his study, Oliver held his excitement in check. He was eager to pack his bags and be off, but first he had to deal with his wife.

"It's been months since I've had any, darling," he lied, and pressed her delicate hands within his own. Better she didn't know the pains in his chest had increased steadily over the last few months, in number and severity. If she knew that, he wouldn't be allowed out of bed.

"Besides, you know how much I've missed the *Jewel*. I need to get her back."

The loss of his ship and the twenty slaves who had run with Samantha were the only truths about that night Justine knew. He'd never told his wife the real reason the girl had thrashed him. It was best she didn't know about his nightly strolls to the slave huts. As employees, he felt it their duty to lie beneath him when his urges became too much for his wife. Only Samantha had ever fought back. He'd managed to convince Justine he was just checking on the girl, who had complained of being ill all day, when she'd coldheartedly bashed him in the head.

He ached for revenge. The girl had done in one night what nobody else had managed to do in his forty years— best him. Since Justine wouldn't understand that, he kept it to himself.

Justine's eyes welled with tears. "It could take months. I can't be without you so long. And what of the plantation?"

Oliver gave his wife a reassuring embrace. He rested his cheek on top of her rose-scented hair. She wasn't bred to handle day-to-day operations of a plantation, and he'd always seen to it she didn't have any worries other than those required by society. A few luncheons, afternoon teas, and the occasional nighttime coupling in their bedroom. Always in the dark, never fully naked. She was a dutiful, loyal wife, if not a passionate one.

"Nathaniel will check in with you daily. He oversees most of the work, and he can do it just as easily without my presence. As for you"—he pulled away and wiped a lone tear from her porcelain cheek—"you and Lewis will be fine, and I won't be gone so long. Now that we know the *Jewel* is nearby, we'll find her."

Worry and, to Oliver's frustration, uncertainty coated her words until they sounded like whining.

"Please stay. I have a terrible feeling about this."

He patted her head and moved to pour himself a brandy. The liquid caught the low light of dusk that filtered into his study.

"It will hardly seem as though I've left before I'll be back. Trust me, Justine," he said, and raised his glass. "A fortnight, at most, and I'll be back. With my ship."

And you, Samantha, will be sorry. Very, very, sorry.

Eight

Luke stared out Samantha's cabin window. He'd dragged a chair over and propped a boot onto its seat, and was nursing his second, and last, rationed cup of rum for the day. There was no need for candles, as he preferred the darkness of the room. His thoughts alone cluttered the space.

He'd known leaving Port Royal that there was something about Samantha that was different. He'd been eager to discover every facet of her body, every curve and delicious taste. Only a small handful of women had resisted his charms, so he'd been confident Samantha would float along like the rest. They'd please each other, enjoy each other. And walk away.

If they were ever lucky enough to meet again, they'd simply take the gift as it was presented and make the best use of it. Only a few had ever lingered in his memories long enough for him to seek them a second time. Mostly, he preferred a variety of women, places, and events.

That had been before Miss Samantha Fine seeped into

his blood. Luke swirled the liquid, the biting smell of the liquor rising from the crockery mug. Still, it wasn't enough to overpower the main fragrance in the cabin. He couldn't describe it in one word. It was a bouquet of scents. Individually the smells of clean bedding, polished wood, sea air, and sensuous woman were appealing. Combined, they made a potent perfume.

Which brought his troubled thoughts full circle. She was no ordinary woman. What she was, exactly, was harder to nail down. Clearly, she could command a ship and crew as effectively as any man he'd sailed under, although her methods were definitely her own. She was strong when she needed to be, and yet she was delicate at the same time. He had no doubt she could weather any storm. It was what would remain after the eye of it had passed that confused him.

"Why do you do it?" he asked the sea beyond the small, circular window. "Why do you force yourself to do something you hate?"

No other captain he'd seen had shown remorse for taking a ship. Not only had he seen the dread in her eyes when he'd announced the merchant ship on the horizon, but she'd wept for the dead afterward. Luke drank deeply of the rum and leaned forward, pressing his forehead against the glass. He needed to find out what drove her. Why was she hunting Dervish? What had he stolen that she'd risk her soul to avenge?

"I don't know, but I damn well will."

Maybe once the puzzle of Samantha Fine was put together, he could get her off his mind. A load lifted off his chest. Yes, that was it. The reason he dwelled on her was because he didn't have all the answers. No other woman had been mysterious. They'd been strumpets, peddling wares he was only too happy to buy. Surely once he'd bedded her and gotten to the bottom of her quest for Dervish, he'd be rid of these nagging feelings that traipsed alongside him day and night.

Feeling much relieved, Luke shuffled to the table where she kept a candle and flint. Tiny sparks shot out and the candle fluttered to life.

Squawk. "Man in cabin. Man in cabin."

Content that the problem of Samantha would soon be solved, Luke dragged the chair from the window to Carracks's cage.

"Now, birdy," he said, "let's teach you some real words."

When Luke woke, cloaked in the smell of woman that lodged in every thread of Samantha's bed, dawn had yet to raise its head. However, if the rattling pans were any indication, Trevor was up and looking to ready breakfast. Luke stretched, easing muscles into wakefulness. The feather pillow was soft. Her bedcovers were just enough to warm a body without being sweltering. It should have been a perfect night's rest. It bloody well would have been if he couldn't smell her with every breath.

Which made closing his eye even worse, because with her scent clouding his senses, it was all too easy to picture her. She'd be naked, of course. The skin he already knew to be soft would heat beneath his touch; a mouth he'd touched fleetingly he now ached to possess. His body, more than ready to deliver what his overactive imagination had created, went hot and hard. The covers, draped low over his hips, slid to his thighs with his arousal.

Throbbing for release, Luke clenched his hands and willed the lust under control. He would have her, damn it. It had been many years since he'd had dreams like those, since he'd awaken with a fierce lust coiled in his belly. He found the clothes he'd left scattered on the floor and dressed hurriedly. Tucking his pistol into his sash, he headed up. It was time to put another piece of her puzzle into place.

The hatch to her cabin was directly in front of the quarterdeck. Though he'd prefer to catch her off guard, there was nothing he could do. She'd see the hatch lift and have a second or two to put up the wall she hid behind most of the time.

The hatch opened without a squeak. One thing about Samantha, she ran a clean ship. He'd never seen one kept so polished. He stepped out and eased the hatch into place.

Samantha wasn't on the quarterdeck.

She'd braced the tiller and it remained pointed, unaided by her hand. The moon wasn't much, but enough to reveal her easily. She was by the mainmast, coiling rope. Luke stood by and watched.

For a small woman, she was efficient. The task, which he knew had been accomplished prior to his retiring, was redone. Luke didn't see a difference, so he assumed she was simply keeping busy to remain awake. She straightened and moved to the bowsprit. He prowled behind her.

He treaded softly, lest his boots alert her to his presence. When she stopped at the bow, long hair flowing with the breeze, and turned to look out the starboard side, Luke's breath left his lungs.

The moon touched her cheeks and nose, kissing her skin with a feminine glow. Her slender neck arched back, revealing the column of her throat. Luke's lips parted. She shook her head, and coils of gold cascaded down her back. There'd never been a woman who looked less like a pirate.

Curves he'd kill to feel in the palms of his hands pressed against the bodice of her simple gown. If only his gaze could burn away the fabric. A picture of her standing on deck, bathed in nothing but moonlight and the slippery trail of his tongue burst upon him. It blinded him with hunger.

Seeing her savoring the night, enjoying the rocking of her ship, scattered every memory from his head. He'd had a woman not long before being hauled into the jail at Port Royal. Rachel? Charlotte? Bloody hell, he couldn't remember her name, but she had red hair. Or was it brown? No, she had black hair, that was it. He was fairly certain.

Luke cursed. What was happening to him? It wasn't that he usually remembered all their names and faces, but he could, when called upon, remember the act. He tried to draw it from memory. And failed.

Annoyed with Samantha and his reaction, he stalked over to the source of his memory loss. To hell if she heard him or not. He had to get her out of his head before he forgot his own damn name!

Sam had busied herself with tidying up a ship that her crew had already organized. The ropes were recoiled, the deck was swabbed again. Everything she could have done to keep her mind off Luke had been done. And none of it had worked.

Her thoughts kept going back to her cabin where he'd held her, where she'd slept peacefully for the first time in five years. After Dervish murdered the *Destiny*, it had been dreams of her family that had haunted her. Later it had turned to nightmares of Mr. Grant. Today, it had been neither. And it had been wonderful.

Now she knew what it was to sleep, just sleep with a man. To wake in strong arms that hadn't harmed her, but had healed a small part of her soul. She stared out to sea. It would be so incredibly difficult not to have that again. But she had to resist him, did she not? He was a pirate. What could he possibly offer her but more pain and misery? And a constant reminder of the loss of her family.

She heard the hard rap of boots on wood and turned. It wasn't surprising to see Luke stalking toward her, although she had expected him to sleep later. It was, however, shocking when he came close enough for his tension to crash over her. The force was tangible and immediately put Sam on the defensive.

"What's happened?" she asked, assuming a problem with her ship or crew.

Luke stopped, but not before he'd invaded her personal space. He was close enough for his every feature to be clear in the moonlight. A green eye, ripe with resentment, pierced hers. An energy, like a hurricane that built and built until its raw power was untethered, pulsed from his pores. His choppy breath blasted her face as he glared.

"When did Dervish rape you?"

The question, so far removed from what she'd expected, stunned her.

"What?"

He aimed a long finger at her chest.

"Don't play stupid now, Samantha. It's a little late for that. How long has it been since Dervish raped you?"

She grabbed at a rope and clung, as much to anchor herself against his verbal attack as to delay answering his question. "What makes you think he did?"

Luke growled, baring his teeth. "I heard your nightmare, remember? I was there. Now you're bent on hunting down Dervish and killing the man. Any fool can put the pieces together."

"Any fool," she murmured and took a deep breath. She hadn't thought of it from his position. Of course it would seem that Dervish had taken her innocence. She had no intention of correcting him. She'd already allowed him further into her life than she should have. Her heart was perilously close to danger as it was. Telling him the truth would further close the distance that was already shrinking between them.

"You're right," she said. "Dervish raped me. About a year ago." She walked around Luke and made her way to the stern, lest he read the lies on her face.

He followed her, his heat prowling closer and closer. Every muscle in her body longed to turn to that heat, to be held and cherished. But pirates didn't stay long enough to build anything lasting. No, Luke would take his pleasure and sail away. Joe was right. She wouldn't be able to live with that.

Luke's hand on her shoulder stopped her. He turned her around. He was calmer now, more like the man who'd held her as she slept and who'd looked at her with smoldering desire. It was that man, not the pirate, she feared more. Because it was that man she couldn't resist.

"When it happens with you and me, Samantha, it won't be anything like it was with Dervish."

She shivered. The certainty in his words should have insulted her, but instead they turned her blood to warm honey.

"It won't happen, Luke. You're a pirate."

His gaze held hers, and within it she caught a fleeting glance of something akin to regret. From anyone but Luke, she'd have believed it.

"Yes, luv. It will."

His arms circled her, drawing her close with the slightest

pressure. She allowed him because her thoughts had washed away with his certainty that they'd be together. Perhaps it was because she'd been starving for affection these last five years. Or maybe it was too many hours in the sun. Surely any man would have this affect on her if she'd only give him a chance.

Luke's fingers teased their way up her spine and into the depth of her hair. His hand found her skull and drew her head back. Knees trembling, heart racing, Sam waited for Luke's next move.

"Very soon, luv, we will finish this."

Before she could argue that it wasn't an end she was looking for, but a beginning, his mouth inched down to hers.

They'd kissed twice before, but neither had the effect of this one. Before, he'd hurried, a quick smack either to keep her quiet or to show his enthusiasm for an upcoming battle. This one left no room for comparisons.

His touch was gentle, lips grazing hers in slow sweeps. Leisurely, he nipped and nibbled, demanding nothing. The beauty of it pressed into Sam and allowed nothing but an honest response. It flowed from her in hot waves. His mustache was soft, and tickled as their mouths met. Sam leaned into him, her hands digging into his narrow waist.

One of them moaned, and then the kiss deepened. Mouths tilted, allowing deeper contact. Sam clutched his shirt, lest she drown in the wave of desire that enveloped her. She'd never dreamed a kiss could be so passionate. There was no room for thoughts, there was only Luke. She arched against him, burning everywhere their bodies met.

His hands snaked down her back to her waist and crept around her ribs. She sucked in her breath and her breasts

filled with wanting, making them heavy in her bodice.
Never had she felt such want, such need to touch and be
touched. She wanted no barriers, just the explosion of sensation.

Her hands found their way to his hair and held on, keeping his mouth fused to hers. When he flicked his tongue
against hers, Sam whimpered and mirrored his movements.
Luke's hands encased her ribs, his thumbs resting just beneath the swell of her breasts. She curved her tongue
around his and felt a rush of triumph when he growled low
in his throat. So this was what being wanton felt like.

It felt like freedom.

Suddenly Luke pulled away. His mouth was swollen
from her kiss. Sam wiped the moisture from his lips with
her fingertips. Luke grabbed her hand and sucked the moisture back into his mouth.

"I want every part of you, every taste, to remain with
me."

The words were intimate and seductive. They pebbled
her nipples and drew her pulse between her legs.

"Luke, I—"

Whistling, Trevor threw open the main hatch and stepped
out with her breakfast. Mortified that he'd see the feelings,
the lust that had her in its powerful grasp, Sam rushed to
the tiller. She threw off the rope and took the helm.

"I have your breakfast, Captain," he said.

He handed her the plate with no more ceremony than
usual. Sam exhaled her nervousness, thanked her cook,
and pretended to eat until he disappeared below.

Luke stepped back from the mainmast, where Trevor
either hadn't seen him or didn't like him enough to acknowledge him. The hunger was still in his eyes. He took

the banana off her plate and peeled it. Then, he ripped off a chunk and held it to her mouth. Innocently, she took a slow bite. Luke's eye narrowed.

"Luv, when your crew isn't around, you and I"—he gestured his finger between them—"aren't going to be interrupted until we're both weak with satisfaction."

He leaned in, his tongue lifting a piece of fruit off her lip.

"And I'll tell you this, Samantha, it'll take me a bloody long time to be satisfied."

He kissed her again, long and deep until the plate teetered in her hand. If Luke hadn't grabbed it, it would have tumbled forgotten to the deck. He pulled away and handed her the plate. She fought the desire to draw him back. Trembling with need, she watched silently as he went back to her cabin. To her bed.

She set the plate aside and placed hot hands on burning cheeks. The kiss had been everything she'd hoped for as a girl—and more. Tongues. Who knew they could mate so wonderfully, could arouse so completely? And she was aroused, from the tingling in her breasts to the rapid beat of her heart. But again, he'd left her wanting.

He hadn't bothered to hide the fact that once her crew wasn't around, he'd finish what he'd begun tonight. Which, she realized with a sharp stab of panic, could be tomorrow night in Barbados. No, she corrected herself, as dawn bruised the sky with purple and indigo, tonight. Desire squeezed in her stomach, and she took a steadying breath.

He also hadn't asked if she'd like to lie with him. He'd assumed. She bit her lip as reality slapped her hard in the face. Of course he wouldn't ask. He was a pirate. Damn it, why did she keep forgetting that? Carracks's scratchy voice carried from her cabin, though the words were muffled.

Like her parrot, she had to find a way to live with Luke. Until Dervish was dead, they needed him.

And after Dervish died, Sam feared she'd still need Luke.

He had managed to stir her desires and then slip away, not caring that he'd left her a tangle of emotions and wants she didn't understand.

Well, Samantha, she thought, *if you needed more proof he's a pirate first and foremost, there it is.*

Nine

It took little thought for Oliver to guess Tortuga as Samantha's starting point. Every vermin who sailed under a pirate flag infested the island. Why should a whore accompanied by one be any different? Besides, Isaac had said his ship was sailing east by northeast. Which put Tortuga right in their path.

The coins in his pockets jingled as he strolled from one filthy tavern to another. He would use those coins liberally for anyone who had word of Luke Bradley. The chance that they'd remember one strumpet from another was slight. He'd decided he'd have better luck asking about one of their own. Sure enough, they'd seen him not two days ago, but hadn't spoken to him. A second coin loosened their memories enough to lead him to the man who had.

Oliver ignored the rotting trash that littered the streets. He casually stepped over broken bottles, shattered cups, and at least three drunks who'd lost consciousness. The smell of stale beer and rum rose from their filthy bodies.

Still, it didn't bother Oliver. Having slaves in his employ, he was used to garbage. And he would do whatever needed doing in order to win in the end.

He stepped into Doubloons and took the first somewhat clean table he saw. Luke Bradley had been there, which meant so had Samantha. Oliver licked his lips eagerly. From his precarious perch on the edge of the scarred chair, he searched the room. He'd been told to look for a bear of a man at least a full head taller than any other around him. He frowned, not seeing anyone of such stature.

He looked again, and this time found the one he'd been searching for. The giant sat with four empty mugs before him. By all appearances, he didn't seem drunk. When he stood, he overshadowed every man in the dimly lit tavern. The floor shook when he stomped to the long bar to get another pint. Oliver scraped his chair back and made his own way over the sticky floor.

"Can I buy you one, friend?" he asked.

The giant looked down on him with clear blue eyes. Oliver figured he often used that look to intimidate. Well, it wouldn't work today. He was getting closer to Samantha, and nobody was going to stand in his way.

"You ain't me friend, but I'll let you buy me one. Yo, Polly, this bloke's buyin'."

Oliver forced a smile and counted out the coins. He followed the giant back to his table.

"What are ya after?" the other man asked pointedly as he guzzled half the cup.

Oliver remained standing so as not to be dwarfed. "Your friend Luke. He said if I ever made it this way, to buy you a drink."

The big man laughed, the sound as enormous as the

mouth it thundered from. Then his dense gaze roamed over Oliver's clean suit.

"That so? Luke been hangin' around the wrong parts again?" He shoved his chair away from the table. "When did you see him?"

Oliver ignored the insult. "A few days ago. Saw him and that girl, Samantha, heading out of Port Royal."

"She's a beauty, all right. I didn't catch her name the other night. Samantha." He sighed, and his mind drifted for a moment before he said, "Luke seemed mighty possessive."

Oliver's fingers curled in his pockets. He'd been sure, but to have it confirmed gave him the fortitude he needed. There would be no stopping him now. He wouldn't rest until he had her. She might be spreading her legs for Bradley, but he'd see to it she spread them for him also. Before he killed her.

He had to focus, Oliver reminded himself, as the giant was now frowning. "Well," he said jovially, "you know Luke."

The man nodded and took another gulp. He slammed the empty mug down. Oliver jumped as the table rattled on spindly legs.

"I have some business with Luke, but wasn't able to catch him before he left. Do you know where he was heading?"

"I ain't stupid, man. You're no friend of Luke's, nor Samantha's." He threatened the life of the chair when he leaned back. Though creaking in pain, it remained surprisingly intact. "And I'll not be tellin' you anythin'."

Since he'd expected that, Oliver shrugged and took a small black pouch out of his pocket. At the jingling noise the other man sat up. Knowing he had his attention, Oliver pulled the strings on the bag and slowly poured out a pile of doubloons.

"I need to see Luke about a personal matter. You tell me his whereabouts and I'll hand you this money." He lifted a coin, turned it slowly before the giant, and dropped it into the pouch. He counted thirty before the man put his anchor-sized hand over the bag.

"All you need to know is Luke's destination?"

"That's all."

His eyes never left the coins as he contemplated. Oliver wasn't worried. He'd used money before to bribe his way through legal matters. Money spoke a universal language. It was only a matter of time until the man listened.

"Luke ain't stupid. He'll kill ya if he smells a rat."

Oliver had no doubt money could buy Bradley's possession of Samantha. If not, then he'd die alongside her. After he'd watched his whore be ridden one last time.

"Let me worry about Bradley." He eyed the man over the coins they both held. "Where did he go?"

Greed filled the giant's eyes. Still, Oliver was restless. This man knew something, and he'd damn well better talk soon.

"Santa Placidia."

Oliver smiled, his heart pounding. Gladly, he released his hold on the money and sauntered out to the sound of a happy man counting easy money.

Captain pocketed the coins. He liked Luke well enough and knew the man's skills. Luke was wily. It would take more than some dandy whose hands looked as though they hadn't seen a real day's work to get the best of Luke Bradley. He signaled for another drink and rewarded the pretty barmaid with a smile and pinch to her arse.

He raised his cup to Luke.

"Good luck, mate," he said, and got back to the business of drinking.

It wasn't until after the midday meal that Sam figured she was tired enough to sleep without thoughts of Luke plaguing her. Sunshine glared through wisps of clouds that did nothing to lessen the sweltering heat. There was no wind to speak of, and the *Revenge* bobbed lazily on the stillness of the sea.

The crew had seen to their tasks and were whiling away time playing cards. The men sat in a circle next to the lifeboat with a mounting pile of coins and other personal effects in the middle.

Willy frowned at his cards, his cheeks flushed over the top of his beard. Joe's hair stood on end and looked wiry enough to scrape barnacles off the keel. His expression showed less than Willy's, but Sam knew by the way his nostrils flared that he had a winning hand. Aidan, skin glowing bright with the joy of being included, was studying his cards intently. Trevor struggled to hold the cards in his gnarled hands before throwing them down to stretch out on his back and await the next deal.

Inevitably her gaze sought Luke, as it had since he'd taken his shirt off in deference to the heat. His skin was smooth, his torso long and lean. When he'd first shed his shirt, she'd been blindsided by a fist of desire. Thankfully, his back was to her now, and by stretching onto her toes, she could see the cards he held. A knave of diamonds, three of hearts, ace of spades, two of clubs, and nine of diamonds. Absolutely nothing.

He threw in another shilling.

Aidan sighed, though the smile remained painted on his face, and tossed in his lot.

Was Luke out of his mind? He had nothing and was increasing the stakes in steady measures. How could he be so bold? She would never—

The thought brought her round. No, she wouldn't wager unless she knew she could win. That Luke risked it all with little or nothing to fall back on spoke to exactly who he was.

Willy grunted and tossed his cards aside. Joe's ruddy cheeks turned a deeper red. His gaze shuffled from his cards to Luke and back again. Sam waited with bated breath to see what Joe would do. There was a hefty amount of money to be won or lost. Strangely, she didn't want either man to lose.

Expectations built while Joe decided his move. Backs were straightened, smiles replaced sleepy expressions as the few who'd lain back to rest caught the excitement and sat up to pay attention. Sam watched anxiously, heart thudding and palms sweating.

Luke examined his fingernails.

After a heavy few minutes of waiting, Joe reached into his pocket, withdrew something silver, and tossed his pocket watch into the pot. Sam gasped. Her crew smiled through yellowing teeth, enjoying the intensity of the game.

Sam wiped her palms on her cotton skirt. There had never been a game on her ship before where the stakes were so high. Luke shrugged, leaned to the left, and reached deep into his pocket. Sam let go the tiller, stepped aside to see what he'd added.

Her breath escaped in a whoosh. He'd thrown in five doubloons.

Willy whistled softly through the gap of his teeth. Muscles in Joe's jaw flexed as he realized he'd lost. Sam knew he couldn't add to it. He was left no choice but to fold. Large, angry hands crushed the cards before he threw them down. Hatred spewed from Joe's eyes as he glared at Luke. Joe wasn't a sore loser. Sam knew it wasn't his losing that angered him, but rather to whom he'd lost.

Luke mildly folded his cards back into the deck, his winning hand remaining a mystery. She'd assumed he'd slowly play each card, one at a time, so the crew could see how cleverly he'd fooled them. Instead, he'd wisely avoided the resentment his farce would have created. Then, with both arms looped around his winnings, he dragged the lot toward him.

"Filthy piece of vermin," Joe muttered. He stood, stretched his arms over his head, and stalked toward her.

Sam, annoyed with herself for being glad Luke hadn't lost, put on a sympathetic smile for Joe. She should have wanted Luke to lose. She should have been feeling worse for Joe's loss. Only crazy men gambled with nothing. Luke shouldn't have won. But the fact that he'd risked it, had the gumption to risk it, earned respect. Even if it was grudgingly given.

Joe was at her side, wide belly heaving.

"Lucky bastard. If I'd had me more money, I'd have beaten 'im."

Wisely, Sam didn't reply to that. She had a feeling Luke would have just kept on betting and Joe would only have lost more.

"I'm sorry about your watch, Joe."

He took a deep breath and smiled at her. "You know me, lass. I don't bet what I ain't willin' to part with."

They watched Willy crawl into the lifeboat, place his hat over his face, and fall asleep.

"Besides, bloody watch ain't worked in five years. I only kept it as a reminder of England."

Sam laughed, the guilt easing off her shoulders.

Then Luke caught her eye and her gaze sharpened while her smile evaporated from her lips. He'd stopped by the cannon closest to them and was watching her openly. Hungrily. It was a bold move with Joe straining next to her, more than ready to go at Luke once and for all. The mistrust between them was as strong as a hurricane. Luke smiled, a sinful curve of mustached lip that sent Sam's stomach tumbling. She pressed a quaking hand to her jittery stomach.

"I'll tell ye again, I don't trust 'im."

"I know, Joe. Just a little longer, and then we won't need him."

"And that'll be a fine day, a fine day."

She fell into troubled silence. In some ways, yes, to be rid of Luke would be a fine day. Yet the thought brought a terrible ache around her heart. She closed her eyes against the sparkling water. Maybe Luke wasn't the crazy one. Perhaps it was her.

"I'll leave her to you, Joe. I'll see you later."

He nodded and took over the helm. Deliberately ignoring Luke's gaze, which hunted her with every step, Sam went down the main hatch to the galley. Since the card game had begun, her throat was drier than sand on a beach, and she hoped to remedy that with her rationed cup of water.

With each step down, the crushing heat eased. Damp air that carried the residual smell of the midday meal cooled her heated cheeks. Sam sighed at the welcome relief. She'd have lifted her gown for a moment to feel the chill on her legs, but the sound of boots overhead changed her mind. Those were Luke's, and she certainly didn't want him to catch her with her skirts raised.

Nearly choking on the thought, Sam hurried to the cask of water, removed the lid, and ladled out her share in a crockery mug she'd taken from the line of clean mugs nearby. The sound of those boots descending didn't surprise her. It did, however, make her stomach leap.

He jumped down the last few rungs and regarded her openly, hungrily. Her hand tightened around the mug. Determined that he not see again how he affected her, Sam held her ground, even though she'd prefer to run. Run before he could plunder her mouth again. Run before she let him.

Besides, fleeing would only encourage a man like Luke. And Luke needed no encouraging.

"I see I'm right on time," he said.

"For what?"

"For you to share that water."

The thought brought back sensual memories of their kiss the other night and threatened her resolve not to get any closer to Luke. He'd hurt her in the end, she needed to remember that.

"You're welcome to get your own."

"I'm afraid I've already had my ration," he said, stepping closer. "And I don't think the crew would appreciate my taking more."

"Shouldn't you be more concerned about what your captain would do?"

His grin was arrogant. His gaze hovered on her breasts, reminding Sam how close he'd come to touching them. Suddenly the galley wasn't as cool as it had been.

"That won't be a problem."

"Oh? And how can you be so certain? I have it on good authority that the captain doesn't like you very much."

The green of his gaze deepened and his mouth once again curved sensuously.

"I fear you're mistaken, luv."

He pressed closer. Still shirtless, his golden chest gleamed with perspiration. It should have been unpleasant. But Sam couldn't help wondering how it would feel beneath her fingers. Even the smell curled her toes. Salty air agreed with Luke.

Her heart drummed behind her breasts. She prayed he couldn't see what his state of undress was doing to her, because if he did and he pursued it, Sam knew she'd be powerless to resist.

"I don't believe I am."

"Are you, now? What about the way you were watching me on deck? You nearly stumbled when I removed my shirt."

"I most certainly did not!"

His eyebrow arched. "You're denying it?"

"I don't have to deny something that didn't happen."

"But you liked what you saw," he said.

"Only in your own mind, Luke."

Sam hadn't thought he could step any closer, but he proved her wrong. Her breasts pressed into his chest. His breath caressed her cheeks and teased the hair that had escaped her bun. His heat was unmatched by even the sun. It burned everywhere their bodies touched, regardless of whether or not there was clothing in the way.

Considering her with an animal's hunger, Luke wrapped his hand around hers and brought her cup to his lips. He drank deeply. Sam's attention locked onto his throat, and she licked her lips. When her eyes met his, she knew he'd seen her reaction. She yanked her hand, and water sloshed over the rim and splashed Luke. Trails of it crept down, lower and lower until they met the waist of his trousers. Sam couldn't help but stare. Luke didn't step back.

"Want to get that for me?" he asked. "With or without your tongue," he offered.

Because she was tempted, she shoved away, losing yet more water in the process.

"You're crude."

"And you, luv, can't resist me."

What could she say? He was right, and they both knew it. She hadn't even attempted to resist him.

"I had a moment of weakness," she conceded.

His fingers brushed her lips before she could avoid them.

"In that case, I look forward to your next lapse in control."

Though her lips were still tingling where he'd touched them, Sam raised her chin, pushed her cup into his hands, and left him grinning behind her.

Stepping into her cabin was like stepping onto land after weeks at sea. Safe. She once again felt safe. The bedcovers were in place, which shocked her. She'd expected Luke to leave her cabin in shambles, yet it looked exactly as she'd left it. She sighed and kicked off her shoes, then lifted them from the floor and placed them directly next to the screen. Since it was warm, she decided to take off her dress and sleep in her shift.

Carracks made scratching noises as she began to undress behind the screen. She slipped a button free. Then another. When the bodice gaped open, she heard an appreciative whistle.

She clutched the garment to her chest and peered around the screen. Luke wasn't there, nobody was. Only Carracks, which could mean only one thing.

"Damn that Luke," she muttered.

Squawk. "Luke is handsome. Luke is handsome."

Sam stepped to her parrot's cage, where he danced side to side on his perch, oblivious to the fact that he'd been manipulated.

"Traitor," she grumbled and slipped into bed. It was all Luke's fault. In a matter of hours he'd corrupted Carracks and managed to make her uncomfortable in her own cabin. She was almost afraid of what else he'd taught her parrot to say. It didn't take long to find out.

Squawk. "You want Luke. You want Luke."

Samantha pummeled her pillow, wishing it was Luke's face. It had been bad before, when her thoughts were impossible to escape. She groaned, turning her face into the pillow that smelled strongly of Luke. There'd be no escaping him now.

"Storm's rolling in," Joe said as Sam climbed out of her cabin five hours later.

She accepted his hand up and scanned the sky.

Angry gray clouds tinged with green tumbled on the horizon. They rolled toward them, seeming to get larger with each blink of the eye. Ragged spears of lightning darted from their mass and lunged for the sea. The winds had escalated during her short and troubled sleep, and snapped the sails. The choppy sea jostled the *Revenge*. It was only a matter of time until they'd be tossed about like a ball of yarn between a cat's paws.

She accepted the looking glass Joe passed her. Land off the port side. Sam blew out her breath. Barbados. She lowered the glass, judging the distance of land against the time they had to escape the brunt of the storm.

"We'll make it, luv. She's a fast ship, she can outrun it," Luke said, stepping to her side.

With a slap, she shut the looking glass. Luke's constant presence, physical or not, was wearing on her. On a ship this size, there was no escaping him. He was in her thoughts, she smelled him in her bed, and now her parrot talked just like him. He shadowed her, never far out of reach, always in sight. And her blasted heart kept fluttering whenever he looked her way.

Her mind warned that Luke was trouble, and she had enough with finding Dervish. But it took only a breath to catch the windy, sea-filled smell of him, to turn and see the teasing in his dark gaze. His desire coiled around her, inside her, and left her blood simmering. When that happened, she forgot all the reasons they were wrong for each other.

"Dervish had best be there, Luke, when we arrive. Or I'll have yer head on the end of the bowsprit by night's end," Joe warned.

Luke cocked his head to the side. "Seems to me, we'd best concentrate on outrunning the storm, or the *Revenge* will be too battered to go after Dervish."

"We'll make it," Sam said. She hadn't gotten this close to Dervish to fail now.

"Joe, I need you up with Willy. It'll take all your strength to hold the sails when the wind picks up."

As though it heard her words, a gust shrieked between the sails, stretching canvas and propelling the ship through the turbulent seas. In an instant the sky went from light gray to charcoal. The clouds were a solid, angry fist poised to unleash their fury without mercy.

Wind flailed in Sam's face, whipping her hair across her cheeks.

Luke's golden hair flew around his head. Despite that, he stood braced on the deck in total control, every inch a pirate. He belonged here. This was his life.

But there wasn't time to dwell on that now. She had to get her ship into port, hopefully still in one piece. Then she could think of Dervish. She tossed a look at Luke, who'd taken a rope and was stretching it back into position. After that, she'd have to decide just what Luke meant to her.

And what she was prepared to do about it.

They arrived in Barbados soaking wet and bone weary. The *Revenge* had lost a foresail, sustained some tearing in the mainsail, and taken on water when the patch Willy had made after their encounter with the merchant ship split open and the hole doubled in size. It was nothing critical, but enough to keep them in port a few days. Luke couldn't have planned it better if he'd tried.

"I ain't seein' Dervish's ship, Luke. Where is it?" Joe demanded after they'd dropped anchor.

Luke scanned the harbor and the collection of ships that rolled with the tail end of the storm. Of course the man's ship was nowhere to be seen, given that it was moored off a completely different island. But now he had an excuse, more believable than the feeble one he'd concocted.

"With the storm, he could be anywhere. He's on his way, though. Captain wouldn't lie," Luke said. He was the one who'd lied. Of course, it was best they didn't discover that yet. First he needed Samantha's help.

Speaking of said lady, she was looking exceptionally lovely in her soaked gown. It clung to her curves, and the damp hair that hung around her shoulders gave her a sultry look. The red stain that had oozed through the sleeve of her gown while she'd fought to keep the *Revenge* on course would help convince her to go along. Nobody knew Luke

Bradley was on board the *Revenge*. He could slip into the forest that surrounded the town without being noticed. Later, he'd meet up with Samantha and finally have what belonged to him.

There was no holding back the grin. Good luck was finally coming his way.

Sam had absolutely no idea how Luke had talked her into this. He'd insisted to Joe that her arm needed tending and that he knew just the person to do it. Since the wound had opened and Joe was concerned about infection, he hadn't argued. Then, before she could do more than instruct her crew, Luke rowed them both to shore. He'd given her money for a carriage and directions to where she was to go.

Now here she stood in the dewy aftermath of a savage storm, with the scent of moss and damp earth all around her, facing a home so grand it could have belonged to the governor.

The massive white house nestled amid trees, tall columns holding up a second-level veranda shadowing a large, stately door. Soft light poured from the windows, and beautifully kept hedges and flowerbeds circled around to the back of the house. The dignified home spoke of money, elegance, and respect. What was she, Captain Sam Steele, doing here?

Thankfully, she didn't look like a pirate at the moment. But what if they could see through her ruse? After all, the dress Luke had barely given her time to change into wasn't much more than what a servant girl would wear. Her hair, still damp, was pulled back with a plain yellow ribbon. She felt like a pauper going to have tea with the queen.

But Luke had said the lady of the house would help her
with her wound, which she had to admit stung like the devil.
He'd been adamant that all she had to do was say she knew
Luke Bradley and she'd be welcomed warmly.

Humph, she thought. *One of Luke's strumpets, no doubt.*
Certainly no real lady would involve herself with Luke
Bradley.

She cast a glance around the majestic trees that stood
sentinel along the lane. Where the devil was he? Too exhausted to question any further, Sam lifted the brass
knocker and gave three sound taps.

Sam counted water droplets falling off the leaves of the
fern nearest the door while she waited for a response. She
shivered, not from the dampness that hung in the air but
from an unsettled feeling that she was being watched.

Promptly, a tall, thin man with firmly pressed attire answered the door. He had gray hair and eyes of such a pale
blue they were almost white. Perfectly curved eyebrows rose
in question as he took in her less than dignified apparel.

Sam felt like a fool. The man looked down a very pointed
nose at her. Only through sheer will did she keep her feet
from shuffling. What was Luke thinking, sending her here?
But since she *was* here and she'd trusted him so far, she
forced the hesitancy from her voice.

"May I speak to the lady of the house, please?" she asked,
drawing upon all the decorum she'd learned as a girl.

Nothing moved but his lips. "Madam is not expecting
visitors tonight. Pray you come back another day. When
you have an invitation," he added pointedly.

He was half Joe's size, yet he intimidated her in a way
her first mate never had. Perhaps because he represented a
life she no longer belonged to, no matter how much she'd

like to. She'd known when becoming Steele that there was no going back. She was no longer a lady. She swallowed the regret and tilted her head to look him square in the eye. Deliberately, she lowered her voice.

"Please tell her I was sent by Luke Bradley."

The man's gaze narrowed, and he looked over her shoulder. Sam turned, expecting to see Luke standing there. The lane was empty, although the watched feeling clung to her like moss to a rock.

"I'll let her know," the servant said, then promptly shut the door in her face.

"Well, that was pleasant," Sam muttered.

Cold fingers crept along the base of her neck as the feeling of being watched heightened. Sam pressed her back to the door. It was never wise to turn your back on a threat, seen or otherwise. Nothing was visible except the palm trees that waved lazily, bright hibiscus thriving at their feet. A thin mist rose from the ground with the arrival of dusk. The sky, still dark gray from the remnants of the storm, added to the eerie feel. Sam swallowed, hoping the servant would hurry back.

Then the door opened and Sam staggered back into the entryway. Mortified and more than a little unsettled, she righted herself and ran trembling hands down her skirt. She looked up into eyes that were the same deep green as Luke's.

The lady smiled warmly, if a bit hesitantly. She peered outside, glanced side to side, then eased the solid door closed.

"I've a nice fire in the parlor. Follow me, and we'll get you warm and dry soon enough."

Sam had little choice but to follow. The woman's navy

blue skirt skimmed the polished marble floor. Her ebony hair was curled and pinned on the top of her head in a fashionable array. Other than her eyes, she didn't resemble Luke, and yet Sam knew they must be related. Why else would he send her here?

The next room was richly decorated with brocade-covered furniture, freshly waxed tables, and thick velvet drapery. Once they entered the parlor, her hostess stepped aside, and the heat of the hearth warmed Sam's cheeks. The curtains were pulled closed for the night, and Sam was grateful for that. Whoever was watching from the trees wouldn't be able to see her now.

She immediately strode to the fire and stretched her hands toward the dancing flames, wincing when the effort pulled on her wound.

The lady coughed discreetly. "Pritchard said you were sent by Luke Bradley?"

Sam turned, unsure how much to tell her. She accepted the cup her hostess offered and inhaled the lemony tang of the tea. The brew was hot, and Sam cradled the delicate cup in one hand, holding the saucer in the other.

"Luke suggested I come," Sam said. "He said you'd be able to see to this."

Sam balanced the cup on the saucer and held out her arm. She flinched as the material clung to her seeping wound.

"You're hurt!" the other woman gasped.

She immediately set her china on the mantle, took Sam's arm, and gently rolled up the sleeve. Her face paled in the candlelight.

"It's so long." She peered closer. "It appears to have missed the main vein. You're very lucky."

Sam raised her eyebrows. "I didn't feel so lucky when it happened."

"Oh, of course not! Forgive me, I'm sure that sounded insensitive."

Everything about this woman confused Sam. If she was a relative, why was she so eager to help Luke? Surely she'd know what he was, and Sam couldn't imagine a lady of this woman's stature associating with a notorious pirate. If Sam was wrong about the family connection, there was a very good chance her hostess and Luke shared a romantic past. Wouldn't she be jealous that Luke had brought another woman to her home?

"It's not a fresh wound."

"No, it happened yesterday. Unfortunately, we couldn't get here any sooner, with the storm and all."

Her arm was turned and examined by hands as gentle as a babe's. "It looks clean, thank goodness."

She gently lowered Sam's arm. Emerald eyes met Sam's. "Tell me Luke didn't do this to you?"

There was both dread and resignation in her voice.

"No, he—"

"Jacqueline, darling, you know me better than that," Luke admonished as he swaggered into the room.

Jacqueline spun around, her skirts swirling around her ankles.

"Luke," she whispered, "what are you doing here?"

Which was Sam's thinking altogether. But before she could ponder that, Jacqueline ran to the doors of the parlor and promptly closed them. She leaned heavily against the tall panels. Luke ignored Jacqueline in favor of the brandy that was on a small cart. The amber liquid circled in his glass before he drank half in one swallow. Then, still disregarding Sam, he smiled at their hostess.

"I've come for a visit." He waved in Sam's direction. "And to see that Samantha's arm is tended to properly."

Jacqueline looked from Luke to her. "Samantha, I'm pleased to meet you." She turned back to Luke. "We hadn't yet gotten around to the pleasantries of names with that terrible gash on her arm."

Luke nodded and poured himself another brandy. Taking his drink, he ambled to the couch, sat as though he belonged, and propped muddy boots on her table. Though their hostess sighed, she didn't appear distraught over his behavior. Of course, if she was on intimate terms with Luke, she already knew his terrible habits.

That thought twisted something ugly in Sam's stomach. Horrified, she concentrated on her tea.

"Dare I ask how she acquired such a wound?"

Luke shifted so he could see over the back of the couch. His smile was brash. "A lover's quarrel?"

Sam gasped, and her cup rattled on its saucer. She set it down.

Before she could speak, the lady held up her hand. "Don't be offended, Samantha. I'm not. Unfortunately, I'm used to such talk from him."

Sam's head was spinning with confusion. Why wasn't the other woman jealous? Granted, she had nothing to be jealous over, but Jacqueline wouldn't know that. Sam took another look at their hostess. A long look. Then she did the same to Luke. Within moments she came to the conclusion that there was no possibility this woman was a harlot, Luke's or anyone else's. She was simply too refined.

Luke set his empty glass next to his boots, both of which remained on the table. Disgusted, Sam shot him a look. He lifted his hands as though to ask what he'd done wrong. Then the lady looked at Sam with a sympathetic glance, and another thought struck Sam. A more horrendous one. If

Jacqueline wasn't one of Luke's harlots, which Sam would wager the *Revenge* on, that left only one thing. She thought Sam was.

She had to correct that at once.

"Excuse me, Jacqueline?" she began.

The woman smiled warmly. "What can I do for you, Samantha?"

She wasn't making this any easier.

"Apparently Luke was wrong in coming here, as was I. If you'll excuse us . . ."

Luke waved good-bye over his shoulder, long fingers wiggling saucily. Fuming that he'd made a fool of her, that she'd let him, Sam headed for the door. She couldn't stay in this wonderful home a moment longer when Jacqueline assumed she'd been with Luke. Even though she wanted to be, which to her mind was equally awful. Truth be told, she spent far too much time thinking and dreaming of being with Luke. Flustered, Sam shook her head.

"Nonsense," Jacqueline said, hurrying to catch up. She stopped Sam midstride. "Luke was right in bringing you here. That arm needs sutures, and I can do a clean job of it. Don't you worry."

She gently led Sam back to the couch that faced Luke's. "Now sit down while I get the bandages and everything else I need. And then"—she turned determined eyes to Luke's mischievous one—"we can find out the real reason you've come."

Luke placed a hand over his heart. "I'm bleeding, Jacqueline. After three years I thought you'd have a better welcome for me than that."

Sam was appalled. What kind of terrible game was he playing with such a kindhearted woman? They were in her home, taking advantage of her hospitality. What would the woman think if she knew the truth about them?

Jacqueline smiled. Then she leaned over the back of the couch and placed a kiss on his darkly tanned cheek.

"You're right, of course. Welcome home, brother."

Ten

"She's your sister?" Sam whispered incredulously.

Luke crossed his ankles, depositing more mud on an otherwise spotless table.

"Had I not mentioned that?"

"It must have slipped your mind. It would be an easy thing, considering there's nothing inside there to hang on to."

Luke's mouth twitched in an attempt to hide a grin. "I promised you someone who could stitch that, didn't I? Seems you should be thanking me, not insulting me."

Sam's mouth worked but no sound came out. He'd never once mentioned he had a sister, and now here they were, two pirates surrounded by money and stature. She jumped to her feet.

"Luke, we have to get out of here! There are people watching this house. I don't know who, but I felt them. If they find out you're here, and that I'm . . . well, we must leave at once!"

"First of all, Jacqueline knows I'm a pirate. So do the

men out in the trees. And you're right, they're looking for me. As for you, you're practically invisible. No one knows who you really are."

"What do you mean you know those men out there are looking for you? How can you be so calm about that? We're jeopardizing your sister's life!" She rubbed at her temple. "Your sister. I can't believe it."

"They don't know I'm here. You, luv, were my distraction. While you were keeping them occupied at the front door, I snuck around back. The house has this little side entrance. No one really knows it's there. You see, it's hidden by shrubs and—"

"You used me?" Sam inhaled deeply in an attempt to calm herself. "You knew they were watching me? What if they knew about Steele? I could've been hanging by morning."

Anger, disbelief, and hurt stumbled over themselves. He'd both misled and embarrassed her. Not to mention he'd risked her life. For what? For a suture Willy could have done? And all the while she'd trusted him, trusted that he was only seeing to her safety and well-being. The pain around her heart stole her breath.

Luke's answer was stalled by Jacqueline's return. The soft tapping of her shoes on the hard floor silenced Luke, but the storm brewing in his eye told her they weren't finished.

Yes, they were, Sam thought. As soon as her arm was sewed, she was walking out those doors. And Luke Bradley be damned.

In the end, she simply had neither the heart nor the energy to leave. Jacqueline had offered her a bath. A real hot bath with rose-scented soap and jasmine bath oil. After that she'd been brought a tray of steamed asparagus, rosemary potatoes, tender lamb, and rice pudding rich with cinnamon. It was a feast and Sam relished every bite, her meal made all the sweeter by being able to eat it in peace. Luke had remained downstairs with Jacqueline, sparing Sam the agony of having to look at his deceitful face.

Exhausted, clean, and well-fed, she hadn't the energy to leave. The four-poster bed that dominated the room had been turned down, and begged Sam to sink into its warmth. But she wouldn't sleep. Couldn't, despite the luxurious room.

Still, there was no sense wasting Jacqueline's candles, so she blew out the flames that lined the dresser, leaving only one flickering on the bedside table. A thin veil of yellow light pooled from its wick and wax beaded down the thick pillar. Sam sat on the feather bed, the softness of which she'd forgotten over the years.

The things she'd taken for granted as a child were now a luxury. Lying on her side, Sam watched the candlelight dance exotically. Dervish had taken her family, and now she was closing in on him. Would tomorrow be the day she found him? Would her family's massacre finally be avenged?

Then what?

She sighed, rolled onto her back. The house was silent around her. She'd heard Jacqueline come upstairs earlier; her room was directly next to her hostess's. Jacqueline. Luke's sister. Married to the governor's brother, she'd proudly announced after Sam had had the courage to ask. A whirlwind of thoughts swirled in her head. They were sleeping in a house they had no right to be in. If they were discovered, they'd hang. So might Jacqueline, whom Sam had come to like very much.

Luke had tricked her into coming to this house. He'd

risked her life. For what? She eased from the bed and paced to the window. Surely Luke had a reason other than her arm for bringing her here. What was it?

Looking out into the darkness that enveloped Barbados, Sam wondered how the *Revenge* was faring. Had Willy finished the repairs? Had they spotted Dervish's ship?

There were too many unknowns for Sam's peace of mind. Since taking Mr. Grant's ship, she'd been in command of her own life. The only question that remained was Dervish's location. But from the moment she'd taken Luke on board, Sam had felt less and less the mistress of her destiny.

Tonight, however, she was too tired to consider it all. Tomorrow would be soon enough to start regaining her control. For the moment, she'd be happy with a small distraction. Remembering the tall bookshelf she'd seen in the parlor, Sam tied the borrowed pale blue robe over the matching nightgown, took the candle, and eased open the door.

Sam crept down the stairs. The doors to the parlor were nearly shut, and she pushed them open. In the corner next to the flickering hearth sat a candelabra with a fistful of burning candles. Next to it, the outline of a man she both wanted and feared.

"Luke."

He raised a glass to his lips and drank. Sam closed the doors behind her. Forgetting she'd come for a book to help ease her mind, she went straight for him.

"Why are we here?"

An unreadable gaze peered at her over the half-empty glass. His shirt gaped open, revealing a chest which for once was free of gold chains. His legs were boldly spread wide, and Sam fought to keep her gaze level.

"How's the arm?" he asked.

"It's fine, but don't distract me. You've strung me along long enough."

She set down her light and crossed her arms, waiting. Luke's gaze slid warmly down the length of her wrapper to her bare toes and back up again. Sam shifted.

"You look beautiful tonight," he said, his voice not much louder than the cracking flames in the hearth.

He was smart enough to know how to distract her, and his strategy hit its mark. A fracture split down the middle of Sam's resistance. He'd never called her that before. Actually, he'd never complimented her without a teasing lilt to his voice or a twinkle in his eye. But as he stood there, his stare unwavering, Sam saw there was no twinkle in his eye this time. In its place was a deluge of desire.

Despite the quiver deep in her belly, despite being drawn to that hunger with all her soul, she refused to be swayed by her feelings. She needed answers. She deserved them, by God. She held up her palm and took a step back.

"No, Luke. You can't distract me. Before any of this goes further, I need you to tell me the truth." Her eyes begged him to understand. "I need to know Luke Bradley."

He brought his left hand to his mustache and combed it with his thumb and forefinger. "You've heard the tales that follow me. What's left to know?"

Wanting to take full advantage of his willingness to talk, Sam sat on the sofa. She tucked her feet beneath her. Luke watched intensely as her bare legs slipped from the folds of her wrap before she hastily tucked them away again. He ran his tongue around his teeth.

"Why would you risk everything to come here? What's in this house you needed so badly?"

His gaze slowly raised from her legs.

"What makes you think I need anything?"

"Three years and you haven't seen your sister. You're not fool enough to risk capture for a few sutures and some brandy."

"Don't underestimate the power of good brandy, luv."

She didn't return his smile, but kept her gaze focused.

"I left something of mine here and I needed it back."

Sam leaned forward. "I'm not a simpleton, Luke. Whatever you've come back for is very valuable or you wouldn't risk your life. What is it?"

He sighed and sat beside her. "I've had treasure hidden in Jacqueline's cellar for years. This was the first chance I've had to reclaim it."

Treasure. She should have known he'd risk both their lives for damned treasure.

"She doesn't know, does she?"

His lips twitched into a grin. "Not even an inkling."

Which was probably for the best, Sam realized. Jacqueline couldn't disclose to the authorities what she didn't know. Still, it wounded Sam to know he'd risked her life for money. His excuse of needing a place to tend her wound, to have a good meal and bath, was not the real reason Luke had brought her here. He was. It was always about him.

He turned and ran a slightly calloused hand down her cheek. "You were never in danger, luv. Nobody knows who you are."

"And if I was? Would it have changed your plans to come here?"

His gaze pierced hers. "No."

Disappointment fell heavily onto her heart.

"*I'd* still be here. You, luv, would be tucked safely on board the *Revenge*. I'd have found another distraction."

There was no doubt he was genuine. She'd seen him

cavalier and obnoxious, could usually tell when he was up to no good. His gaze held no secrets now, and his sincerity let her know it mattered to him whether she believed him or not.

She nodded, and he inhaled deeply.

"When did Dervish take your eye?"

Luke took a slow breath and fingered the black swatch that covered his left eye. "If I tell you, will I get you into bed sooner?"

The twinkle was back, but she knew he wasn't jesting. If she wanted his honesty, she'd have to give him hers. Her heart sped with the words that formed in her mind.

"Maybe. If you tell me that, and a few other things."

His eyebrow arched and his tongue made another quick sweep of his teeth. Sam's stomach constricted. He draped an arm over the back of the couch. The tips of his fingers tickled her neck. He didn't look at her, but over her right shoulder.

"My ship hit a storm, one I couldn't escape. By the time the worst was over, she was sinking fast. I managed to sail her a little longer and got within hailing distance of Tortuga. She sank as I rowed to shore. Next night, Dervish walks into Doubloons, looking to increase his crew.

"As I was without my own ship, I thought I'd sail with him for a while, get some money, and be on my own again within a year. I was on the *Devil's Wrath* for a few months, had myself a nice share of the plunder tucked away. We dropped anchor in Barbados one night, after sacking a very wealthy merchant ship."

His fingers crept into her hair. She shivered, drawing his attention back to her face.

"Dervish's first mate had sailed under me once before,

before I caught him stealing and threw him off my ship first chance I had. Well, it seemed he held a grudge. When we left the *Devils' Wrath*, I made sure I was last off. I took my bag of treasure and disappeared into the forest. I didn't know he'd seen me until later."

"That's the treasure you've come back for?"

He nodded. Sam shifted closer to Luke, her hand drawing his free one into her grasp. Luke watched their fingers entwine and squeezed gently.

"Two days later we weighed anchor. An hour's sail out of Barbados, Dervish and his first mate came to me and accused me of taking more than my share of the plunder."

His gaze burned with conviction. "I didn't take anything that wasn't rightfully mine, but Dervish's suspicion and his first mate's word that he'd personally seen me tuck away more than I should have sealed my fate. Next thing I knew, the whole crew wanted my blood. As I didn't have any treasure with me, or with my belongings, I couldn't disprove their accusations."

He shrugged. "Dervish drew his sword. His crew made sure I didn't have a weapon. A quick slice"—his hand ripped through the air and made Sam jump—"and my eye was gone. Before I could do more than grab a rag to stop the blood, I was being thrown over."

Sam was horrified. "How did you get help?"

Luke rubbed lazy circles on the top of her hand with his thumb. He told the tale very calmly, with little emotion, but that was another of Luke's mysteries. The main emotion she'd witnessed from him so far was desire. Everything else was tucked away, hidden behind indifference and a casualness that belied the storms she'd witnessed in his eye.

"A small fishing boat happened to be nearby, and I hailed it over. They rowed me to port. I shocked poor Jacqueline out of her skin when I turned up with blood pouring down my face."

The image that formed in Sam's head was awful. If she could have crawled into the vision, she'd swim him to shore herself and get him the help he needed, to be by his side so he wouldn't have to suffer alone.

She loved him.

Her heart did a little jig as the truth dawned, but it didn't overwhelm her. The fact that he was a pirate, and what that entailed, she'd deal with tomorrow.

She came to her knees and cupped his freshly shaven cheeks with her hands, then leaned in and laid a soft kiss on the patch that covered what used to be his left eye.

"I'm sorry, Luke. That must have been awful."

When she drew back, a ravenous gaze met hers. If he knew what she'd just acknowledged to herself, he said nothing. The only clue that he suspected something had changed was in the darkening of his eye. As she remained on her knees next to him, they stared at each other. There were things to be said, but they both knew none were going to be spoken. She'd resisted Luke until now, fought her feelings for him. Tonight, a wall between them had crumbled. It was time to see what lay on the other side.

His hands came around her waist, squeezed, and lifted her up. Sam didn't protest as he lowered her onto his lap, her nightgown and wrapper sliding up to her knees. He laid his head back. Heat radiated from his eye, from his whole body, until it seeped into her. The thin wrapper did nothing to conceal the firmness of his grip around her middle, nor the proof of his desire that pressed against her.

"It was worth losing it if you'll just sit there all night long."

Heat swirled where their bodies met. Desire folded in and clouded her mind. Strong hands crept up her back and buried in the waves of her hair. Gooseflesh broke out down her torso.

With the slightest pressure he guided her head down to his.

"Kiss me like you mean it," he challenged.

He needn't have dared her. She'd every intention of doing just that. Too long, it seemed, she'd danced around her burgeoning feelings for Luke. She'd already suffered unsettled nights and days thinking of him, wondering. Wanting. There were many things she'd yet to learn about him, but tonight was no longer for questions.

Bracing her hands on his shoulders, she leaned down, angled her head and poured everything she felt into the kiss. She wanted to take away the pain he'd suffered, to show him how knowing the truth about his eye eased some of the torment within her. He wasn't simply a pirate with a colorful history of pillaging. He was a man who'd been wronged.

Boldly she slid her tongue against his, thanking him for that piece of his past.

He groaned, shifting his grip from her head to her shoulders. His fingers dug into the taut muscles, then eased around to skim down her chest. He stopped at the swell of her breasts, letting his hands rest while their mouths mated. Her heart beat frantically under his hands. She wanted more, so much more. She became the aggressor, gliding her tongue deep into the warmth of his mouth. His lungs filled with air and brought his chest teasingly close to hers.

Accepting the unspoken invitation, her hands slid into his open shirt and pushed the fabric off his shoulders. Then, with fingers tingling, she discovered every lean muscle beneath the silky expanse of his chest.

His heart thudded beneath her explorations. He tasted of rich brandy. She drank as though dying of thirst. Feverishly, she twisted on his lap and gasped when his arousal ground against the wetness that had pooled between her legs.

"I'm no saint, Samantha. Stop, or I'll take you right here."

Then, ignoring his own words, his hands lowered. He cupped her heavy breasts in his hands, lifted them up and pressed them together. His thumbs teased the nipples into tortured peaks.

Sam's neck lost all capability to support her head. Her eyes fluttered closed as hunger ripped through her body. Her head fell back and she arched her neck, exposing both her throat and her breasts to Luke's mouth. He wasted no time. Wet, hot, slippery lips tugged and lashed her nipples while clever hands found the pressure building between her legs. Sam gasped and dug her fingers into his broad shoulders.

"Luke," Sam moaned, licking her lips as his fingers found the center of her lust.

"Samantha." Luke arched his hips, grinding his arousal against her.

His mouth fused with hers in an explosion of untamed desire. Her body had never felt so alive, so incredibly beautiful. She gloried in the way his hands touched her, leaving no area unexplored, unwanted. Following his lead, she buried her hands in his hair, scraped nails across the flat nipples of his chest. Her eyes saw everything, from the way his nostrils flared when her hands neared the waistband of his pants, to the extent of his desire that reached for her when she raised her hips.

It didn't scare her. Knowing the effect she had on Luke, that he was as lost to his needs as she was to hers, empowered her. This wouldn't be a taking, but a sharing.

Drawing a deep breath filled with his musky scent, Sam unbelted her robe and slid it off her shoulders. It fell silently to the floor. Luke's gaze narrowed and his hands clenched around her waist. His head, however, moved from side to side.

"Don't, Samantha."

She stilled. She'd be mortified if she didn't know he wanted this as badly as she did.

"Why? You've said yourself it was going to happen."

He raked a hand through his hair, hair already a mess from her fingers.

"Not here. Not like this, in my sister's parlor."

Boldly Sam reached back and trailed her fingers along his upper thigh. The muscles twitched beneath her palm. His eye wavered, then closed.

"You want me, Luke."

In a quick move that startled Sam, he grabbed her wrist and stopped her actions. His eye opened.

"There's no denying that. But I won't be like Dervish. I won't take you here. I'd pictured at least a bed when we did this."

"I don't need a bed. Just you."

He released his grip. She went for the waistband and began to tug it down.

"Samantha."

The seriousness of his tone drew her gaze from what she was doing back to his face.

"I'm a pirate, remember that. You want to be taken, by God I'll take you. But know who it is that's bedding you."

Passion lay heavy in his eye, but so did something else. She smiled. Luke Bradley was worried about her. Feeling wickedly free, she tugged his pants lower. He accommodated her by raising his hips and the material slid over his backside, down his thighs, and gathered below the knees. The bodice of her nightdress was damp from his tongue, the skirt bunched around her waist. With his arousal in plain view, Samantha looked down at the man she wanted. She'd never have believed it possible, but she wanted to make love for real. With Luke.

"I don't know what to do now," she whispered into his ear, embarrassment adding to the heat that already consumed her, but not enough to deter her from what she wanted most. "Show me."

He did. He loved her with his hands and lips, using his mouth and fingers to tease until she was in a frenzy. Nerves tingled and sang in every part of her body. Open-mouthed, he worshipped her breasts, ran his tongue over her throat, and whispered delectable, naughty words in her ears.

He allowed her only so much of her own explorations before taking her hands, kissing the tips of her fingers, and sucking on each one. It was as though a string connected her fingers to the core of her womanhood. Each slow suction pulled at her and left her restless.

His kisses were long and sensuous, filled with a tenderness that left her humbled and a burning passion that turned her into a wanton. Was it wicked to want this? Was she no better than a strumpet for allowing this kind of touch and returning it with equal fervor?

As he came up for air, his clouded gaze met hers and his ragged breath whipped her throat. Taking advantage of his temporary lack of control, Sam scooted back enough and dropped her head to his chest. His skin was damp and tasted salty. She'd seen it many times, but never like this, glowing bronze in candlelight, rising and falling in heated passion. Bare, for her eyes only. Curious, she licked at his nipples. Breath hissed from between Luke's parted and swollen lips. He allowed one more kiss before he grabbed her.

"I can't wait, Samantha. Damn, I tried, but you're too beautiful. I need you."

He all but ripped off her nightgown and flung it behind him. From the corner of her eye she saw it land on the sideboard. He chuckled, and Sam looked down to see the smile fade as he gazed upon her bare breasts.

His hands came up and reverently caressed the already aching tips. He cupped her and brought her swollen flesh to his mouth. It was beautiful watching him take her in his mouth, seeing his pink tongue flick and lave her nipples. When he'd had his fill, and Sam was begging, he raised her up and slowly lowered her onto him. Instinctively she tensed.

"Easy, luv. I won't hurt you."

It wasn't painful, but neither was it wonderful. Sam looked at Luke, whose face was taut with restraint. Since she'd started it, she'd allow Luke to finish, but she couldn't help being disappointed that she'd pushed him. Especially since it had been more than enjoyable before this point. She sat, Luke completely sheathed within her, and did nothing.

Finally Luke began to move. He rocked his hips and took her hands, placing them on his shoulders. The rocking motion rubbed her breasts against his chest. The contact sent a burst of heat through her. Luke smiled, as though he knew, then slid a hand between them.

Sam gasped and shuddered as his fingers built a storm.

Then, rocking with him, she allowed it to consume her. His mouth found hers and coaxed her lips open. Taking, he lashed his tongue against hers as the pressure built where they were joined. He drove into her as his mouth devoured hers. It was like being in a tropical forest after a storm. The air was heavy, breathing was difficult and labored. Dampness coated their skin and their passionate moans were primal.

Aching and reaching for something yet unknown, Sam returned Luke's kisses with an equal amount of longing. His lips slanted, plundering as though she was some newfound treasure. While one hand continued its torture between her legs, the other claimed a breast. Skin slapped against skin as the thrusts increased.

Candles sputtered and died, leaving only the waning fire in the hearth. Their cries filled the room, creating a concert of passion that resonated around them. It was erotic hearing her soft begging echo around the room. Seeing Luke's chest trickle sweat as he loved her was an image she'd never forget.

Then the pace shifted, became urgent. His hands claimed her hips as her own fingers once again anchored on his shoulders. The wave of need rose with each thrust. She felt it coming closer, getting higher. Her breathing was ragged, his gaze was half-lidded. Suddenly the wave crested and slammed into her. His name slipped from her mouth as every muscle contracted and exploded.

Luke plunged one more time, then strong arms wrapped her back, drew her with him onto the couch as he collapsed. With every nerve singing, Sam lay against her lover. A few sparks spat out as the last of the wood in the hearth was consumed. Darkness enveloped them. They sat entwined, savoring the aftermath of the storm.

When conscious thought returned along with a normal breathing rhythm, Sam had but one overpowering thought.

Pirates were notorious for taking what they wanted and leaving nothing behind. They were blatantly selfish. She smiled against Luke's chest.

When it came to making love, Luke was most definitely *not* a pirate.

Eleven

Sam stood in a haze of contentment and watched Luke gather their discarded clothes. He was dressed in nothing but low-riding trousers. He truly was beautiful. A shadow of stubble darkened his chin as he lifted her nightdress from the shiny sideboard. Muscles in his arms and shoulders bunched each time he tucked another garment under his left arm.

She had donned her robe and waited for Luke next to the cold hearth. He walked to her, arms laden with their clothes, a softness she'd never seen before on his face. If asked, Sam could have walked on water. Surely she felt light enough for it.

"Ready?" he asked, huskiness lingering in his voice.

They both inspected the room once more, lest Jacqueline find something she shouldn't, come morning. Then, a little melancholy to leave the room where she'd known such wonder, Sam nodded.

"Right, then," Luke said. He passed her their clothes, and before she could ask why, scooped her into his arms.

"Take the light, luv, I don't know my sister's house so well that I can find my way in the dark."

He stepped close enough to the mantel that she was able to grasp the lamp he'd lit before going in search of their clothes.

The stairs creaked faintly with each step Luke took. Sam held her breath, hoping it wouldn't wake Jacqueline. What they'd been up to would be only too obvious. It was one thing for the lady to assume they were on intimate terms, it was quite another to be caught nearly naked on her stairs.

Still, with Luke's arms cradled around her, she couldn't help thinking it was worth the gamble. Once he reached the top of the stairs, he didn't turn at her bedchamber, but kept strolling down the hall.

"Luke," she whispered fervently, "where are you going?"

He stopped and looked at her. His eyebrow made a perfect arch over a roguish gaze.

"To my bed, luv. The night's barely begun."

Her body warmed and tingled at the thought. He stepped through the open doorway, nudged the door closed with his hip, and proceeded to a four-poster bed that was as large and commanding as the one in her bedroom. He laid her softly on it and took the clothes from her arms, throwing them negligently over his shoulder once again.

His lips spread into a grin.

"Now," he said, his eye gleaming with the knowledge that he was in full command, "you lie back this time, and *I'll* be the one doing the tormenting."

* * *

A soft breeze floated into the sultry room through the open window and cooled their naked, still entwined bodies. All was silent except for the whisper of palm branches that rubbed against one another. Subtle perfume from the lush flower gardens on the grounds drifted around the bed where Luke lay behind Samantha. Her breathing was even, but not indicative of sleep. Enjoying the companionable silence, he took advantage of the opportunity to run his fingers through her long tresses.

As he knew they would, they slid like silk in his hand. The smell of jasmine from her bath earlier rose with each pass of his fingers. It had never been like this. Usually it was a quick coming together and an equally quick pulling apart. With Samantha, he could have lain as they were all night. He closed his eye, slightly shaking his head. Bloody hell. What had he done?

Samantha turned in his arms, her lovely body rubbing against his, and ignited his desires. Despite the heated lovemaking earlier, he was ready to lose himself all over again.

"I should get back to my room," she whispered, her voice as sensual as the island air.

He leaned on his elbow and propped his head on his hand. The moon was low and full, and lit the room so that candles weren't necessary to see her beautiful features. Her lips were slightly swollen, moisture glistening from his kisses. She clasped the thin sheet in her hand, teasing him with what lay beneath. A pale shoulder, perfectly rounded, caught the moon's light and shone. Three inconceivable truths pummeled him. First, this delicate, sensuous woman was the renowned Sam Steele. Second, he didn't deserve the gift she'd just shared with him. And third, it was only a matter of time before he lost her.

A few days ago he wouldn't have cared. But a few days ago she hadn't let him into her heart. A few days ago he hadn't let her be anything more than another conquest. A few days ago he hadn't realized just what he'd been missing.

She sighed and nestled closer. At rest, if nowhere else, she trusted him. Still, it was only a matter of time until she discovered Dervish wasn't in Barbados, as he'd led her to believe. And when that time came, he knew the loving expression on her face would turn to bitter anger.

He'd known that when he'd formed the plan. At the time, it hadn't bothered him. At the time, he realized, he hadn't begun to care for her. Now, as tender feelings for her engulfed him, he wondered how he could get around the truth and keep her from finding out that Barbados wasn't on Dervish's horizon?

He caught himself. What was he doing? He was Luke Bradley, pirate. He'd never looked back and regretted the decision to embellish the truth, and he wouldn't now. He might be able to fool her about Dervish's destination, but not about who he was. Besides, he reminded himself, she'd known when she'd shared her body. He'd made sure of that.

Still, his conscience scolded him in a distant corner of his mind. He should let her go back to her room. It would be hard enough on her when she learned the truth. Instinctively he drew her against him, hanging on to what he shouldn't. She was everything he'd been told he would never acquire. He was a bastard. And bastards, as his stepfather had preached for years, weren't worthy of anything so fine.

"Get some sleep, luv." *Allow me a few more hours to hold you.*

She shook her head, the ends of her hair caressing his chest. "I don't sleep at night."

He drew back. "Is that why you always take the night watch? To avoid thinking about the night Dervish raped you?"

There was a slight hesitation, and Luke wondered what more there could be. He'd known Dervish had raped her. He bloody well hated knowing it, but had accepted it as truth. Did it go beyond that? He lifted her chin with his hand.

"What happened?"

She scooted up to sit with her back against the wall, the covers clutched in one hand. She held the other out for him.

Humbled, Luke sat before her, taking her suddenly cold hand between his. There was gut-wrenching hurt in her tawny gaze, and a fierce possessiveness pierced Luke.

"I wasn't raped by Dervish. But it *was* Dervish who began it all."

Silently he sat and stroked her fingers as she described vividly the loss of her family at Dervish's merciless hands. It was all too easy to see it in his mind. He felt her pain, her sense of helplessness. Raw anger gnawed at him; he clenched his hands until Samantha gasped and he realized he was hurting her. Forcing himself to calm down, he eased his grip and listened to the rest.

Suddenly so many things became clear. Her fear of getting too close, how she always stepped back to keep a safe distance. Her inability to sleep through the night, her need to be in control. Now he understood Joe's protectiveness. Indeed, he thanked the man for it.

When the tale turned to the plantation and a Mr. Grant, Luke's rage knew no bounds. How could a young girl have been expected to endure so much? It was a bloody wonder she hadn't lost her mind as well as her innocence.

He'd agreed, when she'd sprung him from jail, to help her find Dervish. At the time he'd had nothing else to do, nowhere else to go, nothing to lose. Now, wiping warm tears from an angel's face, his heart heavy with emotions, it became more than that. He wouldn't be going after Dervish just to gain Samantha's ship when Dervish died. Neither was he going to avenge his eye.

He was going to make the man pay for hurting Samantha.

Luke crept down the stairs, watchful for his sister's servants. He was a wanted man and had to keep his presence a secret. Her husband, by sheer luck, happened to be at sea for another fortnight. But if the servants knew he was here, they might feel honor bound to report the fact to the authorities. He wouldn't put Jacqueline at risk that way. He'd hidden his treasure in her cellar, true enough, but she hadn't known it and he'd come back to fetch it as soon as the opportunity presented itself. Using Samantha as a distraction.

The only way, he argued with himself, to ensure his sister's safety. Though she was married to the governor's brother, he doubted that would provide enough immunity against harboring a dangerous and—if he did say so himself—damn good pirate.

Silently, he crept down the empty halls. He appreciated the worth of the ancient Chinese vase set upon a hundred-year-old table. Careful not to disturb it, he moved to the other side of the hall. Bold oil paintings hung on the walls, a strange combination of color and shapes that Luke knew nothing about.

Reaching the dining room, he peered around the corner.

Jacqueline sat at a long, polished table that was covered with steaming dishes and a silver pot he sincerely hoped contained coffee. She raised a golden brown piece of toast to her lips.

"Slide me a piece of that, will you?" he whispered.

She turned in the high-backed chair and smiled. Bloodlines said she was only his half sister, and yet she'd never treated him as anything but a real brother. Which was why he didn't visit often. He wouldn't take advantage of her generous heart by endangering her life. Indeed, if he hadn't needed the treasure, he wouldn't have risked coming at all.

"Come in, Luke. I've sent Pritchard for supplies and assigned the maids laundry duty, with the very direct order that I did not wish to be disturbed today." She gestured to an empty chair. "Please sit and have your breakfast. We have some time before Pritchard comes back." She glanced back the way he'd come. "Where's Samantha?"

Male pride preened like a well-groomed cat within him. He'd managed to do what thus far Samantha hadn't been able to accomplish on her own at night. Since about three this morning, she'd been snoring softly next to him.

"She's sleeping," he answered.

He felt her penetrating gaze and knew her thoughts. Grinning, he helped himself to the silver pot and praised his sister's good taste as ink-black coffee poured out.

"I wanted to lay out a few items she may need this morning, and I let myself into her room. As you know, she wasn't there." She sighed when he made no attempt to answer her. "You needn't look so pleased with yourself. It's a shame to take advantage of such a lovely woman."

"What makes you think I'm taking advantage?" Luke leaned back in the chair and sank his teeth into fresh bread coated with orange marmalade.

Jacqueline stirred her coffee with a spoon too tiny to be of much use, tapped it twice on the side of her cup, and placed it neatly on the saucer. She held the dainty china between graceful hands. Her expression was puzzled.

"She seems lovely. She's polite and courteous, a little reserved."

Luke licked the fruit off his thumb. "But?"

"She didn't sit still. If she wasn't pacing, her hands were twisting, or her feet were tapping." She shrugged and took a careful sip. "I don't know. She didn't appear to be comfortable around me. I didn't offend her, did I?"

"You, my darling sister? Impossible. Samantha's simply . . ." he trailed for a moment until he found the right word. "Distracted."

"That's what I mean, Luke. Are you taking advantage of her kind heart while she's too focused on some other matter to notice?"

Filling his cup again, he picked a cluster of fat red grapes from a platter overflowing with ripe fruit. Jacqueline, dressed in a lovely morning gown of pale peach, was the only person he'd ever felt deserved nothing less than his complete honesty. Today, however, he hesitated. His shirt, with most of the buttons done up in deference to his sister, suddenly felt too tight. Although there were still three buttons opened at his throat, he tugged at the cotton as if it were choking him. Her words were too close to the truth.

"She knows who I am, Jacqueline. I've not lied about that."

"I didn't think you would. But Luke, she's clearly not a pirate, and therefore must be treated better than you'd treat one of your own lot."

She frowned when he choked on a plump grape.

"I don't think she's the kind of woman to take"—she

pursed her lips thoughtfully—"trysts as casually as you do."

"She's made of stronger things than you know, Jacqueline. We both know what we're doing. I'm sure she'd thank you for your concern, however."

Jacqueline sighed. "It's not only her I'm concerned for, Luke."

He snatched a grape from the stem and popped it into his mouth. Then, just to annoy her, he talked around it. "Me? I've been taking care of myself a long time now."

"Yes, but you've never brought a woman to my home before."

He chewed slowly and swallowed. "I've hardly been here more than a few times myself. Besides, she was hurt, and I needed—" He couldn't very well tell her she'd been harboring his plunder for three years. She'd skin him alive. "I needed to see my lovely sister," he announced, hoping his charming smile would convince her it was God's truth.

Instead, she offered a dazzling smile of her own. It set his defenses on edge. She stood, took an empty plate, and began loading it with pastries and fruit. When the plate had enough food on it to feed at least three of Samantha's crew, Jacqueline moved to his side.

"There's more to your bringing Samantha here than a cut on her arm. You've true feelings for her. I know it; you certainly know it, though you've yet to admit it to yourself; and it's only a matter of time before Samantha realizes it. Here." She passed him the plate. "Take that up her. If no one is to get suspicious, I must keep to my usual routine. I'll be back once I've run my errands."

Luke trudged up the stairs like a scolded boy sent to his room. His boots slapped the polished floors while his mind disputed Jacqueline's words. Aye, he had feelings for Samantha. She was beautiful and passionate. She'd managed to carve a name for herself as a worthy pirate while keeping her identity a secret. As a man he appreciated the fact that she was a sensual woman. As a pirate he respected her skill. He'd convinced himself this morning it went no further than that.

He pushed the door open, not enough to slam against the wall but enough to make him feel in control. He was Luke Bradley. He wasn't some heartsick fool trying to woo a fragile maiden. He was a pirate and, as it happened, a man who deeply enjoyed the pleasures only a woman could provide. Feeling better, he set the food on the dresser, took a strawberry, and sat on the edge of the bed.

Samantha sighed in her sleep and turned her head toward him. His heart stuttered. He'd seen her asleep before, and couldn't say why seeing her now had the same resounding effect it had the first time. Jacqueline. She was putting notions in his head that didn't belong there. He shrugged off any lingering thoughts of his sister's words. Samantha had needed sutures. That was all.

Holding the stem of the seeded fruit, he used a strawberry to trace the outline of her lips, lips that matched the berry's color, lips that parted sensuously. Lust slammed into him and coiled tightly. He repeated the motion, circling slowly until eyes the color of spun gold met his.

"Luke," she said. The husky tone wrapped around his loins and tugged.

A healthy flush colored her face. She looked as soft and malleable as heated wax. He intended to mold her to him. Her hair spread golden fire across the pillow and the ripe mounds of her breasts struggled against the confines of the thin sheet. Leaning forward, he lowered the strawberry back to her lips. She took a firm bite, making him groan. Then he took his own bite, threw the rest on the floor, and fused his mouth to hers.

Sweet juice slipped from her mouth to his, mixing with the need that consumed him. Jacqueline's words echoed around his head as he took the kiss deeper, pressing Samantha further into the bed. He couldn't run from the truth. God help him, he'd developed feelings for her. But just then Samantha tore at his shirt and his thoughts scattered along with his buttons. Eager hands stoked a fire that had been simmering below his skin since he'd first seen her. He pulled back to draw a breath, then sank into her kiss again.

He'd think about his emotions later. For now, he had much better things to occupy his time.

"Are you coming with me?" Samantha asked after she'd bathed, dressed, and had her breakfast. Thankfully Luke's sister had the foresight to supply her with a few necessary items she'd forgotten on the *Revenge*. She brushed her hair with the borrowed brush, and although her fingers caressed the ivory combs, she left them on the dresser. She wouldn't take any more advantage of her hostess's generosity than she absolutely had to.

Luke watched her from the window, standing far enough away that nobody looking from below could see him. Over his shoulder the town of Barbados spread out like a fan, and past that lay the docile, sparkling sea with ships of all sizes bobbing in its warmth. Sam took a deep breath, anticipating the salty tang. Had Dervish arrived yet? Lord, she hoped so. She was ready. She rushed to put on her shoes. The sooner she got to the docks, the better.

"Until we're ready to weigh anchor, it's best I stay here. I don't want to chance being seen."

Sam's fingers fumbled with the hooks. Disappointment settled heavily onto her shoulders. Tucked away in this lovely home, having the best sleep she could remember—not to mention discovering the love and passion she had to share—she'd let reality slip her mind. They weren't lovers enjoying a few days' respite from life's duties. They were pirates, hunted and wanted. Preferably dead.

She'd always known that. She'd walked into the role of Steele with her eyes wide open. But never since had the stark reality of her choice been so blatant, so cold and empty. What kind of life was that to live?

Finished with her shoes, she stood and took a long look at Luke. Sunshine beamed onto him. In the bright light the black patch shone with a tint of blue. His shirt was open, revealing muscle and skin she now knew by texture and taste. The chains were once again resting around his neck.

He was intelligent and strong. As she'd seen when he was with his sister and in the tender way he'd been with her, he was also caring and compassionate. Surely there was more for him than piracy.

"Is this how you plan to live the rest of your life, Luke? Hiding?"

He turned slowly from the window where the tops of the trees waved happily in the breeze. A muscle clenched in his jaw.

"If it means saving my sister's life, yes."

"She's your family, all you have. What happens when she has children, and you become an uncle? Are you not going to be here for them either?"

"What I do with my family is nobody's business but mine," he said tightly.

"How can you not want to be a part of her life? She adores you, Luke. I'm sure her children would as well. Is seeing them once every few years the best you can do?"

His nostrils flared and his lips tightened until they were thin as a blade. He moved toward her. With anger seething through him, Sam saw what he had kept well hidden until now. This was Luke Bradley, feared pirate. Even with only one eye and no weapons on his person, the threat was palpable.

She'd pushed too far. There was no trace of the gentle lover she'd known. She backed up. He advanced. Uncertainty began to snake into her blood, curving and winding its way until it consumed her. Her whole body went cold. He wouldn't hurt her; she couldn't possibly have misjudged him that much. Her back bumped the wall; there was nowhere to go.

"Luke." It wasn't pleading. Not really.

Emotions surged in his gaze like waves crashing against sharp cliffs. "You know nothing of my life. Nothing."

"Then tell me, so I can understand."

For a few charged moments he glared down at her. Then he spun away and she sagged against the cool plaster wall. As he went back to stare out the window, Sam took some calming breaths. She closed her eyes until her hands stopped shaking.

"I'd never raise a hand to you, Samantha." His gaze cut to hers.

Her heart gave a small tug, as it would for anyone who looked so dispirited. It was her turn to come to him.

"I know that, Luke."

"Do you?" he challenged. "You went pale as dawn.

Couldn't you feel the shivers that racked your body? Because I bloody could."

Their conversation was taking a different path than she'd wanted, but she sensed it was just as important. She laid her hand on his arm, and though he didn't shove away her touch, she felt the muscles tense.

"It's hard to get over the past. It has nothing to do with you."

He dropped his gaze to his now polished boots. Worn cracks marred the otherwise shiny glaze. He snorted and shook his head, then stared at her in all seriousness.

"It has everything to do with me. You think you can turn me into something I'm not. I'm a pirate, Samantha. It's who I am. Who I'll always be."

She stroked his cheek. "Only as long as you want to be."

He grabbed her wrist and lowered her hand. He'd tightened his emotions, and Sam had no idea what he was thinking behind the cold mask he wore.

"No, Samantha. It's what I am. I'll never be a decent man you can stroll with down the streets. I'm not good enough for that." He released her and took a step back. "Now go see to your ship."

Dejected, Sam nodded. She'd accomplished nothing. She hadn't gotten him to see there were other ways than piracy. She'd learned nothing more of his past or why he believed he was only good enough for robbery. And worse, the tie she felt they'd created last night and that morning had come undone. It scared her just how much she needed it back.

Her hand clasped the latch.

"Samantha?"

She looked over her shoulder. Luke was standing with his arms crossed, his gaze boring into her.

"I never promised you anything. You know who I am."

She did. She always had. Yet somehow, hope had begun to take shape after their lovemaking. They could try to build something together, away from plunder, cannons, and thieves. His words ripped apart that hope; it splintered and fell in a twisted heap. The honest, soft tone he used said it all very clearly. He wouldn't change. She was a fool to have believed otherwise.

Defeat made swallowing painful.

"Samantha?" he asked when the silence grew to a tangible thing.

She wasn't used to having her heart open for another to see. It left her feeling raw. But as it appeared she was to stand alone, she plastered on a smile.

"I'll see how the repairs are coming and if there's been any sight of Dervish. Even with the storm he should be here by now."

Luke frowned and took a step toward her. "It's best not to get your hopes up. He may have sustained some damage during the storm as well. It could set him back."

She met his worried gaze. "He'll be here. After all, it was you who said he was heading this way."

Then, before Luke could say anything else, she slipped out the door.

Twelve

Sam didn't use the driver, despite Jacqueline's note that he was at her disposal, preferring to walk. She needed to clear her thoughts. Holding her head high, she glanced boldly into the foliage, now knowing for certain that men were there. She saw nothing but leaves of varying shapes, some sagging under their own weight, others small with serrated edges. The shades of green were as diverse as the plants themselves. Scarlet flowers pushed through the underbrush, extending stems and thorns for a chance to tilt their velvety faces toward the sunlight.

In the distance, the town was thriving with activity. It was a stew of jovial conversations, horses whinnying, and myriad shouts, barks, and hammering all stirring within the same pot. Any other time she would have enjoyed the chance to linger, to peer in freshly washed windows and gape at the treasures within.

Today, as her feet shuffled along to the quick beat of her heart, she hadn't the luxury. Surely Joe would have seen

Dervish by now. All they had to do was wait for him to sail
out of port. When it was just between the two ships, with
no chance of innocent lives at stake, she would show him
the same mercy he'd shown her family.

Within half an hour she was approaching the bay. Gulls
screamed, either begging for food or simply chatting.
Sleepy water rocked the ships at anchor in a gentle motion
that would have put even the fussiest babe into a deep
slumber. Shielding her eyes from the sharp reflection of
the sun, Sam scanned the harbor.

White sails coiled around booms, leaving masts to stand
bare in the glaring light. Supplies were heaved up on decks,
and men scurried about, unloading and taking them into
the holds. Goats bleated angrily as ropes lifted them off
the ground, chickens scratched in their wire cages. Sam
looked at a ship preparing to sail. Sea water sluiced off the
anchor. Canvas snaked up the masts, enfolded the breeze,
and snapped to duty. Cleanly, the ship sailed off.

The piers bustled with merchants coming to buy fresh
fish from recently docked boats, young boys dashed between men and boxes. Amid them all were swaggering
seamen back on land after long weeks at sea.

Her gaze embraced the *Revenge*. As she generally chose
not to go ashore, the opportunity to see her ship at anchor
didn't present itself often. It brought a smile to her face.
Lord, she was pretty. Sam had chosen the color when
they'd repainted her and she'd never regretted her choice.
She matched the sea now. A much better choice than the
olive green she'd been. Pride and love crept past the hurt of
Luke's earlier words and settled comfortably in her heart.
She sighed.

"She takes me breath away as well."

Sam smiled, having heard Joe approach a scant second

before he spoke. "I'll miss her, Joe. She's been my home, the only one I've had since . . ." She let the words trail off. So many had already been said about her family, what was left?

"Ye'll have yerself another, lass. A fine home with a flock of babes."

Sam tore her gaze from her ship to Joe. "If I survive the encounter with Dervish."

Joe's cheeks flamed. "I won't be hearin' that kind of talk. He's outnumberin' us, but we'll have surprise on our side."

"It will take more than that to win the battle."

"Saman—"

She held up her hand. "No, Joe. We've always known the risks. We've never discussed them, but we've always known." She crossed her arms over her chest, suddenly chilled. "It will take a miracle to come out alive."

Joe wrapped his arm around her shoulders, surprising Sam into stillness. He hadn't done that since the night they fled the plantation.

"Then a miracle, lass, is what we'll have. We didn't survive Dervish and then Grant's abuse to perish now." He squeezed her firmly against his broad chest. "Ye'll see."

A merchant pushing a wheelbarrow of silver fish, a few still flopping about, wove around them. Sam held her breath at the pungent smell. Only when they were far enough away and her lungs burned did she dare breathe. She gazed at the harbor.

"I don't see him, Joe. Has there not been any sign of Dervish?"

He scratched his beard, his voice as confused as she felt. "Not one. I figured he'd be here by now."

It *was* odd. Even with the storm Dervish should have

reached Barbados before they had. Not only was he ahead of them, but taking the merchant ship and the wounds her ship had suffered had slowed them down considerably. Worried, she chewed her lip.

"Do you think he's left already?" She spun around. "Have we come so close only to lose him again?" She didn't think she could take the disappointment.

"He's not been here. We'd know it if he had."

Since everything in town seemed to be as it always was, Sam had to agree. The only reason for Dervish to come here would have been to attack. Nothing was burned, nothing had been shattered by cannon fire.

"What's yer plan, Samantha?"

She kicked aside a rock, watched it tumble across the pier and splash into the water. "We wait until sunrise. If Dervish hasn't come yet, it will mean he's changed his course and we'll have to look elsewhere. In the meantime, Joe, keep your eyes open. I don't want the *Revenge* being attacked with the rest of the town. If you see Dervish coming, get her out of here. You can always come back for me later."

"And where'll ye be at?"

Had it been anyone else, she wouldn't have risked Jacqueline's life. But she could trust Joe. Still, she stepped closer and whispered to protect her hostess.

"Luke has a sister, Jacqueline. She's married to the governor's brother. We're staying there."

Joe's eyes bulged from his head. "Are ye both mad?" he bellowed.

Sam cringed, but a quick glance showed nobody was paying them any mind. "Her husband is at sea at the moment. The place is watched, but I'm safe. Nobody knows Luke is here; he came in through a hidden door."

Joe shook his head, not one of his grizzled hairs moving.

"He's mad, Samantha. How can he be certain he wasn't seen?"

"Because the navy hasn't stormed the house. I'll be back in the morning. How are the repairs coming along?"

He gave her a look that spoke his thoughts plainly; he thought Luke an idiot and Sam a fool. However, he said nothing more about it.

"Willy has the hole almost sealed. Trevor's been flitterin' about restockin' the galley."

"And the sails?"

He nodded. "Good as new, Captain."

The silence stretched as a few navy officers strolled past them. Sam's nerves jumped to attention. She slapped a hand to her heart to keep it from sinking any lower in her chest.

"Easy, lass. They don't know nothin'. Just makin' their rounds."

It took an iron will to move her lips into a fraction of a smile. Joe was right; the men gave cursory nods, checked a few of the boats, and continued on. By then Sam had sweat beading on her upper lip.

"That's too close. We have to leave here. Tomorrow, at dawn, one way or the other." She wiped her hands on her skirt. "When you get back to the ship, tell Aidan to pack his bag."

Bushy eyebrows angled down, creating deep furrows between Joe's eyes. "What in blazes fer?"

"I'm prepared to die for revenge, but I won't sacrifice a young boy for it."

Joe rubbed his large belly. "He'll be mighty upset about that."

"Well, better upset than dead. If a need arises, you can find me at the Kliphorn Manor on Bluebell Street."

"Samantha?"

She sighed. "If it's about Luke, Joe, I don't want to hear it. You've already made your opinion more than clear."

His eyes steeled. "As have ye, lass. But let me tell ye this, I've a bad feelin'. I don't think Dervish is comin', or that he ever was."

Anger straightened her spine. "Luke's lied to me, is that what you're saying?"

Joe stepped back, beefy arms crossed. "Aye. I think he has. And I think he has ye fooled into trustin' him."

It was a thought that had leaped into her own mind, though she'd immediately discarded it. She couldn't explain Dervish's absence, but she knew Luke. He wouldn't lie to her.

"You've forgotten your place, Joe." It hurt her to say it, hurt even more to see the pain in his eyes. But she wouldn't let him accuse Luke or herself of anything less than finishing the task they'd begun.

"Maybe I 'ave, but ye've lost yer senses. Ye've fallen in love with 'im, Samantha. Haven't ye?"

Sam said nothing. She'd never lied to Joe, and wasn't about to start now.

"At least ye'll not be denyin' it," he challenged.

His disgust cut her. He'd never used that tone with her. Chin held high despite the sting around her heart, Sam finished giving her orders. "I'll speak to Luke's sister. I'm certain she'll agree to look after Aidan while we're gone. Have him on the dock at nine o'clock. One way or another, he's not coming with us when we go after Dervish. Luke and I," she said pointedly, "will be back in the morning."

"Aye, *Captain*," he answered icily before trudging away.

Some of her bravery left with Joe, and she lowered her head in shame. She'd known Joe since she was a little girl in the nursery. How could they treat each other this way? With tears burning her eyes, she watched Joe sink into a rowboat. With clean strokes, he cut across the calm bay toward the *Revenge*.

She'd given up so much in order to achieve retribution for her family. Joe was part of that family, and it killed her to watch him climb aboard her ship, hurting as much as she was. All because of Dervish. When it was over, if she survived, she promised herself she and Joe would be friends again. There wouldn't be a chain of command between them, keeping them at odds.

And Luke? She shrugged her shoulders, trying to ease that burden into place. There was only enough strength in her to manage one problem at a time. Luke, and her love for him, would have to wait until Dervish was dead. In the meantime, she had to remain strong for the task at hand.

With renewed determination, Sam strode back toward Jacqueline's. Tomorrow, if life had any justice at all, she'd find Dervish. The sooner he was dead, the sooner she'd be free.

And there wouldn't be a merchant sailor or officer in the navy who would be happier than she to see the end of Sam Steele.

Jacqueline's toes pinched in her shoes, which, though fashionable, hurt like the dickens. It didn't stop her from pacing, though. By the time Samantha's steps crunched on the lane, she'd chewed two of her fingernails down to a stub.

She raced to the edge of the garden, hobbling a little

from the blister that burned on the smallest toe of her left foot.

"Samantha!" she called, and threw open the gate.

Samantha leaped back, eyes wide. Birds scrambled from their roosts, wings fluttering in their haste.

"Oh, forgive me. I'm so sorry. My intention wasn't to scare you to death," Jacqueline said.

"It's fine, really," Samantha answered, though her hand trembled against her throat.

"No, it's not. That was very rude on my part. Come," she said, dragging a stunned Samantha through the gate, which, painted green, blended perfectly with the shrubbery. "I'll have Pritchard prepare us some refreshments while you catch your breath."

She didn't allow her guest an opportunity to escape. Not when it had taken her all morning and cost her two fingernails to have an intimate conversation with her. Now that she had her in the privacy of her garden, had browbeaten Luke into writing their mother a letter to keep him from being underfoot, she did not intend to waste a single moment. Using the polished silver bell Luke had given her for her twenty-first birthday, she rang for Pritchard. Deliberately, she set the bell down with the engraving of the Jolly Roger facing Samantha.

The sun glinted off the image, and Samantha leaned forward, brow furrowed as she studied it. Pritchard arrived and Jacqueline dismissed him quickly, with a request for two glasses of cold tea and a platter of fruit.

"It's lovely, isn't it? It was a gift from Luke."

At his name, Samantha's gaze darted to the trees.

"The guards can only see us. They are too far away to hear." When Samantha didn't seem convinced, Jacqueline tried harder. After all, her idea to corner the woman she hoped would bring Luke out of piracy wouldn't work if said woman was afraid to talk about him. She placed a hand over Samantha's.

"Truly, they can't hear us. I would hardly risk my brother's life, would I?"

Samantha smiled. "No, I don't believe you would." She leaned back in her chair, arranging the folds of her skirt.

Jacqueline took the bell, turning it in her hands. "Ever since Luke turned to piracy, I've pleaded with him to stop. He gave this to me for my birthday—a reminder, he said, of what he was."

Oh, how it had hurt to see such a pretty bell tarnished with a pirate's emblem. To know her brother thought so little of himself, thought he could do no better. Now, as she set it down on the round tabletop, the anger was gone. Sadness, though, remained. There was so much goodness in him, if only he chose to see it.

"It's all he wants to be," Samantha said.

The hurt that choked her words spurred Jacqueline on. She hid her smile at Pritchard's appearance and waited until he'd poured two glasses of tea and left.

"No, Samantha. It's all he *thinks* he can be."

"I don't understand. He never mentions wanting anything else."

"Nothing?" Jacqueline teased. She was rewarded by Samantha's fierce blush. "I'm sorry. That was sinful of me." She pushed aside her glass, leaning across the small table to face the woman she believed had the power to change Luke.

"I love Luke. He's a good man and a wonderful brother. The problem is, my father, his stepfather, told him he was nothing but a bastard. He hammered that idea into his head until Luke believed it."

"Was he?"

Jacqueline sighed. "In the literal sense only. Our mother was raped when she was little more than a girl, and Luke was born of that night."

Samantha went pale as cream. Jacqueline suddenly feared that she'd misunderstood Samantha. Would the woman really hold his past, a past he had no control over, against him?

"How terrible for your mother."

"Luke wasn't terrible," she said immediately, coming to her brother's defense.

Samantha hastened to correct herself, renewing Jacqueline's hope.

"I meant being raped. I'm sure she loves Luke very much."

"Yes, she does. How he was conceived never mattered to her. She had a son and loved him unquestioningly."

"But your father didn't love him?"

Jacqueline sighed, the familiar bitterness rising in her throat. "I don't know why he couldn't. Luke never disrespected him. If anything, he tried harder around him. He did all his chores, helped mother with me." She shrugged her shoulders. "Nothing was enough."

"What did Luke do?"

"He worked from dawn to dusk helping me and mother, even doing extra chores to help bring in more money. Mother was so proud. But when father found out, he sputtered like a boiling kettle. He was embarrassed, you see. By Luke going out and earning money, it made it appear that my father couldn't provide for his family."

Samantha chewed absently on a piece of pineapple. "And then what happened?"

"He told Luke he was a disgrace, that no bloody bastard was going to make him look like a fool."

"But that's horrible," Samantha gasped. "He was just a boy."

"I know," Jacqueline acknowledged, the words of that dreadful day clear as glass in her mind. "Mother cried; I cried. Luke stood proud, said he was only trying to do what was right." She wiped a tear that crept down her cheek. "My father told him that it was too late. He was born a bastard and nothing could ever make that right."

"But your mother?" Samantha gasped. "How could she stand by and let him abuse Luke so?" The horror of it shone in her eyes.

"She admonished my father, but it was too late. The words were spoken. Luke silently left the room. They never spoke again."

She drank her tea, watching Samantha's reaction. The past wasn't pretty, but if the anger and hurt that had Samantha's fingers drumming the table were any indication, it was necessary to be told. She had to know all there was to know about Luke, and Jacqueline knew her brother well enough to be sure he'd never tell her on his own.

"Mother tried to love him enough for two parents, but it wasn't what he wanted. He wanted a father."

"How old was Luke at the time?"

"Twelve."

Samantha sniffed and turned her head, though not before Jacqueline saw her wipe the corner of her eye with her thumb.

"Luke was strong, Samantha. And he knew right from wrong. Despite knowing I was loved more than he was, he never treated me with anything but adoration."

"It wasn't your fault," Samantha said, facing her again.

Tears stung Jacqueline's eyes. *Oh, Luke,* she thought, *you must marry this one.*

"My head knew it. It took my heart years to catch up."

"And Luke?"

"For him the damage was done. By the time he was fifteen, he knew that as long as he remained in London, he'd be nothing but the bastard stepson of Percy Young. He took a position as an indentured servant to buy passage to Port Royal. When his duty was fulfilled, he jumped ship, as it were. Though he loved the sea, he hated being on a merchant ship, hated the formality. He saw the life of a pirate as having the best of both worlds."

"How did you come to be here, then?" Samantha asked.

A warm breeze touched Jacqueline's face as equally warm memories filled her mind. "I was young, hardly more than sixteen years old, when I met Daniel. My father worked for him, you see, and because my father felt it would move him up in the company faster, he invited the Kliphorns to dinner.

"My mother fussed with the house, and by the time dinner was ready, my hands ached from polishing the furniture and scrubbing the floors. But the house gleamed from floor to ceiling. When the bell rang at precisely eight o'clock, I was prepared to spend an uneventful and frightfully boring meal playing the quiet, respectful daughter."

Caught up in the story, Samantha pushed aside her forgotten tea and braced her arms on the table.

"Then Daniel walked in, nearly a head taller than his father, and my mind went absolutely blank. My body, however, sizzled. He was beautiful, perfectly beautiful." Jacqueline leaned over conspiratorially. "Luke does that for you, doesn't he?"

Samantha blushed intensely. Jacqueline laughed.

"I was shocked at first. I'd been attracted to some men before, curious about others, but never with the intensity I felt for Daniel. He did more for me in one look than the others could accomplish with their flowers, romantic dinners, and fancy gifts combined."

"Sounds wonderful."

"Wonderful? It scared the stuffing out of me."

"Really?"

"Yes, and my reaction was only half of it. During dinner his father informed us that his youngest son would soon be moving to Barbados to follow in his big brother's footsteps. I had only five days to convince him to take me with him. Luckily, I can be very persuasive."

"Five days? You left everything behind for a man you'd known only a handful of days?" Samantha asked, frowning.

"Yes."

It must seem odd to her, Jacqueline knew, as it did to most women she'd told, and yet she'd never regretted her decision.

"How could you have been so certain after such a short time? What if it hadn't been a wise choice? It would have taken you weeks to get back home."

Jacqueline slid her half-empty glass aside and took Samantha's hands.

"The only certainty I knew, Samantha, was that I couldn't imagine living the rest of my life without Daniel in it. It may have been a short time, but I knew, somehow, deep in my heart that there would never be another man for me. Did I know for certain we'd be happy, that we'd remain as blissfully in love seven years later as we were when we left England? No, I didn't. And it hasn't all been easy. I miss my family, though it helps having Luke around, even if I don't see him nearly as much as I'd like."

"Yet you left so easily."

At this Jacqueline laughed loudly, remembering the painful good-bye she'd had with her parents.

"Not so easily. There were arguments, tears. My heart was torn in two and my mother, especially, didn't want me to go so far away."

"I'd give anything to have a family, and you walked away from yours."

"I don't pretend to know your story, Samantha, but I can see how you have trouble understanding. Eventually, though, there comes a day when a woman steps from her parents' sides to join her husband."

"I know."

"And really, all I did was extend my family. Daniel is a part of it now, a part of me. As our children will be."

Going on nothing more than instinct, Jacqueline squeezed Samantha's trembling hands.

"You can have it all, Samantha. Luke, children, family."

Bees flitted from flower to flower while Samantha digested what she'd been told. Jacqueline knew she'd been right in telling her. Luke might not see it that way, but in her heart she knew it was right. Her brother had so much to offer, and that he'd brought Samantha to her home and that he looked upon her with tender feelings were enough to make her hopeful.

This woman with tears in her sad eyes was the answer to her prayers. Jacqueline was convinced that if Luke found a reason, one more powerful than anything he'd found thus far, he'd gladly walk away from piracy.

And what, she thought happily as Samantha's gaze rose to Luke's window, could be more powerful than love?

* * *

Luke felt like a bloody fool.

"I look ridiculous," he grumbled into the full-length mirror that graced a corner of his sister's room.

"You look handsome," Jacqueline corrected. She ran her hands over the shoulders of his silk shirt. "You could stand to do up a few buttons, however."

Luke grinned. "And cover something so fine? I think not."

She rolled her eyes. He laughed, then drew her into an embrace. Lord, she was wonderful. It was a puzzle to him that something as good as she came from such an insufferable man.

"Thank you, darling, for everything."

Jacqueline leaned back in his arms and all but glowed. "It was my pleasure. I never dreamed I'd ever have occasion to plan such a dinner for you in my home." She sighed, her hands clasped over her breast. "She'll love it."

Luke stepped away, taking a last look in the mirror. The buff-colored shirt matched the trousers he'd borrowed from his brother-in-law. The knee-high boots were polished to a glossy black. Because it all felt so foreign to him, he'd kept the shirt gaping open, a reminder to Samantha and himself of who he really was.

"She bloody well better, or I'll cast her overboard first chance tomorrow."

"You will not, and you know it." She fussed with his shirt some more. "Because you, my dear brother, are falling in love."

The words had the effect of a rug being pulled from underneath him. He caught the chest of drawers just in time to prevent a fall. "I bloody am not!" he shouted.

His sister laughed—hell, she didn't even try to hide it.

"Yes, you are. You're courting her, Luke. You've planned this dinner, you've cleaned up."

"Just because there's no baths on board a ship doesn't mean I don't enjoy being clean now and again."

"Is that why you shaved twice and spent nearly an hour primping in front of my mirror?"

Luke spun around. "I do not primp."

"Fine, you don't primp," she agreed, her tongue tucked into her cheek.

Taking his hand, she led him out of her bedroom. "Then, since you don't primp, you're ready to face the lady. I imagine she'll be in the dining room, as I've told Pritchard to ensure she doesn't enter the parlor."

"He won't say anything?"

"That you're here? No. He figured it out last night, and I'm sure he won't tell a soul. Still, you know how he feels about you, so better not provoke him."

In the hall, with some unfamiliar demons twitching in his stomach, he kissed his sister lightly on the cheek.

"Thank you."

"You're welcome. Now go, before you lose your nerve."

Luke scowled. "You're not so old that I can't throw you over my knee."

"You've never raised a hand to me, brother, and you won't now." She lifted herself onto her toes and returned his kiss. "Enjoy your evening."

She closed the door in his face before he could detain her any longer. Bloody hell, what was the matter with him? It was just dinner. There was absolutely no reason for him to be nervous. With that thought running through his mind, he wiped his damp hands down his thighs and strode downstairs.

* * *

Pritchard, his face looking especially sour, opened the doors as Luke escorted Samantha inside.

"Oh, my," Samantha gasped.

At her side, Luke smiled to himself. He'd been planning the intimate dinner all afternoon, to undo some of the pain he'd caused Samantha with his words earlier. With Jacqueline's help, Pritchard had agreed to set up a table and serve the evening meal in the privacy of the parlor. The curtains were drawn. Candles glowed on the mantel and a candelabra flickered on the sideboard. In the middle of the elegant table a fat cream candle was encircled by freshly cut orchids.

As this was to be their last dinner together before setting sail tomorrow, he'd decided to make it one Samantha wouldn't soon forget. And one, he thought as he placed his hand on the small of her back and guided her to her chair, that would weigh in his favor when she discovered he'd lied about Dervish.

"What's all this?" she asked.

He unfolded her napkin and placed it on her lap. Her eyes sparkled from the candles and her skin reminded him of a lush peach. He drew his gaze to her lips and had to swallow a curse. Lust heated his blood. They'd made love all night, and damned if his body wasn't ready to do it all over. Never one to resist temptation, Luke knelt at her side, cupped her face, and brushed his lips over hers.

She sighed into his mouth, one of her hands curving around the back of his neck, holding him in place while her clever mouth tormented him. The instant her lips parted, he flicked his tongue over hers, drawing her deeper into his kiss. When blood began to pound in his loins, he pulled back, kissing her lightly one last time.

Her eyes, large and almond-shaped, were full of desire. She pressed trembling fingers to her lips and watched him take the chair opposite hers.

"Well," he said, pouring them each a glass of wine, "I fear anything else will come up lacking after that."

She blushed, and Luke smiled at the red creeping into her cheeks. She'd pinned her hair behind her ears, but had left the rest of it down. Loose curls hung halfway down her spine. His breath hitched in his throat. She was beautiful. And she was his, at least for tonight.

The guilt that had grown all day pressed into him again, reminding him of his deceit and the hurt he knew Samantha would feel. He should tell her now, explain himself and his reasons. She'd understand, he told himself. The longer he waited, the more angry she'd be. But watching her, as Pritchard silently served the soup and then left, Luke knew he couldn't do it. Not now. Not when she looked so at peace, smiling sweetly at him. The way no woman had ever done before.

And that, he thought as he stirred the chowder, was what Jacqueline saw. He didn't love Samantha, although he loved some of the things they did together. She simply treated him the way he'd never been treated by a woman before. She stirred his mind as well as his body.

"What about Pritchard?" she asked.

"Well, he's known I was here since last night. Nothing gets past him, I'm afraid."

"Aren't you worried he'll tell the authorities?"

Her words seeped into him and wrapped around his heart like a warm hand. Christ, she cared. She was truly worried about him getting caught. Except for his mother and sister, nobody had ever given a damn. The knot in his throat surprised him, and he took his time fussing with bread and butter before he knew he could speak without emotion clogging his voice.

"Me, he'd betray without a second thought. My sister, however, he's fiercely loyal to. He hates me, but he won't tell the navy I'm here. He knows it would break Jacqueline's heart."

Samantha pushed her empty bowl aside, leaned over, and grasped his hand. "It would break mine as well, Luke."

Stunned into silence, his chest tight and aching, he squeezed her hand and was relieved of having to answer by Pritchard's arrival with the next course. When he'd once again disappeared, leaving plates of steaming chicken topped with pineapple, roasted potatoes, and green beans dripping with butter, Luke had found solid ground again.

"Well, as I don't plan on hanging anytime soon, we won't have to worry about that."

The meal was delicious. At least he assumed so. Though his plate bore the crumbs to prove he'd eaten, his senses were too full of the woman before him to care about food. Leading her to the couch, he drew her onto his lap. As she cradled in his arms, he traced her cheek with his finger. Liquid brown eyes closed, and she leaned her head against his chest.

"Luke?"

"Hmmm?"

"I've never felt this safe with anyone."

His hand stilled, then dropped like lead to his side. "I'm not perfect, Samantha. Don't make me out to be something I'm not."

She drew back and gazed at him. The affection and acceptance swimming in her eyes scared the hell out of him.

"I already know what you are. You're a fine man, Luke."

He shook his head. "You've drunk too much wine, luv. I'm a pirate."

"For now, perhaps. That doesn't change who you are."

Hands softer than the silk that covered his torso slipped inside his shirt to lie over his rapidly beating heart. "In here, Luke, where it really matters, you're a good person."

Tell her, his mind bellowed. This was his chance to prove to her that he wasn't as she saw him. But he couldn't. Wounds his stepfather had inflicted on him, wounds that were still raw, healed a little at her words. Surely if such a fine woman thought it, he wasn't all bad.

"I'm not what you think," he said instead.

With a firm hand she grasped his jaw and held it. Hard. "Don't you dare tell me you're a bastard. You may not have a father, but that's just parentage. It has nothing to do with what you make of yourself."

Raw anger gnarled in him and he tried to push Samantha off his lap. How dare Jacqueline tell her something so personal! Samantha, though slight, was far stronger than he gave her credit for. She held fast and refused to budge.

"Don't you run from this, Luke," she scolded.

"She had no business telling you," he growled.

"Maybe not, but she did all the same, and I'm glad she did."

Calmly, though her eyes remained wary, she stroked his cheek. "I understand so much more now, Luke."

He'd never felt so exposed in his life. And afraid. Could he really believe it didn't matter to her? "You know it all now, Samantha. The ugly truth doesn't shame you? You've given yourself to a bastard pirate." He didn't know what demon made him say it like that, but he needed it all said.

Then, when he was certain of her feelings, he'd tell her the rest. About Dervish.

Her eyes filled with tears, and one slid from the corner of her eye.

"I love you, Luke Bradley. All of you." She sniffed as more tears slid down her face. "I'm scared of what that means, but it's the truth."

She pressed her forehead to his while her tears left warm smudges on his cheeks. His heart warmed and unfolded within him. He slammed his eye shut. Then, with words choking his throat and burgeoning feelings pressing heavily against his chest, he caught her mouth with his. There was no way to put into words the gratitude, need, and joy he felt. So he showed her the only way he knew how.

His tongue slipped against hers. Her hands stroked his chest and back, digging into his shoulders. He didn't deserve her, his stepfather's voice taunted from the past, but for once Luke ignored him. He needed Samantha, needed her goodness. And dammit, he thought, pulling away to draw a ragged breath, he needed her love.

"Samantha," he groaned, and feasted on her mouth again.

She arched against him. All the hope, love, and tenderness he'd kept locked into his heart poured out. He drew her tightly against him, as much frightened by her declaration as by his own response to it. Their jagged breaths cut through the silence. She stroked his back, he buried his face in her neck and smelled roses. White roses.

"I can't breathe," she gasped into his ear.

"Sorry." He sat up and pulled her beside him. Her hair was disheveled, and he tucked a stray silky strand behind her ear. She stroked his thigh and her eyes glowed.

"We could take this upstairs," she offered.

They could, and damned if he didn't surprise himself by not taking her up on it. But he couldn't. She'd professed her love, and he knew her enough to know she meant it. And though that humbled him, it also made him realize the time had come to tell her the truth. He couldn't lie to her a moment longer. She deserved better. And if she was willing to accept him, she had to know it all.

"Samantha?"

She smiled, and it twisted around his heart.

"I asked you, Luke. You don't have to worry that I'll change my mind."

He raked a hand over his face. "It's not about going upstairs, luv." Then, because he was still coward enough not to face her, he strode to the table and gulped down his wine.

"What, Luke?"

Her shoes tapped the floor as she moved behind him. He lowered his head, his stomach in knots. His hands shook. Damn it, he'd lied not only to regain his treasure but for her protection as well. Still, he knew it would take some convincing to make her see it that way. And it would kill him to see anger in her eyes. Especially now.

"Luke?" she asked, and placed a warm hand on his shoulder.

He took a deep breath.

Pritchard knocked, then stepped into the room. "Pardon me, miss, but you've a guest."

"Bloody hell, man. Tell them we're busy," Luke growled. He'd finally worked up his nerve, and he didn't want to waste it.

The butler frowned. "I've tried. The man is most adamant to see Miss Fine." Pritchard turned to Samantha. "He said his name is Joe."

Samantha turned to Luke. "It must be news of Dervish," she whispered, her eyes filled with hope. Then, louder, she asked Pritchard to send him in.

"Oh, Luke, this is it! We've finally found him!"

Luke took a deep breath, wishing desperately it was true. If Dervish had come, by some stroke of luck, then he needn't hurt Samantha with his lie.

Joe, chest heaving and cheeks ruddy, stepped through the doors a scant moment after the butler opened them. As soon as Pritchard left, closing them behind him, Joe raced to Samantha.

"We've trouble, lass," he puffed.

"What, Joe? What's happened?"

To Luke's shock, she clasped his hand and held fast. Luke squeezed back, telling her silently that he'd do anything for her.

"When I took Aidan to the docks, I overheard some sailors talking." He stopped, swallowed.

Dread crept up Luke's spine like a slithery snake.

"Tell me, Joe," Samantha urged.

"They was talkin' about Sam Steele." Watery blue eyes cut to Luke's. "They was sayin' how word's been gettin' about that Sam Steele isn't what people thought."

Samantha's hand went cold and limp in Luke's.

"What were they saying?" she whispered.

Joe faced his captain, every crease and wrinkle gouged deep with worry.

"They was sayin', Samantha, that it's possible Steele's really a woman."

Thirteen

"My God, Joe. How could they possibly know?" Sam asked, releasing Luke's hand and starting to pace.

She'd been lucky up to now that her identity had remained hidden. Now that it was revealed . . . She stopped pacing, her heart hammering in her chest. Now that it was known, she could hang before finding Dervish.

"I'll tell ye, lass. Bradley's told 'em."

Sam spun around. "For what purpose, Joe? He has nothing to gain by revealing my identity."

An angry flush turned Joe's neck and face the color of overripe tomatoes. His meaty hands curled—ready, Sam was certain, to pummel Luke into a fine powder. Luke didn't move, but kept a steady eye on Joe.

"I'm not knowin' any reason, but there's no one else, lass. The rest of us 'ave been together fer years and word hasn't spread. Then Bradley comes strollin' along an' all hell's breakin' loose."

"What the blazes are you talking about, man?" Luke asked.

Sam and Joe stared each other down. She knew what Joe was talking about. Before Luke, they'd been close. Before Luke, *he* was the man she'd trusted, the one she'd turned to. This was the second time she'd sided with Luke. She understood the hurt pulsing in Joe's eyes. It was the disgust that followed on its heels that hurt her to the bone.

"Joe," she said calmly, "I can't explain it. I've been as careful this voyage as on any other. I don't know how anyone can figure I'm Steele."

"Because he told 'em!" Joe raged, slamming his fist on a side table hard enough to catapult Luke's empty glass across the room. It exploded against the papered wall.

"If I were to reveal anyone," Luke said, stepping toward Joe, "I'd say you were Steele. Then I'd finally be rid of you and your unfounded suspicions."

Joe pushed back his torn sleeves, the muscles on his thick arms twitching. "I'll be showin' ye suspicions, Bradley. Right in yer bloody face!"

Luke spread his legs and braced himself. His hands coiled at his sides.

Sam had had enough. She stepped between a snarling Joe and an irritated Luke. "This is ridiculous. Drawing blood and breaking bones won't accomplish anything. The point isn't who said anything, but what we're going to do about it."

Joe shoved her aside.

"I'll tell ye the point. 'Tis time we're rid of Bradley."

He swung. Luke ducked. He swung again. Luke side-stepped and dodged the hit. With spit foaming at the corners of his mouth, Joe reached out, grabbed the candelabra, and pitched it at Luke. The silver bounced off the wall, leaving a large notch in the plaster.

"Joe!" Sam screamed. "That's enough!"

He ignored her and reached for the bottle of wine. Her screams remained unanswered. Luke, circling Joe like a wolf that had cornered its prey, was no help. Sam knew she had to do something before Joe turned the house to ruins. Taking a deep breath, she grabbed a chair and ran between the men, holding them apart by a mere four spindly legs.

"Out of the way, woman," Joe warned, taking another two steps to the left to keep Luke right in front of him.

"That's enough, Joe. Now sit down and calm yourself, or I'll break this chair over your thick head. Maybe that will knock some sense into you."

"Not bloody likely," Luke grumbled.

"I've had it. Let me at 'im," Joe spat.

Cursing, Sam raised the chair over her head. "I've warned you, Joe—"

To Sam's mortification, that was the moment Jacqueline chose to burst into the room.

"I'm terribly sorry, Jacqueline. There's no excuse I can give you that explains that kind of behavior."

Alone in her bedroom, Sam jammed the few belongings she'd brought into her bag. She'd never acted so foolishly in all her life, and to be caught in the throes of it by a woman she respected was more than embarrassing. It was mortifying.

Jacqueline chuckled. "There's nothing to apologize for. With Daniel away, this house can be most confining. Having you here has definitely"—she paused, biting her lip—"well, it's livened things up, hasn't it?"

Sam winced, tucked the last item away, then dropped the bag by the door. "I'll see to it that all damages are taken care of."

"That's not necessary."

"Of course it is. You welcomed me into your home, treated me better than you should have, considering who I—" Sam caught herself in time and bit her tongue to keep it quiet.

Jacqueline smiled warmly. "I won't lie to you, Samantha. Since Luke brought you here I've been bursting to know just who you are and what you are to him."

"There's nothing to know. Luke is simply helping me with a favor."

To Sam's utter surprise, Jacqueline burst out laughing. "Samantha, there isn't a simple bone in Luke's body." She patted the bed next to her. "Please sit a moment."

"I really need to be going," Sam said.

Jacqueline looked over her shoulder, through the small rectangular window. Outside, night enveloped Barbados in its large black cloak. She faced Sam again. "There's time to talk. If it's the cover of darkness you need, it's still going to be there in ten minutes."

Something in Jacqueline's firm tone unnerved Sam, as though she knew the reason she was running. Which, of course, wasn't possible. However, Luke's sister was right, she could spare a few minutes. With a tepid smile, Sam sat.

"Since time is of the essence, I'll get right to it. What are you and Luke up to?"

It didn't get any more blunt than that, Sam figured. Which didn't mean she had to answer truthfully. She would not further endanger Jacqueline with the truth about the woman she'd welcomed into her home. Still, lying to her face didn't sit well.

Sam focused on the brooch at Jacqueline's neck. "Luke is a friend of my brother's. As a favor to my brother, who is deathly ill at home, I agreed to help Luke get to Havana."

"By way of Barbados? Come, Samantha, an intelligent woman such as yourself can come up with a better lie, can't you?"

Sam gaped, knowing she'd given herself away. Ashamed, she hung her head. Jacqueline shifted on the bed and drew Sam's cold hands between her much warmer ones.

"We've little enough time, let's not waste it lying."

Tears threatened to flow, but Sam fiercely held them back. "I'm sorry," she said. "I can't tell you. I won't endanger you."

Jacqueline squeezed Sam's fingers. "My brother's a pirate and I married the governor's brother. What could be more dangerous than that?"

"I'm sorry. It must be an uncomfortable situation."

"It can be," Jacqueline acknowledged.

"Then I won't burden you with any more."

"Honestly, you and Luke! Do I look like some fragile flower that must be sheltered from all life's turbulent weather?"

Sam raised her head. No, Jacqueline didn't look fragile. Her skin was a light bronze from the tropical sun. Her green eyes shone with intelligence and compassion. And the grip that still held Sam's fingers as prisoners was anything but frail.

"No, you don't."

"Then trust that I can share whatever it is you're doing without my knees buckling."

Sam smiled; the picture of Luke's sister falling faint

wouldn't form in her mind. It was tempting to tell Jacqueline everything, to unburden herself. But that was selfish, and not fair to her hostess.

"You need more convincing, then?" Jacqueline asked. "Very well. I knew, have known all along, that Luke was hiding treasure in my cellar."

Sam gasped again. Jacqueline smiled.

"You knew?"

"Of course I did. Luke would never come here if he had other options. He's always been very protective of me. When he left, I searched through this house, knowing he must have hidden something. It took nearly three days, but I found it." She beamed.

Sam grinned. Poor Luke was so sure he'd hidden the truth from his sister. "You've never told him you knew?"

"Of course not, there's no fun in that. It's much better to watch him scramble, to see which story he'll weave next."

Sam's tension bubbled over in a gale of laughter. If Luke only knew. She looked at his sister then, *really* looked at her. Jacqueline sat, hands folded in her lap, dark gaze patiently waiting. Sam wiped the laughter from the corners of her eyes and took a deep breath.

"What do you know?"

Jacqueline shrugged, the lamplight shining in her dark hair.

"That Luke escaped jail. That the two of you arrived at my home, both trying to hide the fact that you have very deep feelings for each other." She leaned forward. "That you're unhappy."

Air stuck in her chest, making breathing difficult. How could a stranger know so much about her?

"Samantha, I've agreed to take in the boy, Aidan. I've already promised to look after him until you come back, and longer if necessary." She grasped her wrist. "Do I not deserve to know why? Don't you think I could better protect Aidan and myself if I knew it all?"

Every argument Jacqueline had spoken had been like a wave slamming against a dam. With her last plea, the barrier crumbled. Praying she wasn't about to make the worst mistake of her life, Sam told Luke's sister the whole ugly truth, from her family to Dervish to Mr. Grant. She hadn't meant to let it all out, but once she started, it flowed freely. And when it was over, Sam felt as though a terrible weight had been lifted from her shoulders.

Jacqueline wiped tears from Sam's cheeks. Tears she hadn't realized she'd shed. Then, to Sam's great shock, she wiped her own eyes.

"I told Luke there was no way you were a pirate. I'm glad to know I was right." Jacqueline sniffed.

"I think the navy would argue with you that Sam Steele is indeed a pirate."

"Not in here." Jacqueline laid her hand over her heart. "Not where it matters most."

Fresh tears clouded Sam's eyes. She shook her head. "I really need to be going now. I can't thank you enough, for everything."

Jacqueline followed Sam to the door. "Just come back alive, Samantha. That will be thanks enough."

They hugged as sisters would, long and full of unspoken emotions.

"Godspeed, Samantha. Please be careful."

Sam nodded. With a last smile, she went downstairs.

"I'm tired of being left behind." Aidan raged.

Sam had wanted a last word with the boy—the young

man—who had come to mean so much to her. She'd never had a brother, but had she been so lucky, he would have been a mirror image of the lad before her. Only he wouldn't be spitting mad, wouldn't be yelling at her, and wouldn't be refusing to listen to reason.

"Aidan, I've explained all this. You're young; you have a long life ahead of you. So much promise. I won't ruin that."

"Why did you take me from Mr. Grant if you were only going to lock me away?"

Sam counted to three. "I'm not locking you away. I'm keeping you safe."

"I don't want to be here! I want to be on the *Revenge*."

"You will be, when it's all over. When I come back for you."

Blue eyes flashed. "*If* you come back."

Sam sighed and sat on the arm of the thick chair. "I can't promise you I'll be back, Aidan, which is why I won't allow you to come along. You're too young to die, and I won't have you hurt when I can prevent it."

Hands caught somewhere between manhood and boyhood clenched at his sides. "I'd rather die than hide away here. I can do this, Sam. Let me go."

Weary from her confession to Luke, her fight with Joe, and her talk with Jacqueline, Sam rubbed her hands over her face. She knew she was trampling the boy's pride, but pride could mend. A dead body couldn't.

"I'm sorry. My decision is made, and I won't change it. Jacqueline will look after you until we return."

Blood poured into Aidan's face. "Why do you always treat me like a baby? I'm not old enough to go into Tortuga; I can't be left alone on the ship. When will I be treated like the rest of them?"

It was the perfect opportunity to tell him; there would be no better, and Sam knew it. But after years of holding back, blocking memories of her sister and what losing that bond had done to her spirit, Sam found the words sticking like tar in her throat. In her heart he was her family, hers to protect. She'd had no chance to save Alicia, nor her parents. Sam's will snapped back into place. No, she hadn't saved them, but by God she would spare this wonderful lad.

"You're staying," she said.

Tears of anger and embarrassment pooled in his eyes. "I hate you!"

His words, though spoken in heat, sliced through her. Each letter had its own ragged blade that cut into her heart. She hated seeing the hurt and pain in his eyes. Cursed herself for being the one to put it there. It didn't matter that she knew to the depths of her soul that she was doing the right thing. She'd hurt the last person she'd ever intended to. And because she couldn't bear to face him as Samantha, she did what she'd learned to do best.

She hid behind Steele.

"Well, Aidan," she said, standing. "You can hate me all you like. Indeed, I can't stop you. But I can keep you alive. And as your captain, I expect you to listen to Jacqueline as you have to me."

The boy shook with rage. His eyes squinted, shooting silent curses. And though each glare sank into her heart, she bit the inside of her cheek and grabbed her bag.

"Don't bother coming back for me. I won't sail with you ever again!"

Helpless, she watched Aidan race up the stairs, taking them two at a time.

"Please, God, let him forgive me," Sam prayed.

Then, taking a deep breath, she went to the secret door Jacqueline had shown her earlier.

Luke's stomach was in knots. Samantha was on her way to the *Revenge*. As soon as he caught up with her, he'd have to tell her the truth about Dervish. He raked his hands through his hair. Damn! How had he gotten himself in so deep?

"Am I always going to have to say good-bye to you, with no idea when I'll get to say hello again?" his sister asked from behind him.

Luke sighed, turned. "I don't have an answer to that."

Jacqueline nodded, her eyes shining.

"Don't let Dervish harm her any more than he already has."

Luke's head snapped back. "You know about him?"

Jacqueline sighed. "Yes, and about your bloody treasure and how she's the best thing that ever happened to you." She leaned against the wall, arms crossed. "Have I forgotten anything?"

"Bloody hell," he said and mussed his hair again. "She told you everything."

"No, she didn't, Luke. I'm not as simple as you seem to think. The treasure I knew about; she told me the rest. What happens after you find Dervish?"

Luke longed for a drink. Or two. "First I have to tell her I lied about knowing where he was." He told his sister the story, and when he'd finished, he'd never felt so disgusted with himself. He kicked the bag he'd set on the floor. It rolled and bounced off the opposite wall, coins clanging inside.

"Your bloody father was right."

His sister stepped toward him. He knew the slow, controlled movement was a warning that her anger was under tight rein. Her eyes flashed and her lips were pinched.

"You may be an idiot at times, Luke, but you've never been a bastard."

"I am what I am, and you can't change that."

Jacqueline grabbed him by the forearms and shook him harder than he'd ever expected she could. Mutiny flashed in her eyes.

"Stupid is what you are at the moment. I've told you thousands of times you're a good man. When are you going to start believing it?"

"I haven't done anything good for Samantha." The truth of that weighed heavily on his mind and his heart.

"You planned a lovely dinner for her tonight."

He rolled his eye. "With your food, your home, and your hired help. What, exactly," he sneered, "did *I* do that was so fine?"

"You've no intention of fighting for her, have you?"

"I'll help her with her goal; after that, I'm taking my ship and doing what I do best."

She stamped her foot on the floor, narrowly missing his own. "Piracy is not what you do best!" she raged.

His gaze leveled with hers. "Yes, it is. For a few days I forgot that—easy enough to do in such a fine house. But a gentleman I'm not, Jacqueline."

Nor would he ever be. He'd never blend in with the locals, never be content within four walls. For a brief time he'd allowed himself to enjoy a fine woman in a fancy house, to pretend he wasn't wanted by every military man in the Caribbean. But the truth was, he belonged at sea. He was a pirate, and a pirate was the last thing Samantha needed.

With the air suddenly heavy in his lungs, Luke gave his sister a quick embrace. "Thanks for your help. I'll be back . . ." Shame poured through him when Jacqueline's chin quivered. "As soon as I can."

"You can't lose her! She's perfect for you."

"Stop it!" he yelled, though he couldn't have said who he was angry at. "I have to go." He jerked his bag off the floor. "Keep the boy safe, he means the world to Samantha."

Though he turned his back, he could hear the tears in her voice and knew they were coursing down her cheeks. Maybe he shouldn't come back here either.

"*You* mean the world to her, Luke."

He hesitated at the door, bracing himself on the strong wood for a moment. Then, without a glance back, he walked out into the night.

Samantha raced onto the beach, her lungs burning. Sweat clung to her brow. Her hair stuck in damp knots to the base of her neck. She'd run most of the way, keeping to the trees, jumping and darting over protruding branches. More than once she'd slipped on the mossy undergrowth, clawed through the dampness to grab a vine or bough in order to keep her balance. Fear, not one to be left behind, had prowled behind her, its icy fingers stretching toward her. Its cackle had echoed in the squawks and screams of night creatures disturbed from their hunts.

Sam stopped running when her feet sank into the sand. By the time she reached the dock, her breathing was normal. Luke arrived a few minutes later.

"Doesn't look like we were followed," Luke said, hardly gasping at all.

The beach was quiet. There were no gulls scavenging in

the bay, no animals complaining about being lifted onto ships, no sailors with the call of the sea shining in their eyes. Instead, the stars winked down from the clear sky. From the bullrushes down the beach, crickets and frogs played a soothing melody. The water, still as glass, mirrored the half moon above. The few ships that floated just offshore remained dark and at rest, their sails tucked in for the night. The smaller boats tied at the docks rocked sleepily, their oars, like frail arms, crossed over their wooden benches.

"Well, for that, at least, we can be thankful. Let's go."

They pushed the boat away from the sand. The water was warm and sucked at the hem of Samantha's skirt. When they were both soaked from the knees down, they climbed in. Luke took the oars.

"Hand me one, Luke. I'll help row," Samantha offered.

"I've got it," he answered, and cut the paddles into the dark liquid.

Sam huffed out a breath. "I think I can manage a small boat. I can, after all, sail my own ship. Remember?"

"It's bloody impossible to forget," he muttered.

She searched his face but saw no evidence of humor. His jaw was set and he rowed in a smooth, powerful rhythm. He'd rolled up his sleeves in deference to the balmy night, and the muscles in his forearms strained with each stroke of the oars.

There was something going on with Luke, and whatever it was had him in knots. She'd seen him angry, frustrated, and arrogant, but not like this.

"When we get back on the *Revenge*, things will have to remain as they were. Until Dervish is finished," she added when his gaze cut to hers.

The oars finally stilled, though Luke kept his hands

tightly curled around them. His gaze was too dark to read, but Sam felt surrender and pain in the steady way he stared at her.

"Luke." She reached for him.

He shook his head. "We're here."

She hadn't realized the progress they'd made until the small boat tapped the hull of her ship. Carefully, she stood and moved to the ladder. Luke was beside her, his hand a tender aid on her waist as her foot pressed against the bottom rung. She faced her lover, the man she trusted with her life. Placing a hand on his cheek, she wondered at the apology that was all but written in the depth of his eye.

He seemed to pull himself away. "Your ship's waiting."

"I love you," she answered, and longed to wrap her arms around him. To find comfort again in his embrace. To wipe away the gnawing feeling that life was once again going to dump her on her backside.

His gaze bored into hers, his jaw flexed. "We'll see."

Joe's head popped over the gunwale. "It's about bloody time, lass. I won't feel better until we're well away from 'ere."

Sam climbed on board her ship, Luke two steps behind. Joe must have alerted the crew, because all hands were on deck, awaiting her orders.

"Where are ye headed now?" Joe asked.

"Dervish must have sustained some damage in the storm. We'll head back the way we came."

The crew grumbled. They were sailing in circles. They'd never find Dervish. What good was a pocket full of money if they weren't ashore long enough to spend it? But Sam hadn't come this far to tuck her tail and quit now. She stepped away from Luke, past Joe.

"You've all agreed, and I have the signed articles to prove you were in accord. If you've changed your mind, you've only to take the boat to shore. Those of you who still want to sail under my command, you've five minutes to get to your stations. Then we sail back toward Tortuga."

"He's not there," Luke said from behind her.

Sam spun around. "We've got to look somewhere. They must have suffered serious damage in the storm, otherwise they'd be here."

"They were ahead of us. They likely missed the worst of it."

Her temper rose quickly. Her identity was no longer safe. Dervish wasn't where he was supposed to be. Her crew was questioning her leadership, and now the man who was supposed to stand at her side was challenging her in front of her crew. She glared at Luke.

"Then where is he?"

Luke hesitated, swallowed. "Santa Placidia."

"How the blazes could ye know that?" Joe spat, coming to stand next to Sam.

A chill slithered over Sam's skin. Before his lips formed the words, she knew.

"Because that's where he's been heading all along."

The crew's enraged curses rose up like an angry swell. Joe sucked air in great gulps. Though it felt as though the deck had been yanked from beneath her feet, Sam managed to step in front of Joe before he could lunge at Luke. She didn't, however, attempt to hide the betrayal she felt.

"You lied this whole time. Why?" she asked. "For your bloody treasure?"

Luke fingered his patch. It brought Sam back to Jacqueline's parlor, where she'd kissed his missing eye. Where she'd made love to him. Where she'd realized she loved him. Bitter tears burned her eyes, but she forced them back. She wanted to see his lying face clearly.

He hesitated another moment, licked his lips as though he was deciding how much of the truth he had to tell.

"It wasn't all about the treasure, Samantha. When Captain told me Dervish was headed to Santa Placidia, I told you it was Barbados to give you a better chance. A fighting chance." He took a step forward.

Joe growled and pushed at Sam, but she stood firm.

"So Dervish was never coming to Barbados?" Sam echoed.

Luke held out his hand, then dropped it when Sam wouldn't even look at it. "Captain said Dervish's ship was slowing down. He was heading to Santa Placidia to careen it. I knew the best way for you to get your revenge without sacrificing your life was to wait until Dervish had beached his ship. Since that allowed us time to spare, I had you stop here."

Sam stood frozen, trying to comprehend it all. "He's been within a half-day's sail from us for the last two days?"

Luke nodded. Suddenly Sam was desperate for a bath, to scrape her skin raw until there was no remnant of Luke Bradley on it. She'd opened her heart and shared her body. All with a bloody, filthy pirate who'd used her for his own purposes.

"It was all for nothing," she said.

Luke's gaze turned to steel. "It wasn't nothing, Samantha."

He reached for her, but Joe, bless him, moved around to her side. His hand cupped her shoulder, offering his strength.

"Well, Bradley, you must be very pleased. You've got your bloody freedom and your treasure."

Luke's lips were a flat, angry line. Bitterness, hurt, and raw energy swirled in the air between them.

"From the beginning, I admit it was about the treasure. But after—"

Sam cut him off. Her heart couldn't take any more of his lies.

"You're not only selfish, you're heartless, Luke. Joe was right. I'm sorry I listened to the wrong man."

Luke snarled. From the corner of her eye she saw Joe nod.

Cold and filled with a searing pain, Sam knew she had to get away from Luke before she lost her battle with her emotions.

She grabbed one of the pistols that Joe had tucked in his sash. With thoughts of betrayal churning in her mind, she aimed the weapon at Luke.

"Get off my ship."

"Samantha—"

"That's Captain Steele, damn you. And I said get off."

"You'd shoot the man you love?" Luke asked.

It was a dirty tactic. The pistol wavered. Of course she couldn't; they both knew it. "Jump, Luke. We're not so far off you'll need a ship to rescue you this time. I'll even let you keep your other eye."

His jaw flexed. She'd brought up the betrayal by Dervish purposely, and still the mutiny he'd survived on that pirate's ship couldn't have hurt any worse than she was hurting right now.

Joe drew his sword, the blade shining bright and lethal in the moonlight.

"Capt'n may not have the heart to shoot ye, Bradley, but I've no problem with carvin' ye up. Get off her bloody ship before I have the pleasure of doin' just that and feedin' ye to the sharks."

Sam lowered her pistol. Her eyes were swimming now as Luke pleaded silently for another chance. She shook her head.

"Joe, hate me all you will," Luke said, turning his attention to her first mate, "but going into a battle against Dervish, even at his most vulnerable, is a foolish mistake. You can't afford to lose any help at this point."

"Get off," Joe thundered. From behind him the crew chanted for Luke to be thrown in the water.

"Use your head, man. Do you really want her killed?"

Sam's heart and thoughts were racing. It would have done her pride good to heave Luke overboard. But Steele was successful because feelings weren't allowed to get in the way of the goal. And no matter how much it hurt to have Luke this close, knowing she meant nothing to him, that what they'd done together had been little more than a way to pass the time, she couldn't argue. He was right. Dervish was, and always had been, her first priority. To achieve that, she needed Luke.

"Off with ye, now." Joe stalked forward, blade pointed at Luke's heart.

"You could use another gun." Luke tried again, though he was backed against the gunwale and the crew was urging Joe on.

"We'll take our chances," Joe said.

"Luke stays," she said, and every man on deck became silent, every gaze jumped to her.

"But lass," Joe argued.

"Only until we kill Dervish." Her gaze sliced to Luke. "Then, Joe, you can make him walk the plank for all I care."

Fourteen

Squawk. "Man in cabin. Man in cabin."

"Bloody bird," Joe grumbled. Then, belying his words, he poked a thick finger through the bars so he could scratch Carracks's neck. Had the animal been a cat, he would have purred.

Sam didn't bother summoning up a smile. Both she and Joe knew she wasn't in the mood for pretending. Joe came to the table where Sam had been sitting for the last hour, despite tingles that ran up her legs and numbed her backside.

"We're on course, lass. Should be arriving in Santa Placidia not long after sunrise." The chair groaned under Joe's weight as he sat.

Sam spun the empty tin cup Trevor had shyly brought her shortly after weighing anchor. She watched the dregs of coffee make muddy circles in the bottom of the cup. There were too many words, too many apologies stuck in her throat, to answer. She nodded.

"Don't matter what's happen'd, lass. We'll be findin' Dervish now and make him pay for what he done to yer family. 'Tis all that's important."

She swallowed the lump in her throat along with what remained of her pride. "It matters to me, Joe. I believed Luke over you." She slammed her fist down. "I believed a filthy, lying pirate over a man I've known most of my life." She rubbed her aching temples. "How could I have been so blind? And why are you smiling?"

"That's me lass. Ye've never let anyone get ye down fer long. Picked yerself up by the bootstraps, ye have. Glad to see yer doin' it again."

"Joe, I was a fool. I should have listened to you."

"Ahh." He waved a meaty hand in the air. "'Tis over. We've got ourselves more important things to think of than Bradley. Besides," he added with grin, "I've taken care of 'im."

Although she'd already cried enough to flood her ship, fresh tears gathered and fell silently. "I'm sorry, Joe."

He ran a hand down his face, the coarse bristles of his beard scraping the calluses of his palm.

"Don't ye even think on it, lass. We've got a few more hours yet. Why don't ye try to get some rest?"

Sam glanced at her berth, but in her mind she saw Luke lying there, holding her after the battle with the merchant ship. She could feel his arms around her, could smell the sea on his skin. "I can't sleep. I'll be up soon."

Joe unfolded his large body from the chair. "Take the time ye need. I've got yer ship under control."

The stairs protested under his weight but supported him as he raised the hatch and disappeared on deck. Sam took a deep breath, letting her head fall back onto the chair. In a few hours, Dervish would really be dead. Then she'd be saying good-bye to Luke for good. A sob escaped her lips.

"How do I begin?" she asked a twittering Carracks. "How can I possibly forget about Luke?"

Squawk. "Captain fancies Luke. Captain fancies Luke."

Hearing Luke's words from the mouth of her parrot, Sam pinched her eyes closed and wept.

It took all her fortitude to step onto the deck, but she refused to hide in her cabin. And she refused to give Luke that kind of power. He'd wounded her, so much that every breath she took required all the energy she could summon, but he hadn't broken her. It would take more than Luke Bradley to break Sam Steele.

Still, when she saw him standing next to one of the guns, gazing out to sea, her step faltered. She muttered a few curses his way and felt some of her strength come back, even knowing he couldn't hear her over the waves and wind.

"Where's Joe?" she asked Willy, who was at the helm.

"He went below to fetch some coffee and tell Trevor not to bother fixing the afternoon meal. In case . . ." He shrugged.

She sighed and took the helm, forcing herself to look Willy in the eye.

"Thank you."

He nodded, turned to leave, then turned back. "You're a damn fine captain. Luke lied to us; you never did. We know the difference. There's no blame being laid at your feet."

Before she could say anything, Willy was gone, moving to the bow where the rest of her crew were sharpening swords and cleaning their pistols. Extra shots were being divided up and the guns loaded.

Despite her determination to ignore him, her eyes sought Luke again. He wasn't helping her men get ready. Just as well, considering they wouldn't appreciate his services anyway. Instead, he remained focused on the horizon, which was now shifting to a paler blue. The wind caught in his hair and ruffled it about. On a woman it would look a fright. On Luke, it was breathtaking.

"Stop it!" she commanded herself.

She'd changed into trousers prior to coming on deck and had tucked a pistol and a blunderbuss into her sash. She reached for one now, recognizing the pistol when her palm folded around the grip. Feeling the weapon helped her concentrate on what was important. Dervish. Only Dervish.

Still, she knew when Luke finally moved from the gunwale, when he stepped to the bowsprit as pink tinged the sky. And when he turned and finally looked her way, he caught her watching him.

"There it is," Sam whispered, and wiped sweaty hands down the length of her thighs. Her heartbeat rang so loud in her ears she was sure it had moved up from her chest. She rolled her shoulders, the restlessness within her clawing like a tiger tearing apart its supper. All for what stretched out before her.

The *Devil's Wrath* lay heeled over, tilted on its side in the tranquil green blue sea.

"She don't look so good," Joe muttered from her side.

He was right. Even from a distance Sam saw holes in

the hull. Thick green algae clung like leeches to the bottom of the ship. The sails were down and the masts looked as weathered and beaten as the rest of the ship.

On the beach, cannons, barrels, spare sails, and crates had been brought ashore and now littered the white sand. One goat and three chickens complained loudly from their temporary lodgings at the edge of the water.

Some of Dervish's crew were chest deep in the water, chiseling at the layers of muck that impeded the speed of their ship. Others, bare arms gleaming with sweat, hammered as they repaired holes and replaced rotten boards. So far nobody had noticed the stealthy approach of an unexpected ship.

"I hate to say it, lass, but Luke was right. Our chances are much better this way."

Joe stood next to her at the bow, his gaze skimming the beach. Even though Luke wasn't looking her way and wouldn't see it, Sam glared at him. Keeping him from her mind was proving to be an extreme battle, a battle she was losing. Each time she thought she'd managed it, the memories came bounding back. Gnashing her teeth, Sam turned back toward the shore.

"Where do you suppose Dervish is?" she asked.

"Could be anywhere. Oh, damn, lass. I think they've spotted us."

"Stay alert, men, they've seen us," Sam said as she slipped her pistol into her hand.

Behind her she heard the crew move to their positions and the unmistakable sound of hammers being drawn back. A flag of truce didn't guarantee anything, especially with that pack of mongrels.

"How are ye feelin', lass?"

"Like a cannonball just dropped into my belly."

On shore, a handful of men had grabbed their muskets and aimed them at the ship. The rest of the crew remained in the water, hammers quiet, eyes crinkled almost shut in deference to the sun that was beating down on their sunburned faces.

"We're close enough. Drop the anchor."

The loud splash carried in the silent bay.

With a mouth drier than cotton, Sam yelled, "We're coming ashore. We don't want anything but to see your captain. If you fire your weapons, we'll respond likewise, and your ship will be blasted to pieces."

She waited, not daring to breathe, until she was certain they weren't going to open fire, though they didn't lower their weapons.

"Let's go. If anyone moves, shoot them," Sam said loud enough for her voice to carry over the short distance between the ships. She didn't bother hiding the fact that she was a woman. Either she'd die on this beach or she'd have the chance to start a fresh life. Whichever happened, Steele would not be leaving Santa Placidia this day.

"Joe, Willy, come with me. The rest of you, don't let your guard down," Sam said.

"Lass," Joe said, taking her arm. "Ye need to be careful. Ye can't reveal who ye really are."

"Why not? Steele's going to die today, Joe, one way or another."

"Aye, lass. But if we live, ye don't want anyone after ye for revenge of their own. Let me be Steele."

Sam hesitated. God, she was tired.

"All right, Joe. You can be Steele."

He nodded, then with weapons firmly held high, they jumped into the chest-deep water. Another splash followed theirs, but Sam didn't bother looking. She knew it was

Luke. Having finally succeeded in setting her feelings aside for the time being, she was glad Luke had followed. He, too, knew what Dervish looked like and it wouldn't hurt to have another pair of eyes looking for him. Flanked by the three of them, she waded toward the beach.

The water slowed their movement, but the sandy bottom enabled a steady pace without the fear of slipping. Sam's gaze darted about.

"Do you see him, Willy?" Sam asked.

Willy, another survivor who'd actually seen Dervish that night five years ago, looked up and down the beach, then back at the men in the water. Frustrated, he ran fingers through his hair and faced her. Words weren't necessary.

"You don't, do you?"

"No, Captain."

"How about you, Luke? Anything?"

Luke's jaw was set. "No, but I didn't expect him to be sitting on the beach. Even if he didn't see us coming, he wouldn't be making himself an open target. He's here, though"—his gaze penetrated hers—"of that I'm sure."

"That remains to be seen, doesn't it?" she snapped, not about to let him forget the lies he'd already led her to believe.

They trudged ashore, their boots gurgling with every step, and stopped before three of the worst-smelling, vile creatures she'd ever seen. And considering the quality of men she'd come across in the last five years, that was saying something.

If there was such a thing as rotting alive, these men were doing it. Clothes hung limply, so torn and dirty it was impossible to tell their original color. Their hair was as lifeless as their eyes, which had no shine to them at all.

The sun scorched the back of her head. Sweat ran in sticky trails down her spine. Inside her chest a storm raged. Where was Dervish? Was he hiding in the thick under-brush, pistol aimed at them? Since stealing Grant's ship, she hadn't lost any member of her crew. There had been wounds and sicknesses, but nobody had died in battle. She realized then just how unusually fortunate she'd been in that regard, and hoped the day hadn't come when her good fortune dried up.

Sam opened her mouth to ask the nearest corpselike man where his captain was, but before she could speak, he turned to Luke.

"I see the sharks spared ya." He grinned, black teeth poking from between his cracked lips.

Luke shrugged. "It takes a very refined palate to appre-ciate something as fine as me, Copper. Apparently sharks don't have one."

The man named Copper laughed, a sound similar to rubbing two pine cones together. Sam hastened back to the reason she was there.

"Copper, we need to see Dervish at once. Where is he?"

Her words did nothing more than draw the pirate's slimy gaze up and down her body before he once again turned to Luke.

"You're after Dervish? Why?" he asked Luke.

Again Luke shrugged. "I've a proposition for him," he lied.

Something in Sam snapped. It was bad enough she was being ignored by Copper, but to have Luke simply take over as though she wasn't there sent her blood into a raging boil. He was damn lucky she'd allowed him to come along to Santa Placidia, instead of listening to her crew and heav-ing him headfirst into the ocean. Ever since she'd taken him onto her ship he'd refused to acknowledge that she was the captain, a damn fine one. This might not be the place for her wounded pride to stand tall and fight back, but she was so furious she couldn't help herself.

"Actually, it's *I* who needs to speak with Dervish. Luke is only here to—"

"Got yourself a right sassy one this time, eh, Luke?"

"You know how it is, mate. I can't keep them off of me."

If it wouldn't have hurt her cause to do it, she'd have shot both Luke and Copper on the spot.

"I'm Captain Sam Steele"—she spoke loudly but slowly, glaring at both Luke and Copper—"and I demand to see Dervish. Now."

Copper looked at her as though she'd sprung an extra head, but at least she'd finally gotten his attention.

"Nice try, girlie. But Sam Steele is no woman."

"That's right," Joe acknowledged. "I'm Steele and I need to see your captain."

Copper scratched his hair. It surprised Sam that an army of moths didn't flutter out of the mangled nest that covered his scalp. Copper looked back to Luke. "Captain's out of sorts. He don't want no company."

Nerves singing, Sam wiped a trickle of sweat that had crept its way to her right eyebrow. She'd thought to come ashore, shoot Dervish, and get out. Wasting time talking hadn't been in her plans. Feeling as though she'd been standing there for hours, rather than minutes, Sam drew her weapon.

To her left, seemingly from nowhere, two more of Dervish's men appeared, pistols drawn and no doubt loaded as they took aim at Luke and Willy. Luke muttered from her side. She couldn't hear clearly, but the word "impatient" carried through well enough.

"You shoot me, girlie, and the three of you will be dead before me."

"I'll take my chances," Sam said, her pistol never wavering. Actually, it felt rock steady now that things were progressing more as she'd anticipated. "Your guns are on shore, the rest of your men are unarmed. We've got guns and pistols at the ready. You have a choice, Copper. Take us to Dervish or die." She stepped closer to him, despite the smell of rotting flesh that surrounded him. "I've got nothing left to lose. What'll it be?"

Surprisingly, Copper didn't appear too affected by her threat. Luke, however, was rigid.

"I'll take 'em. Luke and Steele only. You and your other man here are to stay back with ours." He grinned. "As long as ye don't do anything stupid, you'll be alive when we get back."

Joe shook his head, worry drawing his thick eyebrows closer together. "No, the lass comes as well."

"Like hell she will," Copper argued.

"We've got ye outnumbered and outgunned. Me ship's ready to fire. If she don't come, I'll give the order now."

Copper glared at Luke, who shrugged his shoulders. Finally Copper nodded.

"Fine, but this one stays," he added, pointing to Willy.

"Agreed," Joe answered. "But if we don't come out or if yer men turn on me crew, me crew will open fire. It's a long swim to Barbados without a ship."

Willy stood as straight and tall as the mast on the *Revenge*. Long as she'd known him, she'd never seen him falter. Come what may, he'd obey her orders.

Sam cast her glance around at what remained of Dervish's men, those on shore and in the water. Though they'd be stupid to try anything in such a vulnerable situation, she'd learned not to predict what a pirate might do. She caught Luke's gaze for a brief moment, and the reality of the situation settled heavily around her heart.

They left Willy guarded by Dervish's men and followed Copper into the thick foliage, Luke taking up the rear. Tall palm trees with leaves outstretched like a giant's fingers gave instant relief from the glaring sun. Sam took a deep breath, inhaling the humidity along with the smell of thriving green plants that ranged in size from low-growing ferns to the towering, scaly-barked, and slightly hairy palm trees.

The underbrush was spongy beneath their boots. Other than the muffled noise their feet created, and the slight jingle of Luke's chains, the silence in the forest was eerie. It seemed to Sam that every creature knew what was coming and was holding its breath, waiting. She knew exactly how they felt.

She darted a glance back at Luke. Though sweat gleamed on his chest and made his shirt cling to his shoulders, he appeared unshakable. His pistol was in his hand, his face showed little emotion. He said nothing as their eyes met, not offering encouragement or warning. And somehow that hurt as much as his lies. Perhaps she'd expected a small word to boost her courage or even a smile. It was silly, she knew, given what she'd said to him earlier. And yet she couldn't deny the stab of pain that his indifference inflicted.

She turned back to Joe and Copper, who was clearly following a path only he seemed to know. Soon the mass of leaves and branches cleared and Sam stepped onto a wide blanket of green moss complete with a small pond that reflected the shapes and color of the shrubbery that surrounded it. Without the cover of the forest canopy, the sun once again burned its way to the ground and slapped those beneath it with a fiery palm. Sam squinted as its brilliance bounced off the green water and cut a path straight for her eyes. She turned her head, and for the first time saw the little gathering of men huddled near the edge of the trees. One was lying down, cussing as the other three fussed with long scraps of ragged cotton.

Luke stepped to her side, his left hand wrapped around her forearm.

"The one on his back is Dervish," he whispered.

He needn't have said it; she recognized his voice from that dreadful night, the night he'd robbed her of her very soul. The only difference was that there was no triumph bubbling through his words. Pain trembled on each word he spoke. It gave Sam a sick sense of justice. The mighty Dervish had fallen on hard times.

And this time it would be he who lost everything. The triumph would finally be hers.

"Captain," Copper said, walking to his leader, "Sam's Steele's come to see you."

Though Luke's hand tightened around Sam's arm, she stepped forward, determined to get to Dervish whether she had to drag Luke along or not. He understood and let go. Joe scowled, but stopped mid-stride when she shook her head at him.

"Copper, you idiot! You were to stay on the beach. Now get back to bloody work!" Dervish yelled.

From between the shoulders of the three pirates crowded around their captain, Sam saw them pulling on long strips of cloth, wrapping it around something. From what she could see between their moving bodies, it was what remained of Dervish's leg. As they drew another length taut, Dervish jerked on the sand, swearing words more colorful than the parrots he scared from their roosts. Sam flinched.

"They have our ship surrounded sir, I had no ch—"

"I made him bring us," Sam said, surprised that the nervousness eating its way through her belly wasn't apparent in her voice.

For a moment silence reigned and everything stilled. Dervish's breath sounded like a rusty saw trying to cut through steel.

"I'm not fit for romancin' at the moment, wench. Why don't ye come back later? An hour should do it."

"You vile—"

"She's armed," Copper warned. "They all are."

"Dammit, man, what's in your head, sawdust?" Dervish struggled to sit up and spewed more ripe words as the effort increased his pain. "What wench dares challenge me?" he growled. "Well, get out of my bloody way so I can see her!"

Three men stepped back, allowing Sam a clear view of her quarry.

Her first thought was that the man didn't match the voice. She'd imagined someone tall and commanding, and though he was sitting on the ground, she could tell he wasn't any taller than Luke. His face was gaunt and had an unhealthy yellowish tinge to it, reminding Sam of overripe bananas. Sweat beaded his forehead and upper lip. He was thin. Frail. Shoulders that should have been broad and strong were hunched and bony.

He'd removed his shirt, displaying a chest the same jaundiced color and the pronounced protrusion of his ribs. Black hair was stuck to his head in oily, matted sections. Time had robbed him of several teeth. Dirty, long fingernails extended from skeletal hands.

Legs thin as bamboo shoots stretched out before him. One ended just below the knee, the stub of which was wrapped with yellowed cloth that was now mostly red. The crimson stain spread as she watched. Just then a breeze coasted over the palm trees and skimmed Dervish. When it hit Samantha, it was rank with the smell of rotting flesh. Samantha's stomach heaved. She curled her toes until the feeling passed.

Dervish took the time to look her over. It was a quick exploration that mostly touched on her breasts and just below her belly. Shrugging, he turned to Luke.

"Luke Bradley. Back for revenge, are ya? I wondered how long it was going to be before ye'd be fool enough to try it."

Luke smiled. "Wrong again, mate."

It confounded Sam that Luke could come face to face with the man who had ripped his eye out and still be able to exchange pleasantries. What was the matter with him?

"Luke was paid to help find you," Sam said.

Dervish didn't bother shifting his gaze her way.

"Luke, Luke." He clicked his tongue. "Ye've resorted to taking orders from wenches?"

His men chuckled, Luke simply shrugged. Dervish turned his attention to Joe.

"Steele, is it?"

"Aye," Joe answered.

"Well," Dervish asked, spreading his arms wide, "What do ye want?"

Joe looked to Sam, then back to the pirate. "Ye killed the lass's family."

Dervish arched his brows then threw back his head and laughed. "Ye came huntin' fer me because of a wench?" He shook his head. "I should shoot ye just for that."

"Ye hurt her," Joe said, taking a step closer to Dervish.

Sam grabbed his arm with one hand and gripped her weapon more firmly with the other. She reminded herself to stay calm, that Dervish would pay. First, however, she had things to say to the man.

She raised her pistol and shot over Dervish's shoulder. A warning only, but a message she hoped he understood. It was her he needed to pay attention to, not Luke or Joe. The crack of the pistol tore through the foliage. Slowly, unlike his men, who'd dropped to the ground at the shot, Dervish brought his lifeless eyes to hers.

"Listen, you loathsome coward, I'm the one who wants to see your miserable life over." This time there was no masking the emotion in her voice.

He sneered at her as though she was little more than a worrisome rat on his ship. "Get out of here. Now."

"You're not in charge, Dervish, and I don't do anyone's bidding."

"She's right, man, trust me," Luke muttered.

Dervish looked her over more thoroughly this time. When his head came up, he had a lecherous expression on his face.

"You're here to kill me? Is that it?"

The clash of wills resounded in Sam's ears. Her throat was dry. The heat pummeled her back, and yet she shivered.

"You killed my parents, my sister, and our crew. You destroyed our ship. Then you turned your back and walked away. How can you be so cold?"

All this time she'd thought the question she wanted answered most was why he'd done it. She realized as she spoke that it wasn't. They looted and killed for profit, she knew that. What she couldn't understand was how the screams of those he'd attacked didn't haunt him. Wasn't there even a slight part of him that regretted it afterward?

"Tell me," he said as he settled himself back on his elbows. "Did I have the pleasure of your precious mother and sister before I shot them? I did shoot them, did I not?" He scratched his head and laughed. "Damn, I can't remember for certain. There have been so many."

Joe sputtered. At her side, Luke inhaled sharply, and she felt his hand on her shoulder as she aimed the other weapon she'd brought at Dervish's chest. She couldn't say his heart because she now knew for absolute certain he didn't own one.

"You murdering son of a bitch!" she growled.

The grin never left his face, though his eyes seemed more wary. His three men, as cowardly as their commander, stepped back, leaving him a clear target.

"Today you lose," she warned.

Dervish rolled his eyes. "Well, then, get on with it."

He didn't think she'd do it. Damn the man and his arrogance! She drew back the hammer. From her right, she felt Luke's stare. He squeezed her shoulder.

"Be sure, luv," he whispered.

But she was. She wanted Dervish to feel the pain her family had felt. To suffer. Perhaps the chest was being too kind. She wanted to kill him, but she also wanted him to suffer. Maybe the knee would be better. He'd be in pain then, the way she had been for the last five years. She looked down the barrel, taking aim at his knee.

Then she noticed the pistol was shaking in her hand. She spread her legs, planting herself more surely. She even brought her other hand up to secure the weapon. Nothing worked. The trembling increased. What was wrong with her? Tears began to well in her eyes and she sniffed loudly.

Dervish laughed out loud, taunting her further. His men followed suit, even going so far as to sit down, clearly thinking she posed no real threat.

She turned to Luke. In his eye she saw herself reflected, saw everything she'd been through for the last five years, and everything she was sorry for. So many things she regretted, so much shame she carried on her shoulders.

"It won't bring them back," Luke said softly.

No, it wouldn't. It would only give her one more thing to hate about herself. With a wailing sound very similar to that of a wild animal caught in a trap, Sam lowered her weapon and turned away.

A resounding pistol shot screamed in her ears, stopping her dead in her tracks.

Fifteen

Sam's eyes pressed closed and she waited for the explosion of pain, the blast of the shot ripping into her back. But nothing happened. Her cheeks were wet and warm from her tears and her nose was running, but she hadn't been shot.

With that realization came a sob of relief. She had done awful things, but she had a chance to set things right, to start again. Her shaking hand wiped away her tears. She breathed deeply, never so appreciative, as she was then, to be able to fill her lungs.

Willy ran into the clearing. Vines were twisted around his ankles. His cheeks were white, his hair held leaves and twigs. He must have thought she'd been shot and had come running. But she hadn't been.

Dear Lord! She spun around, the breath caught in her throat. Luke stood with legs braced one behind the other, his right arm extended straight ahead of him. A pistol—a recently fired pistol, judging by the smoke curling from the barrel—was in his hand.

Dervish's men slammed their mouths shut and scrambled to their feet. Dervish lay dead, a gaping hole in his chest and unseeing eyes fixed on the cloudless sky.

As she stared at the lifeless body, wondering what it all meant, a part of her registered the sound of men yelling and crashing through the underbrush. A flock of birds screeched their way skyward, and the rustling of their wings snapped Sam back to reality.

She spun to Luke. He'd lowered his weapon, but his stance hadn't relaxed. His muscles were tight; he was ready for anything. Dervish's men, however, weren't in any hurry to avenge their leader. They made no move toward Luke or Sam. Luke gave them a warning glare, then moved toward Sam.

"Let's go," he said.

"You killed him," Sam accused.

"I know," Luke acknowledged. "You can thank me later."

"Thank you?" Sam sputtered, rage finally clawing its way through the shock. "This was my decision to make, mine! How dare you!" She balled her hands into fists and came at Luke with all the fury of a hurricane. "He murdered my family. This was my revenge, and I chose not to take it. What did you do? Did you decide that since I couldn't, you might as well? Well, damn you, Luke Bradley, damn you!"

"Lass," Joe said, coming to her side.

"You stay out of this!" she screamed, then refocused on Luke, who said nothing. His eye was dark and troubled, his jaw set. She reached for the pistol he'd used and flung it among the trees. The mossy ground absorbed the sound.

"Years I waited for this. I did things I'm ashamed of and I'll have to live with for the rest of my life. But you were right, dammit. Killing him wouldn't have brought my family back, it would only have given me more reason to hate myself." She drew in a breath, aware that the men from the beach had plowed through the vegetation and circled them, though they only stared at her in stunned silence. "But when I couldn't, when I faced the truth and turned around, you killed him! For your own revenge! You make me sick, Luke Bradley!"

He flinched.

"First you use me to get to your precious treasure, and then you use me again. Are you happy now? You have your fortune and revenge for Dervish taking your eye."

"Lass, list'n to me. Luke was—"

"Luke was only looking after Luke's own interests." Her gaze bored into Luke's. "That's all he's capable of, Joe. He has no remorse for what he's done, do you?"

Luke lifted his chin, his gaze narrowing. "None whatsoever," he said.

Sam felt sick. Sick of herself, of Luke, and of the life she'd been a part of these last few years.

"You know what, Luke? Your stepfather was right. You're nothing but a bloody bastard."

She glared at every man present, daring them to take her on. Since none moved, she dropped her own pistol onto the moss, stepped over it, and headed back to her ship.

As pirates weren't known for their great loyalty, nobody bothered Willy, Joe, and Luke as they made their way back to the ship. The hammering had resumed and the work continued on the *Devil's Wrath*. No mention was made of their dead captain; another would be chosen by the end of the day.

The *Revenge* sailed out easily with a snapping breeze, Joe at the helm. Luke hadn't seen Samantha since coming aboard. The crew was silent as the ship cut through the waves. There was work to be done, there was always something that needed tending, but Luke couldn't summon the energy to tackle any of it. He was below decks, amid the barrels and supplies. The smell of wet wood filled the small space. Luke Bradley was alone. Again.

He needed to think of the future. Samantha hated him so much he didn't hold out any hope that she'd keep her end of the bargain and give him her ship. Not that he blamed her.

Bastard. Bloody bastard.

Her words tormented him, drowning out the sound of waves washing over the hull, the moan of canvas. He'd seen her angry and hurt before, even scared. But nothing came close to the way she'd been in that small clearing. There had been occasions in his life when he'd felt low, felt worthless. But even his stepfather's words hadn't cut him the way Samantha's had. Maybe that was because he knew he'd never had Percy Young's love. He'd tried to earn it, God knew he had, but he'd never succeeded.

With Samantha, he'd done nothing to achieve her affections. He'd been himself, as much as he was capable of. And yet, for some reason he still couldn't understand, she'd given it to him. Love.

He banged his head against the damp wood, drawing his right knee closer to his chest. His left leg lay motionless on the floor, his boot as black as his mood.

Jacqueline said to fight for her. Ha! Even if he'd entertained the idea before, he had no intention of doing that now.

A bastard.

He pounded his fist against the cask next to him, and closed his eye against the pain. Not the hurt in his hand, but the deep despair that had robbed him of breath since he'd heard the word come from Samantha's mouth and seen the belief in her eye.

A bastard.

There was time, an hour at least, to indulge in pity and regret. Sam lowered the hatch and walked dazedly to her berth, through no conscious thought of her own. She couldn't think of anything but what had happened on that island. Luke's betrayal haunted her. She'd thought she knew the man who hid behind the pirate flag.

"How could I have been so wrong?" she whispered. She grabbed her pillow and squeezed it to her aching heart. The soft cotton absorbed both her tears and the sobs she couldn't hold back.

She wept until she was spent and the pillow was warm and wet from her crying. When she thought she couldn't possibly shed another tear, her thoughts turned to her family.

Dervish had taken them along with her happiness. He'd ripped away everything that had mattered to her. By doing so, he'd led her to Grant, who'd taken the only thing she'd had left, her body's innocence. Then, when all she'd had was to take Dervish's life as he'd taken hers, she'd failed.

The wrenching pain came fast and strong. It grabbed at her heart and mauled its way through her body. Tears that started in the depth of her soul surged forward and robbed her of breath. How could this be? She'd given everything, *everything* she was, to finding Dervish. How could it have ended like this? Yes, he was dead, and she couldn't be sorry about that, but when she'd had the chance to avenge her family, she'd finally realized it wouldn't matter. Having a man's blood on her hands wouldn't make the past any better, wouldn't make her any better. For the first time in years she'd taken the higher ground.

And Luke had ruined it.

He'd ripped her heart open with his lies and deceit, and any good that could have come from her decision not to kill Dervish, he'd robbed her of as well. For the first time in a long while she could have felt good about herself. Not for leaving the miserable wretch alive, but for not tainting her soul any more than it already was by taking a life in cold blood.

But now it didn't matter. Nothing mattered. Her family was still gone, and there was no sense of the peace or finality she'd prayed Dervish's death would bring. Aidan hated her, though she wasn't done with him yet. She'd felt a piece of something, something real and good, with Luke, but he'd used her. The hell of it was, she'd let him. She'd known, taking him to Santa Placidia, that he and Dervish had a past of their own. Yet she'd naively assumed he was there only to help her. Now not only was her past in ruins, but so was her future.

Sobbing, she turned onto her side and curled into a ball.

"Mother, Father, Alicia." Her words cracked, but she forced them out. Otherwise her chest was going to explode with the pain. Sam pressed her palms over her heart, and she swore she could feel the pieces of it where once a whole had been. "I'm sorry. I'm so sorry. Please forgive me for what I've done and who I became."

Her cheeks were raw from wiping her tears but she kept talking, needing to purge herself of this overwhelming guilt.

"Please don't hate me," she begged, because if they hated her as much as she hated herself in that moment, she wouldn't be able to bear it.

Sixteen

Sam sat up in her berth, blinking the grittiness from her eyes. She swayed slightly and pressed a hand to her head, which felt fuzzy as a peach. She must have dozed off. Carracks's head was tucked into his feathers and a low snoring was coming from his cage. She turned to the window, but the sun's position hadn't changed much since she came below, so she knew her nap hadn't been long. Nor had it been restful.

She crept to the edge of her berth, but her limbs were unusually heavy and she nearly tumbled over the edge of the bed. Sam righted herself and stood, the room swaying slightly. She shook her head, drew deep breaths, and stretched her arms over her head until she felt more alert.

"Well, I've had my time to feel sorry for myself," she said, waking Carracks, who glared at her before tucking his head back into his feathers. "Now it's time to get some things done."

The first thing Sam did was change into a simple lavender

dress. The light cotton brushed against her bare ankles, swept just low enough to expose the creamy top of her breasts, and made her feel like a woman. From this day forward, she was just Samantha Fine. Whoever that was.

She dragged the burlap sack she'd taken from Mr. Grant's plantation from underneath her berth. Then, with a desire to rid herself of Steele, Sam stuffed the breeches and shirt she'd worn earlier into the sack. With hungry eyes, she devoured every corner, every shelf of her cabin.

The buff-colored cap she'd worn the time they'd raised false colors and taken a galleon heading for Spain by surprise. It had been their most profitable plunder and had enabled Sam to set enough aside for the future. A future, she thought as she crumpled another pair of pants and stuffed them in after the cap, that loomed gloomy and unknown.

There were logs of her destinations to throw away. Destinations her eyes couldn't help but read. St. Lucia, Havana, Tortuga, Portobello, St. Kitts, and enough other names to shame her. So many places she'd searched in her need to right a wrong. So many times she'd failed to find her quarry and yet had determinedly kept going. She didn't realize she was crying until the tears plopped onto the paper and blotted out the words. Unfortunately, her past couldn't be erased quite so easily.

With nothing left in the drawer but maps, she abandoned the table, drawer left open and gaping, to hunt down the remaining threads of Steele. Soon the sack was bulging with books, logs of journeys, and every item of clothing she'd worn while engaging in piracy. Every item but one.

The red silk slid through her fingers, and for a reason she couldn't explain, she drew it to her breast. She'd worn this dress when she'd met Luke. As though it was yesterday, she could easily envision the belligerent pirate who glared at her from behind bars in Port Royal. How was she to have known he'd steal her heart? She sniffed loudly, and this time she felt the tears. Felt their warm progress down her cheeks, a few dropping onto her chest.

"Get out of my bloody way!"

Luke's angry words shoved their way through the hatch and badgered her as surely as if he were standing before her.

"Ye won't be goin' down there. She said she don't want ya near her."

There was a silent moment in which Sam figured Luke was contemplating shooting Joe. They'd be scowling at each other, she knew. Even below decks the air was thick with their hostilities.

"She doesn't know what the bloody hell she wants!" Luke argued.

Well, Sam thought as she wiped her nose on the scarlet dress and tucked it in the sack, for once Luke was right.

Oliver Grant might have made a fortune legitimately, but he wasn't above using means that were a little less pure to get what he wanted. In this case, it was the men who worked the ship and directed it toward the bay. Men who were paid to act without question and forget just as easily.

He was so close, he could all but smell the heat of her skin. One more jut of rocks and he'd finally have the rest of his slaves back, not to mention his ship. He licked lips that carried the salt of the sea. Samantha.

Each wave the ship cut through sent Oliver's heart thudding faster. Sweat beaded between his upper lip and nose.

His hands dug into the gunwale. Another few minutes, and they'd clear the last obstacle. And revenge would be his.

He'd dug into his savings, whittled away at profits. The slaves who were brought back had paid dearly. They were disciplined for their treachery and sent to work with little water and less food. He wasn't going to sit back and allow a few runaway slaves to do what infestations and flooding hadn't accomplished. Nobody and nothing beat Oliver Grant.

He'd spent far more money than he was comfortable with to find his ship, his slaves. He'd spent long hours awake, contemplating. And he was so very close to getting it all back. Standing proud in the bow of the ship, he knew he wasn't going to fail this time.

Silently, the ship slipped around the corner.

Air hissed through his clenched teeth. "Where is it? Where's my ship?"

His lips flattened. His eyes hardened. The ship that lay in the shallow water wasn't his. The men repairing it weren't his missing slaves. There was no sign of a young woman with long, tawny brown hair. Anger exploded like a lit fuse. His breath caught, then sputtered from his chest.

"She should have been here. She was ahead of us, for God's sake!"

"Your orders, sir?" his captain asked.

Oliver opened his mouth. The words died on his lips as a sharp slice of pain ripped from his chest and down his left arm to his fingers. Instinctively, he grabbed his elbow and pressed his arm to his chest. His eyes blurred with a pain as bright as lightning in a midnight sky.

"Sir?" the captain asked, hand outstretched.

Oliver refused the help, took a weak step back while fighting to clear his eyes. Concentrating on breathing, he managed to scrape in a few disjointed breaths. Sweat ran hot down his sides. It soaked his shirt, the thin cotton clamping onto his back. Slowly, the pain receded. He took a deep breath, and nearly shamed himself by falling when his knees turned to water beneath him. His steps weren't pretty, but they got him to the gunwale, where he could lean on the ship for support.

He held up a hand before the man could ask him if he was all right.

"Bring us in, Captain. If she's not here now, I'm sure she was." Because he was panting like a damn dog in heat, he had to take a minute. He swallowed dryly, wishing for a tall glass of brandy.

"And if she was here," he continued, "we can't be too far behind."

Dusk fell in a slow sweep, like a blanket floating down gently. From the chair she'd pulled to the window, Sam watched the sky ripen to the color of the juiciest plum. Darkness hovered on the horizon.

With a small turn of her head, the scene changed. Barbados awaited to the left, newly lit streetlights flickering in the waning light. Sam pressed her cheek against the glass as the *Revenge* glided closer and welcomed the coolness against her face.

Above her, Joe called orders to bring in some of the sails. Hasty footsteps trod above, then stopped. Sam closed her eyes, seeing in her mind the folding of white, the ropes being pulled and tied, the hungry expressions of her crew as the harbor reached out to meet them. She pressed her fists to her chest, where a swelling emptiness throbbed. Lord, but she was going to miss the daily tasks of a life at sea. And her crew. She'd miss them as well. The boat coasted to a stop.

"Lower the anchor!" Sam mouthed even as Joe yelled it.

The stark truth rushed up and slapped her. She wouldn't be calling that command any longer. Dear God, Sam thought, her ship was no longer hers. She'd promised it to Luke. And despite her feelings toward him, she wouldn't go back on her word. Besides, Samantha Fine had no use for a ship.

Still, the hurt choked her. Everything in the cabin that had been Grant's was gone. She'd replaced everything, painted everything, until the ship was hers. Only hers. When she'd promised it to Luke, she hadn't realized, not fully, what giving it away would mean.

It wasn't only a ship and a way of life, it had become her home. The only place she'd felt safe since the loss of her family. She'd made it hers. She'd treasured it, taken care of it. Loved it.

Her gaze feasted on the cabin, taking it all in. By the time it was halfway around the room, her vision had blurred.

"What am I going to do without all this?" she cried.

Seventeen

The water in the bay was serene and inky blue. It reflected the light from Samantha's cabin along with the few lanterns mounted on the gunwale. The *Revenge* drifted quietly on the short lead the dropped anchor provided. The crew, silent and awaiting their captain's return above deck along with her instructions, waited on deck while their yearning gazes darted from Samantha's closed hatch to the night noises that coasted from Barbados. Everything and everyone seemed almost peaceful.

Except Luke.

He'd been simmering so long, he was surprised his head hadn't shot off under the pressure. Damn Joe had kept him from Samantha since leaving Santa Placidia and had all but stood on the wretched hatch to keep Luke away. And the only reason Luke had backed off was because he'd been afraid that the big brute would fall through and flatten Samantha. The fact that Joe kept smiling at Luke, raising eyebrows thick and coarse enough to scrub Trevor's pots, only added to Luke's ire. Well, Luke thought, taking hold of a rope to keep from strangling Joe, it wasn't over. He'd talk to Samantha if he had to drown Joe to do it. Which, for the first time in days, brought him a warm sense of pleasure.

The hatch creaked open. Thirteen men took a step forward.

Luke's first thought was that Samantha looked tired. He couldn't make out every feature in the fading light, but the way she held herself told him as much. Her shoulders weren't quite as straight as usual; her chin wasn't thrust forward in pride. Her hands were still and relaxed at her sides, almost defeated; her voice just a touch softer than usual.

She drew a deep breath. "First, I want to tell you all how much your loyalty has meant. Not many men would have agreed to sail under my command. Not only did you sail, you listened, worked hard, and proved to be an exceptional group of men."

She stopped, ducked her head. Sniffed loudly. When she faced them again, her eyes shone. The men shifted and mumbled, not at all comfortable with the emotional scene.

She cleared her throat, her hands now clasped firmly at her waist. "I appreciate that you kept my identity a secret, and ask only that you continue to do so. Even though I won't be Sam Steele any longer, his identity could still see me hanged."

They nodded and promised, and Samantha gave them a watery smile.

"You can take your things. You're officially relieved of your duties. Thank you, all of you, from the bottom of my heart."

In turns, her crew came forward, clasping her hand,

muttering a few words before they went below to fetch their things. From the boom, Luke watched her say her good-byes. The tears that clung to her lashes as she bid the men farewell were the best damn gift she could give them. Luke hoped they treasured it.

Only Willy and Joe were left.

Willy went first. Luke turned away. He walked to the bow to give her the time and privacy to say good-bye to her friends.

"I'm not so fancy with words, Captain," Willy began.

"It's Samantha now, Willy. Just Samantha." And how long, she wondered, until she knew just who that was?

"Samantha." He nodded. "Suits you better." He shuffled his feet. "Well . . ."

She'd had all afternoon to prepare for this moment, and yet she realized just how unready she was. These men had been her family and friends for the last four years. Willy and Joe even longer. How did one say good-bye to that and not lose part of oneself in the process?

"My father would have been pleased that you've stayed with me."

"Well"—Willy nodded, swallowed—"I figured I owed him no less. He was a good man, Samantha. You'd have made him proud."

She managed a wry laugh. Tears of shame trickled down her face. "I doubt that, Willy."

"You did what had to be done. It wasn't all pretty. But you never made it any worse than it needed to be." Solemnly, he laid his hands on her shoulders. "You were fair. Don't be looking to remember it any other way."

Such a fine man. There had been many times she'd grieved for her family, many times she'd wished for something of theirs that she could hold, hold and remember.

She'd cried over lost trinkets, keepsakes that had drowned with the *Destiny*. So many times she'd ached for a piece of her old life back. And all along here it was. Her father had chosen Willy and Joe as part of his crew; he'd respected them, laughed with them, and worked alongside them. His memory was a part of them. She latched onto the thought and clutched it to her heart. Her father had been with her all along. She might have been without her family, but she'd never been alone.

"Thank you," she managed around the knot of emotion in her throat.

Willy held her gaze for another instant. When his eyes filled, he stepped back, then cleared his throat. "Well, I'll get my things."

Joe waited until Willy was gone before he came forward. Unlike the rest of her crew who had bid her good-bye with different degrees of emotion, when Joe marched toward her, his face gave away nothing. Indeed, it appeared cast in stone.

"Ye may have said all yer good-byes, but don't be expectin' mine." He gave a sharp nod of his head and crossed his arms over his chest.

Sam laughed at his stubborn expression. Of all the ones he'd worn over the years, she'd seen that one the most. It helped ease the fist that was wrapped around her heart. With the back of her hand, she wiped the moisture from her cheeks.

"You always were the most hardheaded man," she said.

The corner of his mouth twitched slightly. "Aye, and that won't be changin' now."

Sam sighed. "You have to move on, Joe. You've given me four years already. It's time you settled somewhere."

She pressed her lips together and gathered her strength. "It's time you had a family."

"*We're* family, lass."

"Joe." She blew out her breath. "You can't stay with me. I've no plans. I don't know where to go, where to begin again. It may take me some time to put the pieces of Samantha Fine back together again."

"Put 'em together. Take all the time ye need."

"Joe—"

"Lass," he interrupted, and the stone face began to crack. "I've nowhere to go meself. It may be that I'll need as much time to think things through as ye."

Over Joe's shoulder she watched Luke turn around. He'd said nothing as she'd seen each one of her crew off. He'd backed away, allowed her privacy. Knowing he'd been there, waiting for his turn, filled her with dread. There was much to say, and yet there was nothing to say. And facing him, saying good-bye, would surely shatter what was left of her heart. He came toward them.

"Joe"—Sam turned her attention back to her first mate in order to keep his attention on her, lest he remember Luke was there and decide to shoot him on the spot—"you can't wait on me. I have no idea how long it will take. I need to find somewhere to stay, and then—"

"You can stay here," Luke announced.

"Now that's just ridiculous," Sam sputtered. Despite the way her heart leaped at his words, she knew she had to leave the *Revenge*.

"Aye," Joe concurred. "I agree with Luke."

"You what?" Both Sam and Luke gaped.

"Ye need a place to stay; this is yer home. Until ye know otherwise, why not stay here?"

"You agree with Luke? Since when?"

Joe shook his head. Clearly even he couldn't believe he was doing it. " 'Tis the right thing, to stay here. Then I won't be worryin' about ye. I'll know yer safe."

Sam met Luke's dark gaze and swore she heard a click as they locked onto each other.

"As long as you want it, it's yours."

"But I promised it to you," Sam argued.

Luke stepped in front of her. His knuckles grazed the length of her jaw. "It's only a ship to me, luv. To you, it's your home. I can wait until you don't need her anymore."

It took three tries to swallow the lump of emotion in her throat. There was something shining in Luke's eye that had never been there before. Something that penetrated to her soul and curled warmly, despite her anger toward him. It might have made a difference had she seen it before. She wouldn't allow it to now. Piracy for her was over. Hadn't she already wasted four years of her life for it? But it wasn't the same for Luke. For Luke it *was* his life.

"I need to get Aidan," Sam said, and headed for the ladder.

"Samantha," Luke called.

A part of her wanted to stop, needed to. But there was so much turmoil within her, she couldn't think straight. Dervish was dead, but she had no more peace now than she had before. Who was Samantha, and what did she want? The questions spun and spun, gathering speed and force like a hurricane.

"Give me two days, Joe. I should know by then what my plans are."

"And me?" Luke asked. "There's things that need to be said."

Still too much a coward to turn and face him, Sam

slipped over the edge of her ship onto the ladder. She kept her gaze lowered. Forced her voice not to crack.

"I have nothing to say, Luke. Come back in two days, then you can have your ship. I won't need it anymore."

"You didn't tell her. Why?" Luke asked Joe.

Joe faced the man he'd hated for the last few weeks. He'd thought Luke arrogant, lazy, and untrustworthy. At least now he knew the last one wasn't true.

"Why didn't ye?"

"Tell her I shot Dervish to keep him from killing her? It wouldn't change anything. Doesn't change who I am."

"Doesn't make ye a bastard either."

Luke snorted, and Joe was shocked to see the other man's shoulders bow.

"Nothing can change the fact that I am exactly that."

Now Joe was getting the whole picture. "And ye think yer not good enough for her. Didn't stop ye from beddin' her."

Luke tensed, clearly anticipating the beating Joe had always threatened. "You'll likely kill me, but so you know, I can hurt you some before you do."

Joe laughed, not believing he was actually warming to this scalawag. "I don't doubt it. But I'll kill ye only if ye don't tell Samantha the truth about what really happened on Santa Placidia."

Luke frowned. "Why in blazes would you want me to do that?"

"She deserves to know the truth. She needs to know it all before she makes her mind up fer good."

"She hates me. And come to think of it, so do you," Luke said.

"She hates that ye lied to her. And in case yer too bloody blind to see it, she loves ye. After all she's been through, if ye can make her happy, then that's what I want fer her. As fer what I think"—he scratched at his grizzly beard—"yer not the same man who boarded in Port Royal. Ye've changed, Luke."

They both turned their faces to the sky, to God's lights that twinkled in the heavens.

"I can't give her what she needs."

Joe smiled at the hurt in Luke's words. There were some things he didn't like about Luke, but he knew as surely as he was breathing that Luke would never let harm come to her. "I'm not sure she even knows right now. Me question, Luke, is do ye want to find out what that is?"

Sam waited in the parlor while Pritchard fetched Aidan. Jacqueline, thankfully, was out this evening, so Sam would be spared a lengthy explanation and a sister's subtle push to pair her and Luke. Since Jacqueline had already proved to be a savvy woman, she'd no doubt realized Sam and Luke were lovers. And that, Sam thought with a twinge in her heart, was a matter she couldn't talk about after such an emotional day. She trailed a finger along the dustless mantel of the cold hearth. It was much better that Jacqueline wasn't home. Even if that did make Sam a coward.

Besides, Jacqueline would have felt it necessary to extol Luke's virtues. Sam knew Luke's good side, didn't need his sister to point it out. But she also knew what lay at Luke's core. Piracy. He'd proven such on Santa Placidia.

No, she shook her head, she had to forget about Luke and any silly dreams she'd begun to spin about the two of them being together. Despite her attraction to Luke, she needed to stand alone, to find Samantha. She heard sullen footsteps tramping down the stairs. This was what she needed, to provide for Aidan.

Aidan dragged his heels into the room and Pritchard silently closed the door behind him. The boy's shoulders were hunched nearly to his ears. His hands were fisted at his sides. An angry flush colored the tops of his cheeks and the tips of his ears that poked out of clean hair. Despite his anger, he looked good. He was clean; his clothes had been washed. He looked as he should, an ordinary boy living in a nice house and leading a common life. She was prepared to fight to see that he continued to live as one. And judging by the battle that brewed in his eyes, it was going to be a hard one.

"I said I won't sail with you again."

"That's fine. I won't be sailing anymore myself."

He crossed his arms over his pressed shirt. "What about the *Revenge*?"

"I have her for two more days, then she's Luke's."

She didn't miss the sweep of sorrow that went through his eyes. Because she understood it, she moved toward him.

"That don't mean I'll live with you. You treated me like a damn baby."

His chin angled up, all but daring her to reprimand him for cussing. Instead, she nodded. "You're right, I did. Now let's sit, and I'll tell you why."

She sat on the couch, very aware it was where she'd spent the best moments of her life, here with Luke. But since she could manage only one hardheaded male at a time, she concentrated on the one who watched her warily from just inside the closed door. The one who didn't trust her to tell him the truth.

"Aidan, you know about my family. About how they were killed."

He nodded. She took that for encouragement and forged ahead. She had a hazy notion of what she wanted to tell him, combined with what a boy his age needed to hear. She'd made mistakes as Steele, and Aidan was one of them. So often she'd held herself back, not going to him as she'd have liked to, not reading him stories more often. All because she thought it best that way. Best not to mother him too much, not to embarrass him. Not to let herself care too much. Now she could see it hadn't been the best thing for either one of them. This time she intended to make things right, no matter the cost to her heart.

"Do you know why I always kept you with me, on board? Why I never let you go ashore with Joe or Willy?"

"Because you think I'm too young. You'd lie and say you needed protection, but you didn't. You just wanted to keep your eye on me."

Oh, dear boy, you're not so very young, are you?

"You're right. And I'm sorry."

He moved to the couch opposite her.

"Why'd you do it?" he asked.

"Because when I first saw you on that plantation, when I saw you hurt and bleeding, I saw my sister." Aidan faded with the tears that swam into her eyes, but this time she let them flow. He needed to know it all, see it all. She'd shielded him enough.

He sat, and she drew a deep breath before plunging into dark, unfamiliar waters.

"My sister was younger than I was, and it was up to me to look out for her, to care for her. If my parents were busy, I was the one who taught her, guided her. I was to look out for her." For a moment, she saw her sister in her mind and smiled through tears at the perfect memory. "I didn't that night. I never even saw her. I was supposed to look after her, and I failed."

Her voice cracked. Aidan, she noticed, had uncrossed his arms. His eyes were bright and focused on her. It helped steady her.

"When I saw you, when I knew I was going to escape Mr. Grant, I promised myself I'd take you with me. That I would do for you what I failed to do for my sister." She wiped tears with her hand, then dried it on her gown.

"I didn't want you in Tortuga, especially Tortuga, because it's such a vile place. Yes, I think you're too young, but it wasn't because I didn't trust you. I was thinking about me, Aidan. Only me."

He sniffed. Sam followed her heart and moved to sit by him. She took his growing hands into her own and held on for life. "What if you got hurt in Tortuga? What if you needed me and I couldn't be there? I don't think I could live with myself for not being there when you needed me most. Can you understand that, Aidan? Can you understand that it was only because I love you so much and that I wanted to keep you safe?"

They were both crying now, and Sam knew he understood. She hadn't pushed him so far away that she'd lost him.

"Why didn't you say so?" he asked, wiping his nose on his sleeve.

Jacqueline might have cleaned his clothes, but it would take some doing to work on his manners. Thankfully, she had the time.

"Because I was afraid. Afraid you'd push me away, afraid you didn't want a big sister watching over you." Too much emotion was pushing inside her to hold it back. She squeezed his hands. "You're the brother I never had, Aidan. I love you."

His face crumpled. "I was scared you'd hate me after those things I said."

His eyes met hers, so full of need it broke her heart.

"I could never hate you, Aidan. Never."

His lips trembled. "Promise? Promise you won't ever hate me so much you give me up? Promise I can stay with you? Forever?"

Her voice hitched. "God, I promise. As long as you want, Aidan, we'll be together. We're family now."

His face shone through his tears.

"I'd like that."

She crushed him to her, smelled the soap he'd used to wash his hair. He smelled of sunshine, youth, and hope.

"Me, too, Aidan," Sam muttered as they clung to each other. "Me, too."

Eighteen

She was beautiful. Perfect. And in two days she'd be nothing but a memory. Losing the *Revenge* hurt more than Sam had figured it would. More than losing the *Destiny*. She'd never mourned that ship, only the people who had been on it.

Sam caressed the sides of the lifeboat with her palm as she strolled the deck. The moon watched her quietly, its soft glow the only light Sam needed. She'd worked, walked, and loved every corner of this ship. A lantern wouldn't show her anything she could easily see with her eyes closed.

Her fingers wrapped around a coarse rope, and she remembered the times they'd been caught in storms, the calluses that had burned from the effort of tugging it. She jerked it to ensure it was secure. Then she stepped over the windlass and leaned against the bowsprit. The water was still as glass, so the ship hardly moved. The ships anchored nearby were motionless and quiet.

The silence allowed her to think.

Aidan was asleep below, in a berth they'd made together

so he wouldn't have to sleep on the floor. She was pleased with their new understanding of each other. Pleased a part of her was finally at peace. She had family again. She smiled up at the stars and imagined their twinkling was a smile in return.

She breathed the humidity into her lungs, held it, and slowly let it out. She had a brother. Now she needed to find a way to provide for both of them.

"Wish I could keep you," she whispered to her ship.

Pushing away from the bow, she wandered back to the helm, around the guns she'd polished until they shone like black jewels, then on to the tiller. The wood was smooth from hours of being held. How many nights, she wondered, had she stood there, gazing out at sea? She'd felt the sea rise up, slap the ship, and spray her face. She'd tasted the salt along with the freedom. There was nowhere she couldn't go, nothing she couldn't see if she so chose.

Dolphins had played alongside the *Revenge*, lean muscles working to ride the crest they made. Wind had both assaulted and caressed her, whispered and raged. Her ship had glided, rocked, and pitched, depending on the wrath of the wind. She'd been soaking wet, shivering, and so cold she'd thought she'd never feel warmth again. There had been wilting heat that had flattened her hair to her head, caused every pore in her body to sweat, and left her throat dry as a desert wind.

There had been times she'd feared for her life, for those of her crew. Times she'd hated herself, and moments she'd been bursting with pride. Those moments, she'd escaped to her cabin, and the triumph had turned bitter with nobody she could run to, nobody so close to her they could feel her joy. She could have turned to Joe, but it hadn't been an uncle figure she'd ached for.

She took the tiller, clasped it as she would the hands of a long-lost friend. Yes, there had been sorrow and pain on board. Loneliness and frustration. But Sam knew that was part of life. And not one of those emotions could shadow the love she felt for this ship. Luke was right. It was her home.

"I'm going to miss it all," she said.

Just then a feeling, nothing more substantial than a chill across the nape of her neck, turned her attention to shore. At first glance nothing was there. There was no movement, no sound. But as her eyes took a second pass across the stretch of beach, she saw a person sitting on the sand. Sam squinted. Yes, definitely a person. A man. With his knees drawn up.

As she watched, he extended an arm and took a bottle from the sand. He lifted it up and out, hesitated, then drew it to his lips.

"Luke," Sam said, and everything inside her curled, then ached.

Though he was likely watching the ship, ensuring its safety, she chose to pretend he was watching her. For tonight, she would allow herself the silliness of pretending he was watching her, that he had nothing on his mind but Samantha Fine. It was ridiculous, but she couldn't help herself. She'd been a captain for four years, men turning to her for leadership. Prior to that, she'd been a naive young girl. Tonight, thinking Luke was there only for her made her feel like a woman loved.

Tomorrow was soon enough to return to her troubles and the stark truth of Luke's feelings toward her. She'd think of a way to look after herself and Aidan, a place for them to live. But it would all wait until morning.

"Good night, Luke."

As if he heard and decided to ignore her, he lay back in the sand and pretended to sleep.

* * *

Oliver Grant could taste victory as surely as the fine brandy that swirled in his glass. He'd known this day would come.

"Enjoy your evening," Oliver said, toasting with his brandy as he watched Samantha stroll the deck of his ship. "Enjoy it while you can."

Cannon fire rocked the ship and jarred Sam awake. Terror clawed at her stomach, stealing her breath. It couldn't be happening, not again! She dashed from her berth, feet scraping the stairs. She slammed her shoulder against the hatch when it wouldn't open. Needle-sharp pain blasted down her arm.

The hatch finally gave way, and Sam pushed her way up. Pirates—hundreds, it seemed—glowed eerily in the moonlight. Their faces swam before her, each one more mocking and more vile than the last. Rotting teeth flashed in cadaverous faces that laughed, the sound a mixture of a screeching cat and an animal dying from a mortal wound.

Despite her terror, Sam knew she needed to act. Her eyes darted, hunting for what she needed most. Panicked, she shoved at the pirates and raced between them. A laugh, high-pitched and taunting, seeped into her bones, drawing her strength. Her legs lost all feeling. She dropped to the deck, unable to stand, no matter how much she struggled.

"Help me," she begged.

Then silence. It was such a sharp contrast that her ears rang with the lack of noise. The pirates shifted, allowed her to see across to the other side of her ship.

"Luke!" she yelled.

He turned to her, blood oozing from where his right eye had been. The patch still covered the other.

"No!" she wailed. Then, drawing everything she had within her, she braced upon her elbows and dragged herself toward him.

"I'm coming, Luke, I'm coming."

Around her the pirates sneered. Then, just when she was mere inches from Luke, pistol fire shattered the silence.

Luke jolted like a puppet being pulled by a dozen different strings from as many directions.

"No!" Sam yelled, feeling the pain to the depths of her soul. But it was too late.

Luke fell, dead, at her side.

She jerked awake, dripping wet. Grief pressed heavily upon her. Her uneven breathing echoed off the cabin walls. Pictures from the dream floated around her head, tormenting her. Luke had lost both eyes. Luke had been killed. She'd failed. She'd lost him.

Sobbing, she scrambled from her berth, ran past a slightly snoring Carracks and up the stairs. Night dampness collided with sticky sweat. Sam shivered. Against the gunwale she craned through the darkness to find Luke. It was a dream. He'd still be lying on the beach. He was alive; he had to be.

Her gaze found the area where he'd been. She blinked. He was gone! How could he be gone? She ran to the bow, her nightgown catching on the corner of the lifeboat. The rip roared in the silence, but didn't slow Sam down. It was silly, unreasonable. But she knew she wouldn't breathe normally again until she saw Luke.

At the front of her ship, she took a deep, if shaky, breath and began her search from one corner of the beach to the other. Her hands dug into the ship.

"Please, Luke, please be there."

Under the moonlight, the sand was dark where the waves rolled in to play. But it was empty. She leaned forward, reaching her torso over the edge of the ship. Praying.

And when she found him, standing on the pier, leaning casually against a post, his attention drawn out to sea, Sam knew glorious relief. It washed like a soft tropical rain down her throat and melted away the last of her fear. Luke was safe.

"Thank God," Sam whispered.

Then, before he could sense her watching, before the energy that had propelled her from her bed to the gunwale evaporated in the night, Sam dropped to the deck.

"Yer lookin' tired, lass," Joe said the following morning.

"I feel it," Sam answered, and tried again to blink away the grit that had embedded itself in her eyes. She hadn't slept a wink after her nightmare, so she wasn't surprised that she looked as exhausted as she felt. "I thought we agreed you'd come back tomorrow. I don't have any answers for you yet."

Joe pressed his girth against the bowsprit. He watched a few dolphins break the surface of the sea, arc, then slip back into the water. When he looked at her, when she could see past the glare of the sun into his eyes, she saw the fatigue in his face.

"I didn't sleep much meself, lass. But 'tisn't why I came. I thought I'd take the boy off yer hands for the day, give ye time to think in peace."

"Aidan?"

"Me?"

Over her shoulder she watched Aidan close the main hatch carefully before stepping to her side. He looked refreshed and exuded enough boyish energy to make Sam, with her weighty limbs and foggy brain, feel a hundred years old. Still, the initial thought of letting him go ashore created a fist of fear in her belly.

"I don't know, Joe . . ."

He held up a palm that had a yellow callous at the base of each finger. "Now, let me speak. Ye need to think, and by the looks of ye, a little sleep wouldn't hurt any. And as it happens, I saw for meself some waterfalls and pools a young lad such as this one"—he ruffled the boy's hair—"might enjoy."

The sun was out and cheery, the sky was as endless as the sea. The temperature was already pressing heat through her gown.

And the thought of letting Aidan go scared her cold.

"I'll be careful, Sam."

It was that, Sam admitted later, that sealed her decision. He'd asked. He'd never asked for anything before. Yes, she'd seen want in his eyes, felt it shimmer off his young body, but he'd never come out and asked. They'd come a long way together, and if he was comfortable enough in their new relationship to ask, she needed to be equally forthcoming. Though it made her heart tremble, she nodded.

"Mind Joe. I'll see you later."

His eyes lit up, and he pressed himself against her, his arms circling her back. She held tight and continued to hold him that way—if only in her mind—as Joe helped him into the lifeboat.

She waved, wiped the moisture from her cheeks. Pressed a hand to her heart, where the ache remained.

"Well, that wasn't so bad."

* * *

It had been a miserable night. No amount of rum—and he'd had more than he could remember—had eased Luke's tumultuous thoughts. He'd tried everything he could think of to rid his mind of Samantha: wenching, drinking, walking, cursing. It hadn't mattered which, he'd failed at them all. Women! It was all their fault; they were the seed of all evil. Damn his bloody sister for making him think things he had no business thinking about. Damn Samantha for her cursed vows of love that were so easily withdrawn. He'd slept little, and his mood was more foul than the rotten plants he'd finally managed to sleep on. And blast it all, someone was going to get an earful.

Though he knew it would accomplish nothing, he needed to release the frustration on the person who had capsized his life. He secured the pistol firmly in his sash, not above using it if the woman refused to sit and listen.

With a barrelful of rum still humming in his brain, he gave a quick glance to confirm the navy was not yet about. He stepped from the seclusion of the forest and wove down the beach to the lifeboat he'd seen Joe and the boy climb from.

He rowed in uneven strokes, each one pushing the blood faster, increasing the pain behind his eyes tenfold. Cussing didn't help his ailment either. It seemed an eternity before the small boat tapped the larger ship. When it finally did, he felt green. It didn't improve his disposition any. Yes, by everything that was holy, he was going to speak his mind and return to the life he knew. Where he was in command, not some woman.

Unfortunately, when his feet landed on deck, and after it stopped swaying, he forgot everything but what was before him.

She'd taken one of the chairs from her cabin and brought

it on deck. It was placed with its back to one gun and its side pressed to the gunwale, which provided her head a support when she tilted it to the left. Her eyes were closed, her mouth soft with lips parted slightly. Elegant arms rested on the sides of the chair, palms up, fingers curled lightly.

She was fast asleep.

She wore no shoes or stockings. Small feet with high arches looked innocent against the smooth planks of the deck. But looks, Luke knew, were very deceiving. He remembered the way Samantha had whimpered when he'd used his tongue along those delicate arches, how he'd done it again and again mercilessly, just to hear that sound.

A warm breeze whispered over the gunwale and through the ends of her hair, lifting and laying them back ever so gently against her cheek. His hand twitched. His loins burned. With the sea holding them in its watery palm, with rum buzzing loudly through him, he was helpless to resist her. Hell, he didn't even try.

He dropped to his knees and pressed his mouth to hers.

Her eyes snapped open and she jolted back.

He grinned.

She glared.

"Miss me?" he asked.

There was no disorientation from sleep. She was very much awake. And, judging from the color of her cheeks, more than a little annoyed.

"What are you doing? You scared me!"

"As I bloody well should have, and you don't have to yell. I'm bloody standing right here! What are you thinking, sleeping on deck? Any scalawag could have come and taken advantage of you."

"Such as yourself?"

He feigned insult by putting a hand to his heart. "Milady offends me."

"What do you want, Luke?"

Despite the ice that coated her words, her warm breath blew across his face and did strange things to his lower belly, which very quickly reminded him why he was there.

"Depends what I can get away with," he said, meaning every word.

"Not a thing." She leaned forward, aiming to stand. "You're in my way," she said.

"It would appear so."

"Move."

He did, sliding closer until her knees pressed against his chest.

"Luke!"

"Yes, Captain?"

Her head fell back. "He says it now," she muttered.

Feeling much more himself now that he wasn't the only one out of sorts, he stood, swayed, then offered her a hand.

She eyed it warily but accepted, then as soon as she was upright, dropped it like a grenade with a lit fuse. The wood, hot enough from the sun to burn the tender skin of her feet, had her jumping from foot to foot as she moved back to the tiller, where she'd left her shoes.

"You've wasted your time. I've nothing more to say to you."

"Then my timing is perfect, as you don't need to speak at all."

She lifted her eyes to heaven, but no divine being came to her aid—which, Luke figured, was only fair. He hated to be the only one whose pleas remained unanswered. There was no hint of humor around her mouth, and her eyes were distant. Captain Steele was back for a last stand.

Lucky for him, Captain Luke Bradley was equally prepared. And he went into this battle as he did every other, with the sole purpose of winning.

He grabbed the chair and lifted it with one hand. He dropped it at her feet.

"Sitting would be more comfortable," he said.

"I prefer to stand," she countered.

"Prefer to be stubborn would be more accurate." He pointed to the chair. "Sit."

She raised her chin.

"Unless you'd take to spending the rest of the day in your cabin, naked in my arms, I strongly urge you to sit and listen."

He watched, fascinated and more than a little aroused, as the gold in her eyes turned molten. Luke gave the chair a slight nudge with his toe. It scraped closer to Samantha. Her mouth opened, but he spoke before any words spilled out.

"Naked in bed, or sitting quietly and listening. Your choice."

Fire flamed her cheeks. "I don't take orders." Her tone could have cut steel.

He shrugged, tugging at his sash. "Fine by me, darling."

Muttering curses he hoped never to succumb to, she yielded and sat down. She crossed her arms indignantly over her chest and stared him down.

It took him a moment to draw his gaze from her breasts, to shove aside the memory of what they'd felt like, how they'd tasted. That was the kind of thinking he'd wallowed in all night, and it was time to purge himself—of it and of her.

But as he looked down at her, beautiful under the glow of the sun, his damn tongue refused to move.

"I'm waiting," she reminded him, her voice that of a queen waiting for a servant to act.

He'd be damned before he became anybody's manservant.

"Why didn't you bloody leave me alone in Port Royal?"

"What?"

"Port Royal. Prison. Me. I was sitting in jail, contemplating when best to make my escape—and I would have escaped in time—when suddenly in you strode. My life was my own and its path the one I'd chosen. Then you sauntered in and everything I'd mapped out splintered and flew into the wind."

The words, most of which were unplanned, spilled forth as he paced the deck. "You make me want things, Samantha, things that I never knew I wanted until the day you sprung me from jail."

He locked his gaze to hers so there'd be no misunderstanding, no escape.

"Last night I sat on a beach and watched a ship float at anchor until I caught myself. I don't need to sit waiting for a woman when there are all sorts of lovely wenches down at the taverns."

"Now you're just trying to make me jealous," she said. "I'm not interested in your conquests, Luke."

He leaned forward. "If I had any to report, I wouldn't be here now, banging my head against a wall, would I?" He ran his hands over his face as he took a few deep breaths to calm himself.

"I went last night, with the intention of proving you hadn't entangled yourself in my life so much that I couldn't break free." His eyes bored into hers. "But every damn harlot that strapped herself to my arm failed to make me feel anything. I couldn't even look at them without thinking of you and remembering how you tasted and smelled.

"I tried to prove you aren't tied to me, luv, but the truth

is, I can't. Everything about you has woven around me, within me. It's not lust, Samantha. If it was, I could have had my fill last night."

She sat frozen as ice, her lips parted in shock. The ship rocked them gently, oblivious to the storm of emotion on deck. Luke's shirt now stuck to his back with a mixture of nervous sweat and the sun's unrelenting stare. In the distance, a lull of sounds played quietly as Barbados went about its daily routine.

"You changed me, Samantha, and I could strangle you for it. I was bloody happy before."

She was trying to be strong, but Luke saw her hands were trembling. "When you get the ship tomorrow, you'll be free to leave. Nothing is holding you here. Nothing ever holds Luke Bradley for long."

"You did."

She shook her head. "That doesn't count. It was all a lie."

His jaw tightened. "You are far too intelligent to believe that. When I had you in my arms, when we were loving each other, that was the truth. The rest is cargo, easily thrown out."

She jumped from her chair. "Cargo? You lied to me repeatedly, let me believe you were an honorable man. You call that cargo?"

He took a deep breath, held it, and slowly let it out.

"Is it really so impossible for you to believe that I can be honorable?"

Samantha stood and went around the chair, holding the back of it. The fact that she used it to keep distance between them wasn't lost on Luke.

"You shot Dervish for your own gain, Luke."

He set his jaw. "Did I?"

"You were holding the gun, Luke. Do you deny it?"

"No, I don't. But that doesn't mean you know the whole story."

She shook her head, her eyes gleaming like the sea. "Luke, let's not make this any harder. Yes, the treasure I could overlook. Having Dervish careening his ship was easier than a battle at sea, but killing him, Luke, that I can't forgive you for."

Her words, her lack of faith, hung heavier on him than any chain he could place around his neck. Joe wanted him to tell her the truth about Dervish, and he'd planned to, but the words turned to ash. Years he'd spent trying to convince his mother's husband that he was worthy. He'd done all the chores asked of him and hours' worth that hadn't been, but it hadn't mattered.

Nothing had been enough. He'd left that life, and it would be a bloody cold day in hell before he put himself back there. Not even for the woman he loved. His stomach clenched at that, and for the first time all day he knew it wasn't due to rum. He loved her.

Well, he thought, looking at Samantha, his heart thumping behind his chains, it wouldn't be the first time he'd left something he loved behind. He'd never begged before, and he'd be damned before he'd do it now. Luke Bradley had his pride.

"You're absolutely right. There's no need to make this any harder. And as I've taken enough of your time, I'll leave you to your ship."

He left without another glance or word.

She didn't call him back, which told Luke everything he needed to know.

Nineteen

Even though his well of patience was deep, Oliver had reached its bottom. He'd waited, planned, taken deliberate steps to get his ship and Samantha back into his possession. To be so close yet unable to make the final move was the most frustrating thing he'd encountered thus far.

But Oliver wasn't fool enough to risk his revenge on an emotional mistake. Not when he'd come this far. So, he settled back and waited. Bradley had left hours ago, but the harbor was busy, and he didn't want to chance anyone hearing Samantha scream.

He smiled. She would scream, he'd make certain of it.

No, he'd wait until dusk, then he'd find her.

He'd always known he'd find her.

"You seem unsettled," Jacqueline said.

"Perhaps because I never thought to have the sister-in-law of the governor on board my ship."

Jacqueline smiled and cast a glance around. "It is a pretty ship."

Since Sam was certain Luke's sister hadn't come to talk about sailing or sailing vessels, and she was afraid that being seen together on the *Revenge* would hurt Jacqueline, she quickly got to the point.

"What brought you by?"

"I was afraid, after I came home and realized you'd already come back for Aidan, that we wouldn't have a chance to talk again."

"I thought it best to leave quickly." *And quietly*, she thought.

"What happened, Samantha? You look sad. Did you not find Dervish?"

"Can we please not talk about that?" Sam asked, her voice cracking.

Jacqueline's eyes filled with sympathy. "I'm sorry. You didn't find him, did you?"

"No, we did."

"Then I don't understand. Wasn't that what you wanted?"

Sam took a deep breath. "Please, I don't want to hurt you. It's best if you don't know."

Luke's sister frowned and leaned forward. It was uncanny, in that one expression, how much she looked like her brother.

"You're as bad as he is. I won't faint or swoon if I hear a bit of bad news, Samantha. Is Luke all right?" She paled. "He's not hurt, is he?"

"No, nothing like that." Taking a deep breath, Sam told Jacqueline the awful story.

When Sam had finished, Jacqueline was quiet for a moment, her brows drawing together as she thought.

"You're determined to live without him, aren't you?"

Sam rubbed her eyes, suddenly weary. "He's a pirate, Jacqueline, and I don't want any part of that life anymore."

"What makes you think he can't walk away from it?"

Sam sighed. "A person has only to look at Luke to see it's in him. He thrives on the sea, enjoys hunting and looting. If he lost that . . ." Sam tried to picture Luke dressed in tail coats and fancy shoes.

"He could do it," Jacqueline insisted.

"He could, but he'd hate every second of it." Strangely, the idea of forcing Luke to conform to the codes of society was criminal. To do that would take away his boldness, his arrogance. However much she'd hated those traits of his at first, she now recognized them as integral parts of Luke.

"You underestimate my brother," Jacqueline said. "Although I agree he'd never be happy as a military man or a politician, he could, and would, live as a respectable merchant." She focused on Sam. "If he chose to."

"And you believe he would, for me?"

"I know it. Samantha, I've seen you together. He loves you."

Sam shook her head. "No, he doesn't. He wants me. There's a difference."

Jacqueline looked at her, and Sam saw the ideas spinning behind her eyes.

"What makes you happy, Samantha?"

Luke came to mind first, but by the twinkle in his sister's eye, Jacqueline already knew that. Life had thrown some terrible things into her path. The loss of her family, the rape, the fruitless ending to finding Dervish. Through it all, there had been good times. Happy times she'd managed to enjoy despite circumstances.

And every single one of them had happened on board her ship. "The sea," she answered, not aware her voice had turned soft and the despair was gone from it. "I love watching the dolphins swim alongside the ship, watching the whales leap in the distance. I love the power of guiding my ship through a storm or listening to her rock sleepily at night."

It wasn't until Jacqueline passed her a lace-trimmed handkerchief that Sam realized she was crying.

"You don't have to give it up, Samantha. It's your choice."

"Piracy isn't a choice," she answered, and blew into the soft cloth. "And I'm through with it."

"Does that includes Luke?"

"Don't," Samantha begged. "Please don't. This is hard enough."

Jacqueline sighed deeply. "Samantha, listen to me. Luke can and will walk away from piracy. I know him. Just as I know both Daniel and I would work very hard to make that possible for him, for him to have a life without running."

She drew a deep breath and squeezed Sam's hand. "We want a family, Samantha, and that includes Luke. I want him to know his niece or nephew, and I want him to be a part of that child's life. I believe it can happen, and you must as well.

"You can have it all, Samantha, everything your heart longs for. Life hasn't been easy for you, but it hasn't been all pain and suffering."

Memories, large as life and bright as the sun, filled Sam's head. Her sister, her mother and father. Their smiles, their voices. Slowly her head came up. The pain still squeezed her heart, but not as tightly as it had. After five years, the healing had finally begun.

"Thank you," she said, her eyes misty. "I needed to remember that."

"You're so much stronger than you believe, Samantha. It's time to put a little faith in life and love. Once you have Luke, the rest will fall into place. You'll see."

Long before she came to the water, Sam heard the sounds. Water crashing onto itself, joyous yells of children. Several birds cocked their heads and watched her march by. Her feet sank slightly in the rich earth with each step.

Sam's steps halted at the path. She felt her mouth gape open as her eyes raced to see it all at once.

"Oh, my goodness," she muttered.

Rock, carved out by years of grinding water, formed a wall of gray that protruded straight up from the surface of the small pond at the bottom, as though reaching for the sky. Thick trees with gnarled trunks poked out of the rock where they dared. The pool below was green and filled with people of all ages. A mist floated above them as the water splashed down from above.

She stood and stared, amazed by the power and beauty of nature.

"She's beautiful, ain't she?"

Sam hadn't heard or seen Joe approach. Though she jumped slightly, it pleased her that after years of always being aware and alert, she was able to forget everything for a moment in time and simply be.

"She is that. I've never seen anything that compares."

"Come closer," Joe said.

He led her down to where the basin of water gathered and where the enthusiasm of the children was decidedly louder. Joe leaned closer to be heard.

"I've tried to get the boy to leave, but he's found another lad and I've had no luck pryin' him away."

In the heart of the small pond, with hair flattened to his cheeks in thick ropes, Aidan splashed a boy similar in age, then howled and dived under to avoid retaliation. Sam smiled when he finally came up for air, only to have a handful of water aimed at his face. Though he coughed up the water, the wide grin never left him.

"It's good to see him with a boy his age," Sam commented.

"Aye. And 'tis just as good to see ye here. I figured ye'd be on the ship."

"I was. I had a few visitors today; they've given me a lot to consider."

"Ah, Bradley."

They sat on the soft ground, and Sam turned from Aidan's antics to her first mate. "You know he came to see me?"

"I told him to. Glad to see he listens ever' so oft'n."

"You told him to? Why? You hate Luke."

Joe nodded his grizzled head, slapped at a huge bug, and grunted when he succeeded in killing it. He picked it up with thick fingers, examined it, then threw it over his shoulder.

"Yer right, I did. Me thinkin's changed now."

"Did you fall on your head?"

He laughed, the sound equal to the roar of the falls. "No, lass, but he saved yer life. I can't very well hate him fer that now, can I?"

"Are you talking of the merchant ship? If I recall correctly, you weren't any friendlier to him after that."

"Not that, lass. It's Dervish I be talkin' about." His gaze narrowed. "Didn't he tell ye?"

Confused, Samantha shook her head.

"Blast him! I told 'im to tell ye." He muttered curses

under his breath and didn't stop until Sam grabbed his meaty arm.

"Tell me what, Joe?"

"If it wasn't fer Bradley, lass, Dervish would've killed ye."

What happened on Santa Placidia floated through her mind. "Joe, Dervish was bleeding and unarmed. How could Luke have saved me from him?"

"When ye lowered yer weapon and turned away, the scoundrel drew a pistol from behind 'im. Me heart bloody stopped. Dervish was goin' to shoot ye in the back. I had no weapon. Nothin' I could do. But Bradley did, and thank blessed Jesus he did, or we wouldn't be talkin' now."

Like the clouds parting after a fierce storm, everything Luke had said suddenly made sense. Hadn't he told her she didn't know the whole story? He'd admitted to killing Dervish and yet he never explained his reasons. Why?

"Oh, Joe," she muttered, shame spilling over her. Luke hadn't explained because she'd never given him a chance. The first thing she'd done was turn on him and accuse him of killing for his own purposes. She buried her face in her hands, remorse making her ache. He'd saved her life, and what had she done? She'd called him a bastard. She'd used the thing she knew would hurt him the most.

She remembered the coldness that had swept over his face, and the betrayal in his eye earlier today when she'd refused to allow him to defend himself.

"He was suppos'd to tell ye."

"Well, I wasn't very eager to listen to his explanations."

"It ain't too late, lass. Ye can listen to him now, let him explain."

She shook her head. "I don't know where he is."

"Ye know Luke. Ye know where to start lookin.'"

Hope, bright as any sunrise, made her smile. Yes, she knew Luke. She knew he was honorable and gentle, loving and brave. She knew she loved him, and if she didn't find him today, she'd wait on the *Revenge* until he came for it in the morning.

"Thank you," she said, excitement racing through her blood. "Will you be all right with Aidan?"

He waved a big hand at her. "The other boy's mother already invited us fer supper. If that's to yer likin', I can keep the boy until it's time to bring him back fer bed."

She thanked Joe, waved good-bye to Aidan, and picked up her skirts, running as fast as she could.

Dusk spilled over Barbados in a bounty of pink and purple slashes. Across the darkening sky, the balls of clouds had melted into a mixture of lavender and blush. The sea, an exotic shade of blue green, breathed in long, deep breaths that crept a little further up the beach with each exhale.

Pelicans glided over the water, hunting for their dinner. Gold ribbons crept from the horizon, where the sun was nestling into the sea, to the *Revenge*, where Sam waved at one of Jacqueline's servants who'd been kind enough to row her to the ship, leaving the boat on the beach for Joe and Aidan's return.

Upon leaving Joe, she'd searched every tavern she could find, all to no avail. Though she was careful of who she spoke to, she left word everywhere she went. If anybody saw Luke Bradley tonight, they would tell him it was imperative that he make his way to a ship called the *Revenge*. She didn't expect Joe and Aidan for another few hours, and hoped Luke would come before they arrived. For what she wanted to say, what she needed to apologize for, she wanted privacy.

She leaned her forearms on the gunwale. A few people milled about the docks, and though she could tell they were talking by the arm gestures, no sound carried to her. She was alone and, for the moment, glad of it. She'd need some time to formulate how best to tell Luke she was sorry.

Her stomach clutched and she slowly breathed through it until it relaxed again. She could only hope it wasn't too late for them, that she hadn't cut him too deeply with her lack of faith. She pushed herself away from the side of her ship, her hand caressing the ropes and tiller as she made her way to the hatch that led to her cabin. The future, however uncertain, did hold something very bright in it. Luke and Aidan. And her ship. How they would all work together was something they'd have to work out. As a family. Her heart was so full, it was a wonder it didn't burst. Who would have thought springing a pirate from jail would be the best thing she'd ever done in her life?

Because her mind was elsewhere as she climbed down into her darkened cabin, she didn't notice something wasn't right. She didn't recognize the pungent smell that had haunted her nightmares, nor did she hear the shallow breathing. Not until it was too late.

With a snap, sulfur singed the air and the intruder lit a candle. Her worst memory, very much alive, leered at her.

"Good evening, Samantha. My patience has finally been rewarded. I can't tell you how satisfied I am to see you again."

Twenty

The scream that formed in Sam's head sputtered out in a shocked moan. Her knees buckled. She landed hard on her backside, then scurried up as fast as she could, staying as far from Oliver Grant as possible.

"No, it can't be."

Her hands gripped the ladder, which helped support her shaking knees. There wasn't a part of her that wasn't trembling. He couldn't be alive. She'd killed him. He couldn't have survived that assault to the head. No, it was a nightmare.

But then he expelled cigar smoke in a languid breath that filled the small cabin and constricted around her throat in wispy fingers.

"I assure you, dear girl, it is me. Although I imagine I look far different than the last time you saw me."

He rolled the fat cigar between fingers that were just as fleshy. His predatory gaze never left her. Even as he rose from the chair and trailed a sallow hand over the pale blue cotton blanket that covered her berth, his eyes remained fixed on hers. Evil oozed from his satisfied smile. It slithered to the floor, across the distance between them, and curled around her ankles. Sam shuddered and staggered back, only to come up hard against the wall.

"You won't be hiding from me again," he said, arrogance squaring his shoulders. "Indeed, I haven't waited all this time only to come up empty-handed again. You, my dear, aren't going anywhere."

The past came barreling back. She was helpless again with nowhere to turn, nowhere to go. Grant could easily grab her if she tried to run. And this time, she had no weapon. Fear turned her skin clammy and cold. Her heart galloped, making her breathing loud and uneven in the otherwise silent room.

"Yes, you understand, don't you?"

From the inside pocket of his jacket, he pulled a black blunderbuss. Its reach wasn't meant for great distances, but in the cabin it was more than adequate. He purred as he sat on the edge of the berth, the weapon aimed at her heart. Sam moved behind the table. The back of a chair slid through her slippery fingers as she tried to hold on to something, anything, to keep from falling to pieces. He would take her again, she knew it. Already bile was churning its way up her throat. She couldn't live through that again.

"I remember the night I had you. You were so young, so scared. Kicking and screaming, your nails clawing at anything you could find." He laughed. "I'd never had such a boisterous girl before. Heavens, you all but squeezed the life right out of me." He slapped his thigh as though it was a forgotten jest.

Shame jumped onto the fear and brought tears to Sam's eyes. To Oliver it had been fun. He'd found entertainment in taking her innocence, in hearing her screams. Screams that even now echoed in her ears. Even with the small table between them, she could feel his hands on her body. Sam pressed her hand to her mouth and forced herself to calm down, forced the disgrace away. *Think*, she told herself. *Stay calm, there has to be a way out.*

With tears burning her eyes and her jaw aching from holding back emotion, her life raced through her mind. The *Destiny*, her parents, Dervish. The plantation, the rape. Captain Steele. Luke Bradley.

She couldn't hold back the moan that slipped through her fear. Luke. She'd come so far, so much farther than she ever would have believed possible. For the first time in years, she was contemplating a future, a real future. She'd found a man to love and share a life with, a man who knew everything about her and loved her in spite of it. She released her jaw and took a fortifying breath. The tears dried, and she wiped away the last trace of moisture with a steady hand. She'd been a victim twice in her life. By God, there wouldn't be a third time.

"I may have failed the first time, but if you touch me again, I won't make the same mistake. This time, I will make sure you're dead."

The smile died and his gaze struck. "Mighty big words. How do you propose to stop me all by yourself?"

"Any way I can," she answered between clenched teeth.

"I think I'll enjoy your efforts," he said.

Taking his time, he slowly removed his jacket. He folded it in half and draped it over the screen.

"This must go," he muttered. "You've made yourself at home on my ship, I noticed."

"She's mine. You don't deserve her."

His gaze narrowed and he stepped forward. She smelled

the whiskey on his breath. Her gown was already damp under her breasts and arms. Grant must have felt the heat, too, because his upper lip was dotted with moisture.

"That table won't stop me," he taunted.

"Maybe this will." She grabbed a chair and tossed it at Grant.

He ducked, and although it caught him in the shoulder, he avoided the worst of it. Sam didn't waste a second. Running around the table, flinging chairs in her wake, she dashed for the ladder. If she could get above deck, she could jump into the ocean.

While fear propelled Sam, anger pushed at Oliver. He caught her as her hands pushed open the hatch, his grip iron tight. Moist evening air fell like a light rain on Sam's face. Stars twinkled brightly, but didn't offer the help she so desperately needed. No amount of kicking, wiggling, or struggling helped. Sam screamed and thrashed, using the edge of the latch to pull herself up.

"Let go of me!" she yelled. "Let go!"

With a heavy grunt and a strength she couldn't match, he pulled hard enough for Sam's tenuous grip on the hatch to give. She fell down the ladder, her cheek hitting the rungs, and landed in a heap on the floor of the cabin.

"Damn you," Oliver wheezed, his face now the color of uncooked pastry. "You always were more trouble than you were worth."

Her face throbbed. Her fingers stung and bled where her fingernails had ripped. The blunderbuss he'd somehow managed to hold on to was once again pointed at her. Moonlight fell from the open hatch onto Grant's shoulders. The candle he'd lit earlier was only bright enough to draw out the angles and planes of his greedy face. While she fought to control the fear that raced up and down her body in cold waves, she tried to formulate another plan. As Steele would. After all, it was Grant who'd created Steele. It was only fair that he die by him.

Taking every speck of control she could muster, Sam drew herself up. Oliver sneered.

"Always were too damned willful for your own good."

In a move that revived one of her worst nightmares, Oliver reached for his belt. "As I was saying . . ."

Sam's hands clenched into fists. She was ready to use them. "You'll never have me, or the ship. You're not worthy of either one of us," she said.

"Oh, you are mistaken, my dear girl. First you, then the ship. You are both very much mine. However, much as I enjoy your screams, I don't think the whole bay needs to hear them."

He moved sideways, keeping Sam in his sight, and took two steps up the ladder to reach for the hatch.

Warm water dripped onto Grant's head, and he froze.

Wet, black boots landed hard on the hatch, narrowly missing Oliver's fingers. She knew those boots! *Oh, thank God*, she thought.

"Luke, it's Grant! He's got a weapon!" Sam yelled. Even as she shouted the warning, Grant fired toward the opening. The sound ripped through the stillness. Luke stumbled out of sight. Sam screamed.

"Luke!" she yelled.

Grant cursed and hurried back to her. His meaty fingers dug into her forearms and he pulled her past the table. He then slipped an arm around her waist, took a blunderbuss she hadn't realized he had in his other hand, and pointed it at her head. He backed them into a corner.

"Now, let's see how badly your lover wants to help. Bradley!" Oliver yelled. "If you can still walk, you'll have to come down here to get your precious Samantha. I'm not fool enough to go chasing after you."

Each breath felt like forever while Sam waited to hear sounds from Luke. Any sound to prove he hadn't been killed. Grant's breathing rasped past her ears. His hold was as firm as the weapon that rested coolly against her temple. Sam felt violated just being in his grip. She turned her head aside.

"You've got one minute, Bradley, or your little strumpet here will know what it's like to be with a real man. Again."

His vile laugh crawled over Sam's skin.

Sam counted the seconds in her head. If Luke hadn't come by the time she reached forty-five, she was going to take her chances. Her hands were free, and she had every intention of using them.

Twenty. Twenty-five. Thirty. Sweat trickled down Sam's forehead. She blinked away the sting. Her fingers curled into fists. Thirty-five.

"Let her go, Grant," Luke called from the opening.

Sam sobbed and uncurled her hands. Grant tightened his hold.

"If you want her, you'll have to come down here. I don't need anyone else coming aboard and interrupting my evening. But," he added as one black boot hit the top rung, "I want your weapons thrown down here first. No surprises, Bradley, or Samantha dies."

Two pistols, a sword, and two daggers flashed silver in the moonlight and clanged to the floor. Luke descended. Wet hair lay heavy against his head and trickled in small rivulets down his hard face. His shirt and sash were missing. And thankfully, there was no blood in sight. His eye searched Samantha's. The worry in the murky depths of his gaze gave her strength. He'd come down empty-handed.

Neither of them had a weapon. And yet Sam had never felt so confident in her life. She and Luke had each other. Together they'd be all right.

"Well, well. If it's not the infamous Luke Bradley. I imagine the navy will be very, shall we say, appreciative when I hand you over to them."

Luke leaned negligently against the wall, his weapons at his feet. "That's a grand goal for someone who was once overpowered by a seventeen-year-old girl."

Grant snarled and pushed the pistol harder against Sam's head. Though she felt confident, she didn't underestimate Grant's power.

"I've been looking for her since she left me for dead and stole my ship. Her and every other slave that escaped that night. Years it took to gather them up again, but find them I did. All except for Samantha, the boy, three men, and my ship. Thanks to you, Bradley, I have the two that matter most."

Luke frowned. "Me?"

"My solicitor thought he saw my ship the day of your escape. Since he's hardly ever wrong, I decided to look into the matter. The governor was very forthcoming with the details of your escape. It seems a certain young lady had tricked the guards into eating something they shouldn't."

His grip pulled tight enough to hurt her ribs, and his rancid breath prowled over her cheek.

"You see, Samantha, I have a very long memory. I remembered you doing the same to me and figured it had to be you. Since I hadn't had any luck finding you, I decided to follow Bradley instead."

Grant straightened. "You, my friend, are much easier to track than she is. I'm in your debt."

Luke's upper lip curled back. Sam could only stand

stunned as she assimilated it all. Grant had been looking for her all those years? While she'd been concentrating her efforts on finding Dervish, he'd been trying to find her? The thought sickened her.

"Now," Grant said, "I think I've waited long enough. And you, Captain Bradley, are in my way."

Sam felt the gun slip from her temple and saw it point at Luke. Luke stood tall, his body alert and aware. His eye never left the barrel of the gun. The hammer cocked.

Sam didn't hesitate. She jabbed her right elbow deep into the softness of her captor's belly. He let out an *oof* and his gun wavered. Sam rushed for Luke. He grabbed her and tossed her to the side. He reached for his pistol but wasn't fast enough.

Grant's gun exploded, and Luke fell. Oliver smiled in satisfaction. Sam didn't question what needed to be done. She'd been haunted before by thoughts of having killed him, but she had no qualms now. He wouldn't stop. He'd keep trying, as he had been for the last four years, and Sam wasn't going to have any part of that. It was ending today.

She didn't spare a glance for Luke, who lay still on the floor. She took the other pistol he'd dropped and spun to Grant, who was in the process of reloading.

"Drop it," she warned.

He ignored her. Her hand wavered, and she needed to bring up her other to steady the pistol. "I said drop it."

Grant was wheezing now and sweat poured down his face. He wiped it with a sleeve and finished reloading. He aimed at her.

"I haven't come this far to fail now," he said through gasps. Saliva had gathered at the corners of his mouth.

"Yes, you have. I won't let you ruin the rest of my life."

"You should have thought of that," he said as he staggered slightly, "before you stole my ship."

He cocked the weapon, and though his hand shook, she knew he wouldn't miss. Luke moaned, drawing Grant's attention. Sam pulled the trigger.

The shot was true, and Grant staggered back. Blood spurted from his shoulder. He dropped the blunderbuss and stared in shock from the wound to Sam. Then his face twisted with fury and he ran toward her. She took a step back, despite the arsenal that remained at her feet, but Grant never reached her. Midstride he jolted back, clutched his chest. His eyes widened in pain or shock, Sam wasn't sure which. Then he fell to the floor.

Silence hung heavily.

Luke rose, staggered across the floor, and pressed his fingers to Grant's throat. "He's dead."

Sam dropped the pistol. "I killed him," she muttered.

"Not with a shoulder wound, luv. My guess is his heart stopped."

Sam couldn't look at Grant. She turned and sat on the bed. "He's been looking for me for years. He hunted me like an animal. Just like I did with Dervish. Oh, God, Luke, I'm as bad as he was."

He winced as he knelt before her. "No you're not, luv. You turned away from the man who shattered your life. It's not in you to be mean. Not a damn thing wrong with that."

Sam wiped away the tears that spilled down her cheeks and looked at the man who'd saved her in every way that mattered. "I'm sorry, Luke. I'm sorry I called you a bastard. I was hurting inside, but it was wrong to throw those words in your face. I was just so lost. To have come so far, only to turn my back, was inconceivable. Why couldn't I have seen the futility of it before then?"

Afraid he'd reject her touch, Sam wrapped her arms around her middle. "When I heard the shot, my first thought was that you were killed. But when I turned and saw you'd fired the shot, nothing made sense. But I was wrong, Luke, so desperately wrong to accuse you without ever letting you explain. My only excuse is that I haven't had much reason to trust pirates."

This time she did reach for him because she needed to touch him, needed to feel him and know, for now, that he was with her. "I know I can trust you, Luke. I do trust you. And I'm sorry that I was the one who proved to be untrustworthy. I told you I loved you, and yet at the first sign of trouble, I abandoned that love."

Her voice cracked. "Please tell me I'm not too late, that I haven't lost you."

Luke's gaze bored into hers. "When you turned from Dervish, I knew in that moment that I loved you. You think that was your weakest moment, but I believe it was your strongest. It made me want to be a better man, to be worthy of being in your life."

Sam sobbed, and her hands clasped Luke's. "I don't care how you came into this world, Luke. Your parentage is of no consequence."

He inhaled deeply and sat next to her. "Bloody hell, that hurts!" he cursed. He leaned back, then, since that didn't seem to help, rolled onto his stomach.

That's when Sam saw the blood. "You're hurt!"

He looked over his shoulder, then back at her. "So it seems."

"Don't move. I'll get a rag and some water. The shot must still be in you."

Luke grabbed her hand and tugged her down next to him.

"It's just grazed. At any rate, there's some things that need finishing before I let you out of my sight again."

Despite being wounded, his gaze was strong and his voice deep. Both touched her very soul. His hand reached out and held her hip firmly. "I'll not have my children go through what I did. If you're sure you can tolerate me, we'll need to be married."

Sam's heart soared, but her voice trembled. "I think that can be arranged."

He almost looked surprised. "I swear I'll see to it you're happy."

"Just don't leave me, Luke, ever. That's all I ask."

"That, luv, I can guarantee."

His kiss wasn't soft. It plundered the way a pirate kiss was meant to. He pressed her into the mattress, his hands curling in her hair. His tongue sought and conquered. She gave back all the love that swelled in her chest. Pirate or not, he was hers.

When he drew back, his gaze was heavy with need. For her. She smiled.

"How do you feel about building ships?" he asked suddenly.

"Building them?"

Funny, how the picture came so easily to her mind and made perfect sense. Who better to create a work of precision and passion than two of the best pirates the Caribbean had ever seen?

"I can't think of anything more perfect," she said.

"I love you, Samantha."

"I love you, Luke, with all my heart. Just as you are."

He grinned wickedly. She'd never felt so at home as she did in that moment, with the man who'd captured her heart.

"About my wound," he began.

He was up to no good. She knew it. She loved it.

"Yes?"

He leaned closer, his breath caressing her face, his lips hovering over hers. "I think it can wait a moment longer."

Don't miss the next swashbuckling romance
in Michelle Beattie's pirate series

Romancing the Pirate

Available October 2009
from Berkley Sensation!

Enter the rich world of
historical romance
with Berkley Books.

Lynn Kurland

Patricia Potter

Betina Krahn

Jodi Thomas

Anne Gracie

Love is timeless.
penguin.com